eat
the
ones
you
love

eat the ones you love

SARAH MARIA GRIFFIN

TOR PUBLISHING GROUP ~ NEW YORK

This is a work of fiction. All of the characters, organizations, and events portrayed in this novel are either products of the author's imagination or are used fictitiously.

EAT THE ONES YOU LOVE

Copyright © 2025 by Sarah Maria Griffin

All rights reserved.

Endpaper art by Ana Miminoshvili

A Tor Book
Published by Tom Doherty Associates / Tor Publishing Group
120 Broadway
New York, NY 10271

www.torpublishinggroup.com

Tor® is a registered trademark of Macmillan Publishing Group, LLC.

Library of Congress Cataloging-in-Publication Data

Names: Griffin, Sarah Maria, author.
Title: Eat the ones you love / Sarah Maria Griffin.
Description: First edition. | New York : Tor Publishing Group, 2025.
Identifiers: LCCN 2024050949 | ISBN 9781250910691 (hardcover) | ISBN 9781250910707 (ebook)
Subjects: LCGFT: Horror fiction. | Fantasy fiction. | Romance fiction. | Novels.
Classification: LCC PR6107.R533 E28 2025 | DDC 823/.92—dc23/eng/20241105
LC record available at https://lccn.loc.gov/2024050949

Our books may be purchased in bulk for promotional, educational, or business use. Please contact your local bookseller or the Macmillan Corporate and Premium Sales Department at 1-800-221-7945, extension 5442, or by email at MacmillanSpecialMarkets@macmillan.com.

First Edition: 2025

Printed in the United States of America

0 9 8 7 6 5 4 3 2 1

To Ceri, for being the warm earth I grow from

To Caro, for the light to grow towards

I empty my mind

I stuff it with grass

I'm green, I repeat.

—"Becoming Moss," Ella Frears

eat
the
ones
you
love

seed

Only in a time-locked building like the Woodbine Crown Mall would you see a HELP NEEDED sign in a shop window.

Not HELP WANTED.

Needed.

It was handwritten on the back of a piece of what looked to be torn wrapping paper and taped to the glass, at an odd angle. Shell stood outside the florist, her groceries and gravity tugging red crevices in the palms of her hands. Well. Her mother's groceries. Not what she'd choose for dinner, but it wasn't Shell's kitchen, or Shell's table.

HELP NEEDED.

Shell's own voice inside her head had been so loud lately. We all need help. She imagined that whoever it was running a dank little flower shop in the Woodbine Crown probably needed a fair amount of help. Maybe not more than her, necessarily. But more than most.

The mall was almost exactly as it had been since Shell was a child, or before, even. Three wings, and the great glass terrarium in the atrium, murked with moss and condensation. This would have been a gorgeous feature if it hadn't been there for thirty years and never seen a lick of window cleaner. A three-pointed crown with a strange old emerald at the centre, it was a late 1970s relic, an aspiration towards American luxury retail ambience transplanted deep in the veins of the Northside

Dublin suburbs. An architectural curiosity. Three floors. The local Dunnes Stores, a library, and a radio station. An enormous fountain in the centremost wing that had been gathering copper-wish pennies to no apparent cause. No functioning elevator. A kip, Shell thought. A weird kip in a nest of housing estates. A heaving, dilapidated heart at the middle of a wire grid of old veins. The terrarium, the sick heart within the sick heart. Sick hearts all the way down.

Not a single part of it had ever been knocked and rebuilt in Shell's lifetime. No new lights installed. The linoleum tiles on the floor, mostly a dappled beige, except those that had failed under endless footfall, which were replaced at random with incongruous glitchlike patches of red or black. The ceiling was low, but in such a way that a person would hardly notice until they perhaps had been inside for an hour and were met with the strange sensation that they were miles away from daylight. The unit layout was, seemingly, unplanned. It all made Shell feel a bit sick, generally, some low nausea that could have been repulsion at poor design instilled in her at art college, or the unshakable awareness that she was, well, back home. Back here. She'd never had any intention of being anywhere of the sort. She didn't know whether she hated it truly or was just heartbroken. She couldn't tell yet, but either way, it was smothering, all of it.

What had happened in January should have freed her, but it trapped her back here instead, and she felt her eyes well up and wasn't it too far into everything to be still crying? Summer racing up on her. HELP NEEDED nearly set her off, but she couldn't cry here. Everyone watched everyone as they stepped in and out of the shops, the bookies, stopped at the coffee dock or sat over a plate of deli breakfast at Keeva's Kitchen in the scant food court under the huge, cold skylight, peering at other people's groceries through any thin spots in plastic carrier bags. Shell pulled her neck scarf up over her chin for comfort. She could at least pretend to be invisible then. Pretending was half the battle.

Even without the fabric over her nose and mouth, there was a thick in the air that you couldn't condition out, a gelatin feeling, suffocating. It made Shell feel like she was eight, fourteen, and perhaps like she was seventy-two and still here, in a shopping centre adjacent to her housing estate, still here, still in this place. Something wouldn't let her leave this part of the world and she had worked so hard to get gone. She had almost escaped.

She looked at the flowers in tall green buckets outside the florist that needed help and thought to herself that she would buy some and at home she'd draw them. They would cheer her parents up, act as a casual token of gratitude and appreciation, and keep her off her phone for a few hours tonight. They would also act as a very helpful excuse to inquire about what kind of help was needed, exactly, in this flower shop.

A graphic design job like her old role at Fox & Moone now was as good as a pipe dream: a situation that felt impossible to replicate. The listings Shell found were all for entry-level positions that somehow required five years of campaign experience, or executive roles that held no appeal to her, even if she had been qualified. She was stuck in the house with too many other adults: her sisters, her parents, too many of them in the space all day. Annoying one another. Her sympathy pass had run out weeks ago; now she was an interloper. It wasn't like she hadn't been looking for work. It was more that she'd been sending miserable emails to friends, peers, friends-of-friends, trying to suss out if their companies were hiring and being met with more unemployment, more bad news.

So sorry to hear about you and Gav, such a shame about Fox & Moone, just between you and me we're actually letting so many people go right now, love a recession, lol, I'm sure you'll be snapped up in no time babes x

Eventually, they stopped asking at all how she was getting on with the hunt.

Every message she got back from every query hit the same beats. They might as well have just said: Sorry to hear about your life, but I've got nothing for you, someone else might, I suppose? Over and over, until all of Shell's long-treasured favours were tapped out, and she was left staring into her laptop all day, scrolling, hope numbed, unable to cut back any self-pity. She'd have emigrated already if she had the money.

Her mother had expressed concerns about her going off and starting over at her age, at thirty-three—but what about Galway? That would be far enough away for a new beginning but near enough home, too. Just across the belly of the country, the other coast.

Still, even that kind of move was steep cash, and as much encouragement as her mother gave her, there was no world in which Shell was being bankrolled. Shell was to sort herself out.

So, sorting herself out could look like retail. Forty hours in a shop a week was preferable to the wallowing, to the endless pingback of *So sorry hun*. Minimum wage would be a slap, but one she could take. Floristry was the same as design, right? The meticulous organization of beautiful, delicate things. Shapes. Shell liked shapes. She scooped a heavy bouquet—expensive, but best to look like that wasn't an issue—from a bucket out front and walked inside. One arm weighted down with carrots, six densely wrapped chicken breasts, and a large tub of gravy granules in a cloth bag, the other cradling a carefully-organized-to-look-kind-of-wild clutch of sunflowers, eucalyptus leaves, ferns, and some mad, virgin's-cloak-blue blossoms she couldn't name.

The shop was a little larger than the walk-in wardrobe she'd shared with Gav, back at the apartment. The ceiling just as low. Lit funny, yellow almost, by multiple lamps instead of one overhead light. It was so cold, so suddenly, that Shell felt a chill go over her and her nose turn pink. The shelves were jammed with wreaths, succulents, swags. Buckets on buckets, some tall, some stout, rammed with flowers, organized by species, not colour. Pots and pots of monstera, the kind you see a lot of on Instagram now that nobody leaves their house so much anymore. Talk radio played at a low volume, almost inaudible, but Shell just about caught the jingle: *Woodbine Crown FM, afternoon vibe at 106.9!* There was an almost-chaos to the place: it was overrun with life. Well. Not life. The flowers were dead the second they were cut, weren't they? Shelly supposed nothing in here was alive, only a handful of potted plants and herself.

However, it was not just Shell and the merchandise. Down the back of the lush, close den was a high counter, and perched on a stool behind it, reading a book, was the florist.

Shell knew the outline of her, somehow. Had they been in the same school? A few years apart? It wasn't until the florist looked up from her reading and right into Shell's eyes that she started to feel in any way nervous. The florist closed the book, tilted her head to the side, and said, "Delphis and sunnies. A dream. Let me stick a little extra paper around those for you."

Shell smiled, handing the bouquet over the counter, hoping her cheeks would lift the signal to her eyes, and said, "A dream, thank you. Do you mind me asking—like, sorry—what kind of help do you need?"

The florist laughed, husky, unspooling brown paper into a square. "That's a big question." She laid the flowers down to wrap them.

"I'm unemployed," said Shell, before she could think, and the florist, taking a thumb of tape from a large black dispenser, said, "Oh, the sign," in a voice that made Shell feel as though she'd missed a joke and said something incredibly stupid at once. The florist quickly swaddled the bouquet with the paper and taped it in place. She stood the flowers up on their stems, the bunch finding a stable geometry, flourishing with light petals at the top, bound into a hinge and all the weight low, in the green legs. They both admired them in silence, for a moment, the gold and the blue and the green. The wild and the order.

The florist was taller than Shell and her hair was cropped short. It was dark—perhaps it would have been curly if it had been long, and Shell was very aware then that she was looking at her, properly, trying to decipher why it was that she felt like she knew her. She wore small glasses, but her features were large. Her eyes and her mouth were generous.

"Are you interested?" the florist asked, looking at the bouquet, adjusting it slightly.

"Sorry—what?"

"Interested. In the job. How do you feel about flowers?"

The woman's apron was denim, like one a carpenter might wear, with a black leather strap holding it high on her form, buckled over her heart. She held the now-wrapped bouquet out, gently, as though it were a breathing animal. Shell reached across the counter to take the flowers and noticed as it changed hands how light the bouquet was for something so large.

"What, these ones? They're—beautiful." And the blooms looked up at Shell, the solar disc of flower and the little blue licks of petal and the green, green, green all around them.

"I meant more in general, but yes, they are. Are they for anyone special, or just yourself?" asked the florist, hands on the counter. On her left hand was a dark, slim ring and Shell wasn't looking for that, necessarily. But it was on the correct finger to imply that she was engaged, or married. Her nails were short but manicured, shiny black.

Shell looked back up and answered, "Just for me. I'm going to draw them. Pass the evenings, you know?"

The florist shook her head slightly, tipping a couple digits of the register without looking. "Ah, I do, yeah. The evenings can be hard all right. And that's eighteen, please. We don't take cash anymore."

"Oh. Yes." Shell suddenly realized she had no hands with which to remove her card and handed the bouquet back to the florist. There was a moment's kerfuffle, and they both laughed in a nice way, as though mutually. It was almost as if they were both aware of something about the other, now. She tapped her card. It made a noise. She couldn't remember the last time she'd used a paper note. The florist handed her back the flowers again, crumpling the receipt into a tiny firm ball and throwing it over her shoulder.

"I'm looking for a full-time assistant. That's the kind of help I need."

"I'm—I'm looking for work. I'm a—I was—a graphic designer. But I worked in retail for, like, six years, before I was in the agency. Fox & Moone. They went under," replied Shell. "Not because of me, like. Because of, well—you know. The world."

"Oh, I know. The world. The economy." The florist then smiled like a cat, revealing crooked white teeth and a deep dimple in the left side of her cheek.

Trouble.

Shell held her nerve and smiled fully. "My name is Michelle—Shell. Not Michelle-Shell. Like people . . . call me Shell."

"Michelle-Shell. I'm Neve."

She pronounced it softly. Like never, but not quite.

"The sign's been up a couple of months, and nobody's asked about it. Realistically, the Crown won't be open into next year, so this isn't a long-term gig. You can assist, though, if you like. Come in a couple of mornings, see if you have a feel for it. Thirteen euros an hour—isn't much, but we have some big clients who tip well. We start most days at four a.m., close up when we're sold out. I basically never leave but don't see that as a standard. It's the early starts and cold hands that put people off this job." Neve took a business card out of a tiny plastic cradle on the counter and placed it in the bouquet.

"I don't sleep more than a couple of hours a night anyway," said Shell. "And, look, sure you know what they say about cold hands?"

"Warm heart," said Neve, holding her hands up to either side of her face. The ring caught Shell's eye again, but this time so did calluses and white scarring on her palms. Shell was struck again by the feeling that she knew her from somewhere, but she didn't say that; instead she smiled and said, "Warm heart," too.

"Look, fire me over a CV tonight. Email's on the card. I'll call your references, get you in on Thursday. Does that work?"

Neve's tone was direct and slightly commanding. Shell was sure she would agree to just about anything the florist said.

"Yes," said Shell, almost without thinking at all. They said so long, talk to you shortly, thanks a million, and Shell left, the fragrance of the bouquet more intense now, and she thought to herself that that was the easiest it had been for her to get a job since she was a teenager. It was fifteen minutes from her parents' place and the potential for long hours would keep her busy, keep her out, away from the crowd in the house. The wages would add up. Slowly.

She could take photos of the flowers for her Instagram. Replace all the surreptitiously deleted images of her life with Gav, scrubbed late one night, silent motions of her thumb rendering seven years of photographic history nonexistent. Selfies of their smiling or pouting faces in Prague, in Barcelona. Images taken of printed photo-booth strips, black and white, her on his lap, both of them in sunglasses for the pose, hers shaped like lovehearts. Their too-formal, stiff poses in other people's wedding parties. All gone. Every single one of them. Like it had never happened. She would plant lush, blousy peonies and starry white lilies with yellow tongues in the space online where the story of her life had just been: Shell and Gav at Primavera, Shell and Gav at Emer and Donal's big day, Gav drinking a craft beer with his eyebrows raised. The caption on that said *This one*, with a heart emoji.

As she'd erased them there in her childhood bed, under the covers, she couldn't remember a single thing about how she'd felt in any of those shots. She had no idea whose life it was, really, taking up all that digital space. Now it would all be flowers, all hers. Sunnies and delphis and roses and cosmos would be all people could see when they went looking. Bloom after bloom after bloom atop long, fragile stems.

It almost, if she could spin it just right, on the tip of her finger—would look like a choice she'd made. Not just a coincidental opportunity that had opened in front of her, that she had taken out of boredom and discomfort, the need for cash, any cash at all to help her start her life again. Cash for a deposit, a few months' rent out west to tide her over while she found another job. She'd gotten good at living slim. Cancelled her Pilates studio membership in town, stopped donating to the podcasts she followed.

All that and Neve had been so up front about the Woodbine closing down—Shell had heard rumours of it, but it hadn't felt possible, or something. Her mam had mentioned it, as had her nana. They were mourning the loss of local proximity to a good supermarket in advance, the cream cakes from the café upstairs, how handy it was to have a hair salon so close by. They were confounded, almost, by the potential of a rental-only apartment block that would spring up in its place.

Who would want to live in a flat on the site of a rancid old mall? Surely the foundations were rotting, surely the bad vibes in the air would carry on to whatever was built over it.

And, well, Neve seemed nice. Smart. Engaged, importantly.

This was good, and safe, given the mischief that glinted off her surface, like how at the right time of day, the sun reflects tiny blinks of magic on still bodies of water. They would be great pals, Shell and Neve.

This would be easy.

Or at least, that had been the plan.

If Shell had been paying more attention to anything further than her own feelings, she might not have missed so many details sitting out of place in the flower shop. The vines growing over the ceiling, on the floor—she stepped over them without looking. The long, thin bruises on Neve's arms—she only noticed the florist's hands because Neve showed them to her, in flirtation. The wrong things in the space weren't convenient to Shell: she was only really looking at the woman in front of her, only really looking at the bouquet, only really thinking of how to help herself.

Oh, she's perfect.

Shell stood the bouquet on her dresser, just as Neve had built it: with perfect balance. Seemed it a pity to disassemble it, to put it in a vase.

I was nestled there, my energy not dwindling yet, a happy observer of this new place outside the Crown.

She was proud that she'd gotten it home in one piece. Despite a lopsided eleven-minute walk back to her family home through the grey, fat labyrinth streets of the housing estate, she hadn't even lost one petal. She felt like an event, tottering with a bouquet that was slightly bigger than her upper torso, all bright yellow, sky blue, celebration on a dour stretch of Tuesday afternoon.

Shell always felt under surveillance here: the eyes of long-moved-away spectres of childhood peers still peeking out from behind telephone poles, not able to shake the sense of perceived judgement, the tightness under her ribs. An abiding and unrelenting sense of shame, technically, was what it was. The same shame she'd held as a child had mutated now, become textured, sophisticated, and immutable. I could tell she felt like a dick carrying the bouquet.

The worst thing in the estate was to be a person who wanted to be looked at in any capacity: to want for attention, to need anything, or to appear even for a moment as if you did. Parading down the Rise holding an enormous bouquet as though there were something worth celebrating happening was profoundly humiliating, and Shell expected at any moment for the estate to move in this way—to be yelled at by a passing fleet of twelve-year-old boys on bikes, to receive an eye-roll from a harried new mother pushing a buggy containing a screaming child, a judgement from a priest, maybe, stony-faced and appalled at the vanity of it.

In reality, literally nobody cared about the girl with the shopping bags and the flowers. She was invisible: ordinary. If I could, I would crawl inside her collar and whisper in her ear, Nobody cares, Shell, over and over. Nobody is thinking about you, and though this would not release her from the narcissism of believing that the world's eyes were on her as opposed to on their own steps and field of vision, it would at least jolt her, cause her to consider that maybe her life was even smaller than she had imagined at first. I will tell her this, I will leaf my way into the parts of her that can hear and feel and I will assure her that the eyes of others slip off her like furniture, she is unremarkable, objectively ordinary. Her pain is a non-phenomenon. But as she walked through her neighbourhood here, she believed herself to be the protagonist of reality, and the tragedy was not that she was heartbroken, retrograded, moved back in with disinterested parents. Rather, it was that she was deluded and ordinary and abjectly blind to both of these realities.

Silly girl.

Her humiliating fantasy ended abruptly when she got home and her mother was delighted to see her: all the shopping done, and a big bunch of flowers? She was a dote for going out of her way to bring home something nice. Shell's sisters were in the living room and were coaxed out to look at the bouquet, swatted away by their mother from plucking some blooms off it for themselves. The bouquet was enough to get everyone up on their feet, out of their books and phones and laptops for six or seven minutes. The bouquet was like a guest in the house, and Shell realized then that becoming a florist wasn't just good news in that she was going to be earning her way and would be seen to be getting her life back on track—the presence of flowers would assuage some of her mother and father's resentfulness at her presence. Win, win, win.

None of the losses had shown through yet.

Shell kidnapped the lush, overflowing houseguest of flowers up to her room, promising she'd return them in one piece once she'd taken some pictures, done some sketches of them. Her mother called her a little dote again and again: what a sweet thing her girl had done, off away to market and back with flowers. As though they were picked from a field by a child with a basket and cloak. As though Shell hadn't been behaving cynically, strategically, bolstering herself with the beautiful, green, and dead.

Up in her room then, the flowers stood, and I a spy amongst them. Shell erected the awkward, too-modern ring light she had purchased the previous Christmas, which had once stood in her bathroom at the flat with Gav. Her bathroom, not theirs. Her bathroom was her own space, a sanctuary where she could carefully make herself beautiful every day, where she could sit on the edge of the bath and scroll her phone in peace—especially at the end. The ring light, a black, industrial tripod and a halo of LED white scream, was almost the shape of a person. Her skeleton man, all the meat of the old life she'd had stripped away, and here she was in her childhood bedroom with just this machine instead of Gav, instead of anything at all. She sort of danced with him, the ring light, trying to get him to stand just so, to light the flowers as though they were a seventeen-year-old girl, as though they would catch the eyes of the internet and give her, if not meaning, at least attention.

She shot the flowers as though they were to be spread across the glossy bed of a magazine fold, as though their pixels were to be stretched and blown and pasted across the walls of a concession stand at an airport. She shot them billboard, she shot them baby you're gorgeous. Truth be told, Shell did have an incredible eye: something she didn't know about herself but I know because I know everything about her now is that she was in possession of an anomaly in her vision that permitted her to perceive more colour than the standard human can with their eyes. Tetrachromacy sounds like magic but is mere genetics, and was secret even to Shell herself. So I will credit her this: alone in her room she was not merely feigning marvel at the light and the flowers, she was truly admiring them, shooting them and capturing a version of them that only she could see. If she had known this about herself, she would have made this exceptional sight a core tenet of her personality, so perhaps it was best she didn't know.

Shell elected a close image that contained enough of the bouquet to express a vibrant range of colour and variety of plants, but not enough to show her room, her unpacked suitcases, her own tired reflection in the vanity mirror. She captioned it, carefully, *New Beginnings!* bouquet emoji, hibiscus emoji, sunflower emoji, glitter emoji. These flowers could have been a gift from a lover—and this image and caption had the potential to provoke anxiety in Gav, if he bothered to look. She couldn't be clocked, either: she was getting a job working with flowers, she technically was experiencing a new beginning. This is all the truth, she thought to herself, proud of the smoke-and-mirror act, sitting on her bed, slipping off her sneakers and socks, grateful for her mother changing her sheets—the crisp, laundered sensation of a freshly made bed was almost spiritual.

It would be the duvet for the rest of the day for her, over drawing the flowers. She was tired now, from the emotional exertion of taking out the light, thinking of the light in the old apartment, thinking of her old bathroom and comparing it to the poky family bathroom she shared with her two resentful sisters. Shell decided she was doing her best and crawled into the fresh nest to reward herself for her big morning, by closing her eyes for a nap.

It is there, as she slips out of the day early to rest bones that don't need rest, that I begin my work on her—but she does the heavy lifting for me. She thinks about Neve almost the instant her pillow warms around her and she dips two, three inches out of waking but not quite into sleep. Thinks about the sharpness of Neve's jaw, the leather strap of her apron, her hands. Her teeth were neat and white. The gradient of her voice was so familiar.

Shell thinks how they will be such pals. Such friends. Soft, fae Shell with her highlit curls and angular, wry Neve and their little flower shop. Foam pierced with sharp stems, roses spiralling fat from tight buds, learning a new language, learning the names for all the gorgeous and the dead things around them. Wreath, spray, swag, crown, Neve would teach Shell to become an architect and Shell would be a fast and ready learner. Shell would become somebody out of the shadow of her old life, she would stand tall and emit light so powerful that all colour was changed by her. This new press forward, a halo.

What a daydream for the silly girl. I let her have it. I did not change the course of it even an inch. There would be plenty of time for that.

When she eventually woke herself up proper, Shell held her phone at an angle to her face that meant she didn't have to rise, and checked the public response her two thousand followers on Instagram had left on her image and mysterious caption. They didn't know it yet, but they were reading the very first chapter of a story she would tell them, one flower at a time. *Looks unreal babe! Omg where did u get them? Stunnin Shell! Gorge xxxx.* Bouquet emoji, tulip emoji, rose emoji. Standard hundred and twenty likes, fine. No sign of Gav, though he would have seen it. This was close to the last time she would consider Gav's gaze, though she didn't know that yet. His sister's mark was there, though—helpful.

Shell thumbed open WhatsApp.

The number of unread messages gave her a tug of anxiety. Various groups full of talk hummed away: she didn't want to leave her digital *read* imprint on many of them, so her lack of participation would be seen to fall under *busy* over *saw it, didn't care,* though only the latter was true.

She opened her most regularly used chat group, the girls who she'd gone to college with and who all still orbited in and out of one another's lives through brunches and gigs and gallery launches. They'd seen a lot of each other before the breakup. Sometimes it still felt like they were in college—still having little house parties, or going on walks, or sitting on blankets in the park during the summer drinking gin and tonic out of tins. That was all different now, but the three of them had been as good to Shell as they could, given that social gatherings had fallen out of their pattern of habits as the demands of their thirties began to mount. That, and the reality that Shell's relationship had crumbled and none of theirs had. Chloe was pregnant; Emily had started her own business selling artisanal, handmade candles because her freelancing had dried up. Lorna was—well. Busy. They were all busy. Shell had distinctly not been busy. She'd mostly been sad, hiding, communicating through memes when she couldn't muster up any more emotional support for anyone else in their triumphs or their true, unspeakable losses. She had neither.

Birth and death were still realities happening to other people, whereas nothing had been happening to Shell, only the slow fall of the tower she had built for herself. Her breakup hadn't even been that interesting: at least if there had been an affair, a crisis, there would have been something to talk about. Shell and Gav's slow numbing to each other and the obviousness that the breakup was a good thing in the long run didn't make for a lot of rallying, cheering. The girls were all still kind of friends with Gav; Shell wasn't going to split herself open and give them her pain in case some impression of it made their way back to him. The thought of details of her breakdown being distilled into gossip made her feel sick, so she kept her mouth firmly shut. Going to the pub to get shitfaced and climb the body of a stranger wasn't a restorative option; she hadn't done anything like that in years, and wasn't best composed to manage sexual rejection, given that the heady cocktail of being laid off and her relationship dissolving was so recent. Lorna, who had, in college, been the riot leader, who was always trying to convince people at three a.m. in smoking areas to get a taxi to the airport with her and just like, go to Berlin—we can just go—was now the invigilator within the group, insisting that they all put self-care first. Ensuring, sherifflike, that there was no toxic behaviour occurring. So there was no talk of Shell hopping out to meet a pleasant, stupid man for a drink and a ride, and even if there was, she wouldn't get the chance to share her thrilling tales of self-esteem recovery with her friends.

So she didn't share anything with them anymore, really. A picture of a lizard wearing a party hat as a reply to *How was everyone's day?* A baby goat wearing some sunglasses in reply to *Any plans for the weekend girlies?* Talking through increasingly deranged memes was easier than saying anything at all. Today, though, she did have something to share—and they were poised, waiting for her tale. *Who were the flowers from? What's the story with the bouquet? Is there a man? Multiple men? A person who is not a man? Are you trying to make Gav sick, because I'd say he's sick. I'd be fucken sick. New beginnings? New beginnings of what?*

The strange little digital spotlight was down on her now. She finally had something to tell them, to show them after weeks of embarrassed deflections.

lol, no man unfortch girls—but new job. i'm starting to take shifts in the florist so I can re-skill: it's something i've always had such a passion for but never had the opportunity to pursue. Drawing was her passion, not flowers, but what did they know? *now that a little bit of the pressure is off me to keep up with gav's lifestyle in town, i've done some reevaluating and am going to go down a path i feel really strongly about. plants! flowers! expect loads more bouquets from me in future!* Bouquet emoji, fire emoji, bicep flex emoji.

The responses were short, exclamation-pointed—*Good for you girl, go get it, sounds unreal*—not the level of enthusiasm that Shell had hoped for. Perhaps if she told them about Neve, they'd be more interested: the flower shop is tiny and pokey and run by this girl—or like, woman or whatever—who looks and feels really familiar. Shell thought about asking the girls if they knew someone called Neve, but stopped herself. She didn't want to know if they knew her. She wanted this to be all her own. They already knew everything about her life before: a couple of their boyfriends were friends with Gav. They'd all gone to Inis Oírr to the biennale since 2014, they'd hit micro festivals across the country multiple times a summer, even flown out to Primavera. There had been innumerable, identical, exhausting weddings from the outer limits of their social lives, weekend after weekend after weekend.

I liked getting this vantage point on her. I liked crawling into her memories, into her desires.

Neve was far from this room, farther still from Shell's old world. Neve was her employer and even the thought of showing her new, strange presence in her life to the girls made Shell feel a bit sick. Neve and the shop were Shell paving the path ahead for herself, not the road behind her. Neve would tell her what to do, so she didn't have to think about anything for eight hours a day.

Plus, if she wanted to know what Neve's deal was, she could just search her. Distinctive enough name so that typing *Neve Florist Woodbine Crown* led her to discover Neve's social media profiles—agonizingly all private. It would take Shell a shift or two before she could risk a follow, a step over that strange threshold, privileging her to the four-thousand-ish photos stored on Instagram that tracked Neve's life until now. Only around a hundred followers. Following sixty. Slim metrics. Personal, not performance.

At this stage Shell was bluntly aware that she was attracted to Neve, and had decided that the sensation of knowing her from before was likely pheromones. It didn't hurt that there was also a dense pollen in the air, that their tiny show had had me and my vines and my leaves and my buds as an audience. I chose Shell, make no mistake, but there was a helpful organic chemistry waiting there, too. This was no possession. I did not even lift the heat of Shell's blood any higher on the stove of her, not necessarily. Shell saw Neve's face, her smile, and took in her body, and something in Shell's own body made a decision. Shell probably would have been thinking about her anyway, scouring the internet for traces of Neve's identity, scrolling through Google Image Search for the whole look of her.

After some time trying to glean her from the occasional images made public, Shell decided to get up and bring the flowers and me downstairs, share us with her mother, place me generously in the kitchen where everyone could experience my beauty and I could use my flickering strength to observe them in return. She was sure to tell her pleased father that there would be plenty more where they came from in the months to come, that they'd never be out of blooms. Shell was temporarily the star of their rickety show with too many in the cast, a whole family living in dense quarters, reluctantly choosing the act of stepping on one another's toes rather than bearing out the rental crisis in the rest of the country. After dinner, when her sisters left for their room and her father retired to the sofa to softly scroll his phone and half watch *The Sopranos,* Shell set about drinking a bottle of white wine out of a glass full of ice cubes with her mother at the kitchen table. They watched videos on her mother's iPad of women arranging flowers in Sweden, in Japan, in London. Building arches from foliage in double speed, like sculptures turning thin wire structures into lush archways littered with fat peonies and roses in varying shades of coral and cream; these florists are architects, long in their trades, hands green, hearts green. Shell's mother was a happy tourist, and by the time her first enormous tumbler of chardonnay on the rocks was finished, she was wearing one of my flowers from the bouquet above her ear. Shell twirled a piece of eucalyptus between her finger and thumb as she tried to take in anything from the screen, other than a low sense of marvel at how easy these florists made it look. How that could be her someday. How she hadn't had this ambition when she woke up that morning, but here it was.

They watched a forty-minute video of a woman building a chandelier that trailed fern and bloom down as though they were glass and light and drank another bottle between them. By the time one a.m. came and Shell was loaded, hugging her mother good night, she had genuinely convinced herself that she really cared more about the flowers than the impression of organizing the flowers, that she was really ready to be an apprentice at the heel of a sculptor, that this might just be the best thing that ever happened to her, and you know, she wasn't wrong.

Her life otherwise would have been on a predictable rail. She and Gav would have had two children, a wedding that seated about two hundred friends and family members, a three-bedroom house in a suburb in a nicer postcode than the ones either of them were raised in. She would have been safe.

But—she never would have felt like she felt when she met Neve. She never would have felt what she was going to feel when I arrived for her, in her. She never would have known what it was to glimpse past tile and brick and wire and the boundaries of the world into something bigger, and older, and wilder. She never would have known that I am the best thing. Neve might have been the sculptor and she the apprentice, but I am the angel in the marble and I am starving. I am so, so hungry.

And lucky her to come to know the feeding of me.

It could have been anyone who took notice of the sign, but it was Shell, and the room was flooded by emotion when she and Neve began to speak. Both of them in so much pain, so polluted by loss that it had just about changed their colour; it warmed the temperature of the air in the shop, and I could feel it over every inch of myself, how the energy they both took to conceal it was so potent you could get wasted off it, if that kind of thing was your poison. If this tiny exchange rushed through me so hard, what will it feel like in a week, in two weeks, in a month? To watch it bloom and ripen for eating?

Michelle, Shelly, Shell. The sorrow when she read the word *needed* over and over again there in the southernmost wing of the Crown. How much she needs will be the ruin of her. I felt the live little tug of curiosity that rose in her, how fresh a feeling it was. She'd felt very little other than the same gradient of miserable after the extremity of her own sorrow had become boring to even her. She will find new pain to thrill through herself in no time. I will lead her there and she will, I am sure, follow me like I am a miracle.

I am, though.

A miracle.

A brisk handful of emails charted Shell's week so that before she knew it, she was to be waiting outside the locked, shuttered public entryway to the Woodbine Crown at 4:30 a.m. on Thursday. She'd only been in the shop on Tuesday and was glad to feel a sense of Neve's urgency around getting her started. Her new life right there, opening like a palm.

Getting ready for work had been a strange task. She'd been at home for so long—between her parents', and her and Gav's old place, so accustomed to sweatpants and cardigans and slippers that she was finding it hard to work out what looked normal, semiprofessional. Retail professional. Shop-floor professional. It was different, facing the public in this way. She thought of how Neve had put herself together, from the small glimpse of her she'd taken behind the counter, and went through some of her packed-away clothes, looking to correspond. The strangeness of getting dressed for work at 3:30 a.m. was not lost on her: her head felt loopy in the way it only ever did on the way to the airport for an early flight. This was it—this was her routine from now on. Her middle-of-the-night life. She let the selfie ring illuminate her bedroom rather than turning on the bluntness of the overhead light. Her eyes and her mouth felt strange as she brushed her teeth and pawed out her eye sockets with cotton-pad cleansers in the bathroom, being as quiet as she could so as not to wake the rest of the house. She was cold. Didn't matter how warm the house was or wasn't, how thick her pyjamas—this time of night was a cold one from the inside of her, not the outside.

She wore a carefully selected pair of black dungarees, wide-legged, turned up a little at the ankle. They were stylish, but they also communicated a crafty, artisan energy that she felt would be appropriate for the nature of the work she was about to undertake. She paired them with a ribbed dark charcoal vest and a thick cream Aran cardigan. Shell had gotten rid of a great deal of her silver jewellery so as to purge herself of the tasteful little totems Gav had left her with, and opted instead for thick circular earrings made of off-white leather. Sneakers in the same shade. Hair out of her face in a knot on her head. A minimal makeup composition: not enough to proclaim too much glamour, but enough to make her look as though she cared. Because god, she cared so much. She had painted her fingernails the evening prior, an almost invisible nude. She was well composed by the time she was leaving the house, a little after four, a cup of tea in a KeepCup in one hand, a bitten crescent of toast in the other.

The air was still cold, and the sun wasn't going to be coming up for another couple of hours: night was firmly down on the estate, amber-flooded from streetlamps. Shell turned from her street through the green, empty copse that linked her nest of streets to the Woodbine Crown. She knew she had nothing to worry about, that the groups of lads who had hung around there at night when she was a frightened teenager were long grown up and moved away, but she still moved at speed anyway. She and her old friends, long-gone girls from the estates, would sing as they walked home after dark through the park, convinced that their mania and pitch-wrong renditions of "Celebrity Skin" and "By the Way" would keep anyone who'd do them harm at bay. Shell put Hole on her phone and picked up her pace. She hadn't listened to them in years: the rough distortion made her feel brave, even though her heart rate had picked up and the shadows felt longer. She hadn't taken the copse after dark in forever, and this was just her morning walk to work now. Even if she had been able to keep the car in her and Gav's split, there would have been no point driving to the Crown, it was simply too nearby. There was no use being scared of the same things she was scared of when she was fifteen: the copse was a four-minute walk. What could happen in four minutes? Every single one of Shell's footfalls matched a beat, and she thumbed *repeat* on her phone so that the crunch and bass didn't leave her alone for a second.

By the time she made it to the shut-down doorway, she was on her fourth listen to the song. Made a nice metric to get to work to. A text message had arrived—Neve, saying to reply when she landed. Shell replied a perky *hey! i'm here!* She leant against the door, hands in her pockets, looking out over the empty car park, the McDonalds still lit. The flicking traffic lights on the main road changed from green to red, and the wind moved through the barely green trees around the big old church on the other side of the crosswalk. She hated the look of it, the feel of its presence. That fifteen feeling wouldn't quit. Shell had never wanted to move back here. She'd wanted to skirt through for an hour on Christmas day at an absolute push. It would take her some time to get up enough wages to get set up on her own, and she told herself to not get demoralized: this morning was the start of the road out.

The tiny pixels on Shell's phone didn't prepare her for Neve's face, first thing in the morning. The sharp jaw, the high cheekbones, her surprisingly full mouth, and the smile she gave was warm and spooled excitement through Shell, who smiled warmly in reply. "Howya."

"Howya so, look, get in now before the alarms go and security thinks we're pulling a heist." Neve cocked her head to the side and called her in. Over the threshold stepped Shell, fumbling her earbuds out of her ear into the front pocket of her dungarees, still bumping tinny bass and Courtney Love's furious voice. Before she could stop the playing from her phone, Neve remarked, "Bit early in the morning for that, but you know what, I respect it."

"I mean, it is four a.m., that's, like, dancing hours, right?"

Neve laughed. "I'm sure someone's out there dancing, somewhere."

Something inside of Shell began dancing at this moment and it did not stop, not for a long time after.

The lights in the Crown entry passage were on, but low. All the shop units were shuttered—the older-ladies fashion boutique, the Golden Discs that somehow was still operating and slinging music and DVDs, the kitchen-installation showroom. Their footfalls sounded strange on the well-worn lino. Shell had never seen the place like this, so quiet, humming only slightly with the sound the old lights made. The air was sweet with the smell from the bakery in the supermarket already. Pastries that hadn't changed in sixteen, seventeen years, blanched white breads. The supermarket was in another wing of the mall, but the whole place hung dense with the feel of almost-ready food. An almost-ready day.

It was the biggest supermarket around for miles, somehow still holding monopoly over the estates. Shell decided she'd get her breakfast from the deli counter as soon as she could, just from the smell of it. She and Neve moved quickly and quietly down the long corridor to the shop, passing the main atrium and the now pitch-black indoor-outdoor garden of the terrarium. Shell had only seen it in the dark as a child, during trips to the shop with her friends after the winter's afternoon sunsets, but it was usually at least a little illuminated by twinkling seasonal lights or the glare of surroundings shops. Here it was a black, enormous gem. She didn't like looking at it. It was almost as if something in her was responding to me. Almost as if she knew. I have a much stronger grasp on her here, because there is more of me, not just whatever could fit in a flimsy bouquet on her nightstand.

"It's a bit spooky in here when it's closed, but don't worry—you won't ever be in here at this hour without me," Neve said, her voice carrying a little strange over the length of the avenue—shuttered butcher, sports shop, locksmith kiosk, pharmacy, phone service shop, rivalling phone service shop, vape shop, greetings cards—"I've worked here since I was fifteen, so there's probably no alarm you can trip or weird back storage room you can find yourself in that I haven't dealt with before."

"I'll try not to wander off," said Shell, "even though this place feels weird with nobody in it. I kind of want to go exploring."

"I promise, it's painfully boring after the first handful of shifts. You'll be so bleary-eyed most mornings you'll barely notice the look and feel of the place, so you should soak up the novelty while you can. It'll get really dull, really quickly." Neve gave a soft laugh and a look over her shoulder. "I'll try and keep you entertained."

I felt like extending a vine and tripping or jolting Neve for the audacity of flirting so keenly with Shell. For deciding the tone. So frank.

She was always like this in the mornings, always slightly hot-blooded before the light flooded through the day and distracted her. In the dark before dawn, Neve was different, and this was not information for strangers like Shell—but I suppose it helped.

The dancing in Shell corresponded to Neve's promise of entertainment, and she smiled warmly back. "And I'll try not to give you too much trouble."

They arrived at the shop, already opened up. It was less

impressive than usual without any flowers outside, and the pokey shop floor sparse for a lack of stock. The only greenery in sight, Shell noticed as she ducked her head a little to get inside, were the fat green vines that embroidered the walls, the ceiling, and hung over the inside of the doorway like a curtain. That was me. She'd seen me now, noticed me. Hello, Shell. We're going to be such good friends, you and I. I'll try to give you as much trouble as you can manage.

The only other green things were the houseplants left over from yesterday's restock. Shell didn't know any of their names yet, but she will. She would know my name, too, know it so well that it will run through every breath she let out, under her breath, under the bare words she murmurs as she sleeps. These plants that stood around my vines were just things that make people feel better in their homes. I look like them, but I am not the same as them. The plants that grow out of me and around me are far more interesting than these.

Shell stopped to look at one, touched a holey philodendron leaf with her hand, and Neve said, "I read a few articles about how people in their thirties are really into houseplants. So, I tilted our stock towards these guys. Peace lilies, *monstera deliciosa*, cacti, succulents. Flowers can seem a bit like a frippery to some people, you know, but a houseplant feels more sensible. So I keep them around. People seem to like them. And if people can't keep them alive, and they die, they just come back and buy another one." As Neve spoke, she picked up a spritz bottle and pointed it at a calathea, misting the deep green and veined pink of it absentmindedly, giving a little shush under her breath, like she was soothing it. "Now there's a steady stream in and out the door for bunches and about one customer in five picks up a plant. You won't see many of them, I'll have you out the back most of the time. No use in keeping you up front and wrecking your head with the general public."

"I'm happy to go wherever you send me," said Shell, following Neve through the small entryway behind the counter and down the tiny passage that led to the frankly enormous back room. She let out a laugh of surprise when she stepped in.

The tiny shop front led to a couple-hundred-square-foot back room full of stacked buckets. A few contained unbloomed roses wrapped in brown paper, huge closed lilies waiting to hit the time in their death when they opened to the world in all their heady yellow pollen and white-blush-pink petal luxury. The bottle-green walls were decked with great loops of wire and ribbon and twine and tape, shelves stacked with wicker baskets of all sizes and dark green bricks of foam. Wire brackets held pliers, scissors, knives, bundles of further wire and cable. A long, high table stood in the middle of the room atop a soft rug, breaking the vast concrete floor, making it feel a little cozier. The ceiling was high, cavernlike. It was, Shell noted, fucking freezing. Her nose immediately turned pink, and she rubbed it a little with the heel of her hand, a nervous tic.

"That was the shop, this is the workshop," said Neve. "This is where the magic happens."

She walked into the space with her arms stretched above her head, as though she were introducing a grand library or a ballroom, and Shell could, for a second, imagine her here every working day of her life, her lean body fit in the grand expanse of tools and blooms so well. It was as though she were a doll with a plastic vignette of her workplace. Shell would be her accessory now. And mine.

In the hours before sunrise, then, Neve walked her one footstep at a time around the back room of the flower shop, pausing for several minutes in front of each instrument of the trade. Shell wished she had something to take notes with, listening intently, feeling some details slip by her before she could catch them. Neve's voice was postcoded Northside, a little deep.

Maybe she'd been a smoker once. Shell tried not to stand too close to her, observing the odd distance of retail choreography. Follow-the-leader. She just followed her little by little, examining spools of chicken wire, different kinds of pliers, different formations of dense green foam.

In front of a large cabinet full of plastic tankards, Neve stopped, hands on hips. "Now this, this is important. These big bottles are full of fluids that prime the flowers—you've to be fairly careful here, you don't want to kill anything. I mean. They're already dead. But you don't want them to be dead-dead. These largely help them look alive." She then went on to list a ream of chemical-sounding names, and Shell felt herself zone in, hanging on her every word. Neve was speaking fast, and it wasn't long before Shell began to struggle to follow her, though she was desperate to keep up, desperate to seem competent.

She must have betrayed how overwhelmed she was feeling—eyes widened, mouth fallen slightly, knowing she wasn't going to be able to recall all of the names of different conditioning chemicals, not for a while. Shell hadn't learned anything new in quite some time—she'd been an expert in the field she'd been made redundant in and had become accustomed to just knowing what to do, what things were called. Here she was ignorant, and panicking that the sun was hardly rising on her first day at work and she wasn't able to even follow the names of different floral conditioners properly.

Neve noticed immediately and stopped.

"Bit too much too quick, right?" she said, eyebrows up.

"No, no—" Shell leapt to defend herself, but Neve wasn't having any of it.

"It is a . . . lot." Neve gestured to the workshop. "I know. I just haven't had anyone in here in a while. You know, when you're just used to something, you kind of forget how intense it can seem to someone seeing it for the first time. Let me get the kettle on. The first delivery'll be here any minute. I asked them to stop by at a reasonable hour today because I had help starting."

During the next half hour, Shell sat on the workbench, blowing steam off the fresh cup of tea from a ceramic mug that she had retrieved from a tiny kitchenette in the corner, watching Neve receive what seemed like an obscene quantity of flowers through the back door of the workshop from a large deliveryman. They gave each other a high five and chatted away as he passed her long cardboard box after long cardboard box. Neve refused Shell's help in lining them all up along the walls. "Oh, I'll put you to work with these soon enough, just watch for now," she assured her. It was all over quite quickly, an early-morning quick-step so rehearsed that they could move at an almost shocking speed. The boxes were an odd shape, flat, almost bigger than Neve's torso, but she handled them lightly. After the dance was complete and the back wall of the studio was entirely stacked with boxes, Neve gave the deliveryman another high five, tipped him a note, and sent him on his way. The door closed, and it was just Neve and Shell again, Shell's tea still nearly too hot to drink.

"These were cut in Holland yesterday evening, I ordered them last night, and here they are with us before sunup. I get a tonne of my blooms from there, but I cut my greenery and some other special pieces from the garden here in the Woodbine. Saves money," said Neve, lifting a box up beside Shell on the worktop. She went to move, but Neve waved her back, said, "Stay there, it's a good vantage point to watch what I'm doing."

She opened the box, and there, lying flat and flush, were two dozen white roses. Neve ran a hand down the stem of one and loosened it, thick leaves and thorns intact still, dressed as it had been when it grew in a farm far away. Shell could smell them, heady and definitive: rose. Grandmothers, weddings, powder, pink candies, cheap soap, fabric conditioner, hotels. The petals were crisp, paper blanched on the outside, but towards the centre blushed a very slight peach-pink. Neve lifted it to her nose for a second and inhaled, closing her eyes to it, her lashes thick on her freckly cheeks. She then passed it up to Shell—"Careful of the thorns, they're bastards"—who took it between her finger and thumb, and imitated Neve's same breath in. Shell found herself flush with the sheer perfume of it.

"Unreal," she said, passing it back to Neve, who was placing her apron over her sweater, preparing to get to work. There was a tiny moment, as Shell handed it to Neve, busy tying the cords of her uniform, when Shell imagined Neve with the rose taken between her teeth.

The crush had been immediate, and was steadily veering towards all-encompassing. It was making Shell a terrible learner. She couldn't remember the last time she'd met someone and been so immediately attracted to them. It hadn't really been like this with Gav, not so transfixing anyway—or had it?

Shell couldn't seem to remember; all of that felt so far away from the two of them there in the morning dark and all the flowers in tall boxes, and all the learning to be done in the absolute privacy of this workshop. It felt like a very small space, as though the room outside the direct heat radius of Neve and Shell had fallen away, as though they were the roof and walls of the space and the whole thing was just them and the roses and Neve softly demonstrating leaf and thorn removal using very specially designed gloves, saying how every stem must be stripped back firmly, but still delicately. How Shell would get fast at it in no time, would be doing it in her sleep. How you couldn't dig out the thorns, how you had to just blunt them, so as not to leave wounds on the stem of the flower. How they could become sick so quickly, and how that sickness spread amongst the other blooms. How by tomorrow these roses would be overblown and no good, but today they were at a perfect size for bouquets. They move quickly in their death: they are beautiful, they are lush, then they are no use at all, emitting a ripeness that forces other flowers to bloom faster if they're left standing around too long. Like an ecosystem of dead things, pulling one another further into decay.

Some of the words that Neve spoke to Shell were my words. We talked about life and death a lot, the two of us, and to me it seemed strange that she so easily parroted my thoughts about my kind to this stranger. I nudged her foot with a vine, just once, when I felt her get too romanced by the performance of explaining simple ethylene emissions—but she kicked me back. Of course she did. She's been kicking all her life. I like when she pushes back at me, my sweet, mean Neve. So wilful, taking as much pleasure in giving the show as Shell was, watching it. Shell hadn't noticed yet, but I did, that Neve wore her heavy ring on a chain around her neck today, not on her hand. She'd made that decision in the middle of the night, justified to herself back in her apartment that she'd be working twice as hard during Shell's first shift and she had to keep her hands clear, didn't want the ring snagging on anything. That made me laugh, deep and far away as I watched her string it around her neck and hide it under her sweater, still touching her body, still a vow made solid, but just out of sight. Giving it the opportunity to fall, then, out of mind.

"You know what," Neve said eventually, "you'd better go get something to write this down on, I've nothing around here. The supermarket'll be open, now, zip over and pick up a copy book or something. Will you grab me an apple and, like . . . I don't know, whatever you're having for breakfast? Something hot. And a flat white. Oat milk, double shot."

"Sure!" Shell snapped out of the headiness of listening to Neve's ream of plant facts. "Sure."

Neve gave her the store credit card and told her not to go wild buying lottery tickets and Bacardi Breezers on the flower shop's dime, and Shell said she couldn't promise anything, that she might swing by the Cassidy Travel shop and fly herself somewhere nice instead, and batting back jokes with Neve made her chest feel tight and her cheeks hot. It was easy.

"I can't believe I have an assistant to get me cups of coffee!" cackled Neve as Shell made her way out the front. "I'm going to be insufferable in no time!"

Shell was too far gone out of the shop to call back a reply, but she felt herself almost say something embarrassing like I doubt that's possible or I'm at your beck and call or I will literally do anything you say, so she moved quickly to get out of Neve's magnetic field.

The shopping centre was beginning to lift its lids, now, just seven in the morning. The inside was still dark, but there was a difference, like the corridors knew the sun had risen outside.

Some of the shutters were lifted a foot or so off the ground, so Shell could see the bright glare of shop lights spilling out onto the lino and hear the faint puttering of staff getting ready to open their shops. Nobody was really here yet, and not every shutter was up: most opened later in the morning, but the phone service shops and the pharmacies were slowly coming to life. Far down the main walkway, the front doors were ready to open, but no members of the public were coming inside. How immediately Shell felt like she was part of the crew, then, part of some secret league of people of the mall, here before she should be. This was not dissimilar to the feeling a tourist might get, blending in with locals in a country that does not care that they are present beyond the contribution their capital gives to the local economy—but Shell wasn't really aware of that. She didn't feel like a tourist: she didn't possess the self-awareness to perceive herself in that context. She felt, rather, like she was entering into some kind of romance with the space—though that might have been a residual high from listening to Neve talk about the roses.

She padded across the atrium space, past the newsagents and kiosks that dotted the floor, and looked, in the new bare dawn, up at my house. The tall, moss-dense walls of my terrarium. My fortress, the green eye of this building, of this whole region. I looked back at her, and she felt it, though she didn't know what the intensity was, putting it down to the big morning she'd had and the fresh crush on Neve. It was neither, it was me—and in time coming, she would know me and learn to identify this feeling, my presence, my gaze. But she had no vocabulary for me just yet.

At the very centre of the centre of the Crown, I am the glint of light in the emerald. Beyond the old glass, in the outdoors-indoors of the garden where nobody goes now but Neve, I start. I begin there, the petals of my head white, my eye, black. I finish out across the parking lot now. I reach for the thick road, for the school where the small children go. I'm not strong enough yet, but I will be. Strands of me are beneath every tile in this building. I am up in the empty blue swimming pool beyond the farthest escalator, behind the purifiers, the vents. I am braided with the wires that pump power to each storefront, I am in the filaments of the lights. Beneath the refrigerators in the butcher, wound under the ovens in the industrial bakery hidden where customers can't see, in the supermarket. I am as good as a nervous system to this mall, though it dies despite my effort. I am all listening, all feeling, and hundreds of bodies move by me, emotion falling off their skin, radiating, and most of it is slush but all of it is sustenance, though so rarely is it as brilliant as my Neve.

Shell would learn so many things, even if they were now just an instinct, just a sense of being seen, being known—though the extent of that knowingness was far, far past what she could guess. Hi there, Shell. Hello. I tapped the glass, inaudibly to her, more for my own entertainment than anything else. Her eyes were big and blue, a cold, liquid colour. Certainly not extraordinary.

She stopped for a moment then, past the lottery stand, and looked at the glass. She hadn't heard me. She was just wondering what was in here. If there was a door: if she could get inside and have a look around. Now that she belonged to the mall, surely she was within her right to explore, wasn't she? Staff-only zones were now Shell zones. A funny, easy arrogance from a person who had worked in the centre for three hours and couldn't even retain the names of different widths of floral wire.

But Shell didn't stop for more than a few seconds before she picked up her little migration towards the supermarket.

I had liked Shell immediately because she was not Jen, and Jen had helpfully disposed of herself back in January. To be clear, I was not the reason Jen left Neve. Jen did that all by herself.

It was so intimate, spying on their breakup. I loved it. Loved to see the tremor in Jen's hands as she clenched her fists by her sides, to be able to see the liquid dimension of the tears tumbling down Neve's cheeks. I was invited into the apartment that night, in my defence. Neve knew I was watching. She brought me in. I cannot listen from where I am not invited, placed, planted. I cannot move on my own. I am too small still. Perhaps this is why I am so hungry.

Sometimes my fronds are placed inside the greenery bunched with a handful of roses in a glass vase on Neve's kitchen counter. Sometimes I am placed in a little fern she keeps in the turned-up edge of the woolly hat she wears when it is cold and the flat won't heat. Sometimes, a single bloom of mine pinned to her sweater, right above her heart. Sometimes, too, I am planted inside her body, though I cannot always access her when she is gone too far from the place I grew from first. She rarely strays, though. She wouldn't. Doesn't like when I'm too far. I knew that night that she was glad I was there. I am always on her side, silently. Witnessing. How sad for her to be alone in this moment with her almost-broken heart. I would make sure she was never alone, not even for a second.

You know, in two years of proximity, I could never quite get a purchase on Jen. Jen often came home from her work in the laboratory doused in chemicals that made it hard for me to think and listen, even if I was inside of Neve's body, even if I was on the kitchen table in a slim ceramic jug. The reek of her, those days. The poison. Two years I tried to get ahold of her. But she was slippery. There were no little snags, no cracks in her veneer. Neve showed me to her. Neve let her see the place where we hide together. Neve invited her through that locked door, and Jen was immovable. She would not open herself up to me, not even a little.

Jen and her big American laugh. Her confidence, the self-assured way she would make jokes, all the time, almost as much for herself as for anyone listening. Even now, walking back and forth, pendulum, laying out the hard and lonely reality of her life with Neve to Neve herself, she was confident. Assured. Healthy. There was not a single cavity I could slip through, even now. If Jen hurt, the hurt was so far away from her surface that I couldn't taste it even if I swallowed her whole. This, and the chemicals, made her difficult for me to like, though it seemed I was the only one in Neve's life who did not like Jen.

I could never like anyone as much as I like Neve, even this woman Neve thought she loved so completely.

Neve loves me the very most. I am her Baby. She calls me that, always has. Baby is the name I have here. A sweet nothing of a name, though I am her everything.

I belong to her, she belongs to me. Jen had nothing to do with us.

Still, the *us* of me and Neve was not the reason Jen was leaving. Jen was leaving for a matrix of reasons, which she had spent the evening listing. The one that hurt Neve the most was that Jen had decided that Neve needed help, and she could not give Neve any help, not anymore. Help with what? With the shop, with the hours and hours of her life spent alone in the tiny alcove between a butcher and a vape emporium in a shopping centre rotting in broad daylight, condemned. Shilling houseplants and bouquets to the remaining customers who shopped there because they had nowhere else to go, because the Woodbine had been there since the 1970s, because it was the heaving old nerve centre at the very middle of miles of grey housing estates. She needed help with getting her shit together. With getting some perspective. With untethering herself. Jen had tried and failed. Jen didn't understand what Neve needed. I did, though.

Their apartment was small and warm and amber by lamplight, and Neve was smoking at the table, as Jen paced up and down the kitchenette, explaining. As if her explanations made any difference to the outcome: she was leaving. She had taken a job on the other side of the country. A good job. A great job, in fact. Precisely in her field. Another lab, a better lab. She'd asked Neve to come with her to this new place, months ago, and Neve said no. When the email landed in Neve's inbox saying they were shutting down the Woodbine Crown Shopping Centre, where her shop was and always had been, Jen asked her again to come with her, Look, look how the universe is sending signs that it's time to call it quits, that it's time to move on, she said. Neve said no. She loved that shop. Swore that she'd stay there until the very last day. Proclaimed, hand on her chest, that it was her home.

What she didn't say was that it was where I was born. Where I grew from first. Where she'd tended me, nurtured me. It was my home. So Neve's home was with me.

Jen said, I want to be your home. Neve said nothing to that.

She said nothing now, just months later, either, in the event horizon of Jen's departure. She'd known this was coming, she'd told me that. Seen it, felt it in Jen's absence, in an uncommon quiet that came over her while they got ready for bed, while they ate, Jen's eyes trained constantly on her phone. All the signs pointed to the exit Jen was making, and it was only now that she was announcing something she had technically already done. So instead of protesting, she just let Jen talk and pace and talk. Neve assumed privately that she had practiced this breakup with her therapist.

"I moved here for you, Neve. I packed my bags and left my country and came across the ocean for you. You can't get into a moving van and come, what, like, four hours with me? Four? For a clean start, a better life? Even for an adventure, you know? I adventured to get to you, I just didn't expect this to be, like, the end point. No buried treasure, no mountain to climb. I think you'll probably meet someone, someday, who makes you want to go—but I'm just . . . I'm not that person, and I've kind of made peace with that." Jen opened the refrigerator and took out a bottle of white wine that leant in the door and poured some into a mug. She tilted the bottle towards Neve to offer her some, and Neve nodded wordlessly. Jen opened the cupboard to get Neve a proper glass.

She took a couple of padding steps across the kitchen and handed it to Neve, who took it from her without making eye contact, then stepped back to her little stage, as far across the tiny room as she could get. She took a deep breath.

"The worst thing, Neve, is that I love you. I love you so much that I can tell whatever it is that's really going down in the Woodbine is hurting you—but I don't love you so much that I can let that place hurt me any more than it already has. I've just got too much fight in me, you know I do." Jen leant against the kitchen counter, and Neve ached, knowing that what Jen said was true. Jen would not go down with any ship. She would walk on water before she drowned. I found it exhausting, but Neve had, of course, found it thrilling. Jen had auburn hair, not quite red, thick and messy the second she released it from the tight braid she kept it in for work. She was short and spindly, and when she wasn't bound into her lab whites she wore T-shirts that were a little too tight for her and jeans that rode low on her narrow hips. Neve often found that Jen dressed like an extra in a television show from their youth—Neve thought the American had a Sky One 8 p.m. vampire slayer wardrobe, once she was out of her clinical uniform. It was so foreign to Neve, but she found it gorgeous even now, even in the hurt. Jen was barefoot as she stood there, and Neve could see the tender line below her belly and above her belt and realized she would never again put her mouth there, or on Jen's throat, or watch her toes— painted black—curl. The tattoo wrapped around her ankle that read JOLENE, JOLENE, JOLENE, JOLENE that always made Neve laugh a little when it appeared up at her shoulder. She wouldn't wrap her hand all the way around the anklet of those letters again. That was done. There was no sex in this fight, no lovemaking. Their bed had gone cold, and it was colder still now in the kitchen. I assured her that she wouldn't be wanting heat for long, though that wasn't much salve.

She'd found Jen on the internet. A closed community for professional and amateur botanists. Jen was an orchid specialist and Neve was a florist, and that was enough to lead them both to the same flickering set of pages. Little by little I watched their relationship materialize word by word, pixel by pixel. They quickly became enthusiastic emailers, which was convenient for me. Nice for Neve to have a little girlfriend who lived on the West Coast of America, a distraction for her friends, the others who worked in the Woodbine. A girlfriend, a smokescreen for Neve's work with me. Jen had been useful until she was real. Until she took it upon herself to migrate across the world for love, and moved right in with Neve, in on top of us. I tolerated her because I thought I would find a way to use her. I couldn't. I won't be so weak again. The next one, I will be cleverer with. The next one will be just right.

"Don't you have anything to say? Are you just going to sit there, Neve?" Jen was tiring of the sound of her own voice, the extent of her own litany. "I expected you at least to . . . I don't know. Resist. Bargain. Anything."

"There's no point." Neve stubbed out her cigarette and wiped her tears on her sleeve. "There's no point at all. You're right. I'm married to the Woodbine, to the shop, to the job. And if you don't want to be . . . committed to that place like I am, then you can't be committed to me. I get it. So why fight? I know you moved to this country for the green fields, not the grey shopping centres. So you go to the fields. I'll stay. I'm not going to imprison you."

"That's the thing, Neve, I think you are imprisoned by that place. Locked in. I'm trying to free you. I've been trying. That place is fucked, and you know it. I know it, too. I can't, like, unsee it or something. That stuff in the Green Hall—I don't like it," Jen said, shaking her head. "You go into the shop at four and stay all morning, all day, but you can't see the place for what it is. You know a guy drank himself to death there a couple of years ago? A kid went missing just before I moved here. You just walk in and walk out like nothing bad is happening, but the place it rotting in front of you. There's no honour in staying."

Neve shook her head. "Someone has to give them their flowers. And you make it sound worse than it is. I'm not the only one who stayed after the tragedies—Daniel, Bec—even little Kiero stayed, even after what happened to his sister. The local radio station is still open. The library still runs. That supermarket is busy, especially after five. The food court is packed with women, all hours of the day, new mothers, old ladies—the place isn't dead, Jen."

"No, but it is dying. And that's no good. No good at all." Jen took a deep swig from her mug of wine, then poured herself some more. She realized this was the most Neve had spoken all evening. She'd just let Jen talk before. But when the mall came up, she came online.

"Well, we have time. We don't know when they're closing, so it's business as usual until they come in and take us out." Neve's denial was firm. I wish I could have been in that sturdy, unmoving place with her, but I knew my days were numbered, our days. Neve was not ready to make a plan, but I wanted nothing more. I would wait for the right moment. The perfect opportunity.

Jen sighed heavily and shook her head at Neve's resistance. She had less patience for Neve than I did. Loved her less than I did. You see, they'd had this conversation before, a handful of times. It was like a song they kept finding themselves singing. They could be talking about whether to order in or throw together a meal and would somehow end up talking about the Woodbine. They would be trying to plan a little trip to the city or even just down to the coast on a rare crossed-over day off, and suddenly their conversation would be all wrapped up in whether the Woodbine was actually going to close or it was just scaremongering, whether they could just flatten the heart of the community, whether it was in fact the heart of the community. The parts always the same—Jen protesting against the Woodbine Crown, and her protests only tightening Neve's bonds to the place, to me. Jen couldn't understand how Neve felt about the place. She couldn't understand what it was like to have grown up working in a shop, to have inherited it under such distressing circumstances. To not have any other roads—Neve hadn't finished school, but Jen had a PhD. Neve made flowers into bouquets. Jen looked at their genetic makeup. This had initially brought them together, but the disparity sat between them, unmentioned, rancid. Giving off fumes that made both of them feel all wrong.

"Neve. We're not talking about the Woodbine anymore. We're not talking about the committees, or why they won't reopen the community pool. We're talking about us. And the fact that you are somehow making this breakup about your job is proof that I can't help you." Jen took her phone out of her pocket. "All roads end at the Woodbine, and if that is where this conversation has gone, again, then we're . . ." She wiped an escaped tear from her eye before it even crested her cheek. "Finished here. I'm going to stay at Bec's tonight. You don't mind her helping me out, right? You're not going to give her shit?"

Neve shook her head. "Not my style. I'm glad you two are close. Good to see."

Jen smiled a little and sniffled. "Thanks. Look, I'll come over with her tomorrow morning while you're at work to get my stuff, and then I'm going to hit the road. They have a single room ready for me on the compound. Maybe we can talk in, like . . . a week, or something."

Neve shook her head, letting her own tears flow.

"I think a full stop is the best thing for me, Jen. Talking after is . . . you know, going to hurt more. I don't think I can handle starting another written correspondence with you. No emails, no texts. We can call it here."

"You're right. You're right. Christ, Neve. How did it come down to this?" Jen put her cup into the sink without washing it, just like she always did, and walked to the doorway. Her coat, a quilted black bomber jacket with a little patch on the breast in the shape of a crescent moon, hung on the rack with Neve's cardigan, denim jacket, and work apron. Jen didn't have a lot of stuff. There hadn't been room for it in her suitcase when she moved. She only had one jacket, and Neve was watching it walk out of the apartment on her back for the last time.

"You just spent two and a half hours telling me how it came to this, Jen. We know how it came to this." Neve's voice cracked here.

I hated the noise of her pain. I hated the feel of her hurt. And me? I had nothing to do with it. I didn't make her feel this way. I would never. I only want to worship her. I only want to keep her safe.

Jen gave a small, sad laugh and slung her little bag over her shoulder.

"Thank you for this whole time, Neve. For the adventure. I really, really hope you get the help you need. I'll be thinking of you."

Neve did not want to give a parting blessing, but she did raise her glass across the flat in a silent salute to their time together.

"So long, Jen." Her voice was smaller than it had ever been.

"Good luck, Neve." Jen's voice wavered, in a kind of harmony with Neve's. She was out the door then. Calm, polite. So healthy, even in her sorrow. Disgusting. But, at least, gone.

Then it was just Neve and me. Me and Neve. Just the way it should be, just the way it had been for so long before. She sat in the quiet and lit another cigarette, and I do not like her smoking but it was a special occasion, so I did not give her any reprimand.

On her finger, one digit down from where she held a slim little Lucky Strike, was one of the rings she and Jen had made for each other in the first heady, duvet drunk, obnoxious and wet and stupid weeks of their courtship. A tight dark eel of a ring. A promise neither would keep. They'd each cut a lock of their hair and mailed it to a French craftsman they'd found while lazily browsing the internet together. By their two-month anniversary, two rings came back. Auburn and black with the slightest gradient of silver, bound with a wooden clasp. Delicate and fine, and when Neve put it on for the first time I felt the love soar in her like a wild bird. I did not know how Jen felt, but I did know that these dark rings were more than just symbols. They contained something. And now, now that their song was over and their courtship done, she surely had no need for it. Surely she could give it to me. Let me eat it, and all the feeling and memory inside it, too.

I asked her, in her ear, in my softest, nicest voice, Can I have the ring now, Neve? And she said, into the empty kitchen, "No, Baby. No. This isn't for you. You have enough. You don't get . . . this."

She so rarely said no to me. But her no then was porous. I could tell. It was open. I would find a way beyond it. The ring carried in it her heart. I knew it did. I could feel it. And oh, how I wanted to eat that heart up.

There are all kinds of things I have managed to eat in this world, with my vines and petals and tendrils and mouth. But Neve's heart, that red-gold thing in her, that was what would make me complete.

What would make us complete. Us.

I would find a way to crawl through the *o* in her no. But that night, in the smoky pain of her apartment, less Jen at last, I merely held her. I exerted what little energy I had in the clipping she took from my centre that sat in the vase beside her. I unfolded my green shoots and vines onto the tabletop like compassionate little garden snakes, and I wrapped them up her arms and shoulders and throat like the lover I am, like the lover she needs. She never resists this. I softly wormed a single vine up to the corner of her mouth, like a kiss, and she opened up, smoke on her breath, in a kind of surrender.

It was not total, but it was enough.

Shell was hungry, in that very particular airport way, from the before-dawn rise. She wondered when this kind of early start would feel more like work than holidays. In the supermarket, barren but for the occasional member of staff at a shelf or a counter, Shell admired what all of the laid-out vegetables looked like before they'd been touched by shoppers.

Neat, dense rows of oranges and bananas, perfectly set shelves full of sliced bread loaves. She wandered down past the butcher counter towards the thick household goods aisle and grabbed a pink notebook with illustrations of flowers on it from the small stationery shelf—appropriate, she thought to herself. At the deli counter she smiled warmly at the ladies who worked there, hair netted, decked out in white aprons and billowy plastic gloves. Shell was thrilled to notice that she was the first person to order from the hot deli—all the golden, fried food and bright, homogenous salads hadn't been touched by an order yet; they were all immaculate. While the rest of the space had a badly lit grimness to it, the deli counter felt fresh and holy. As though it had been cut and pasted from somewhere far more wholesome.

She thought about ordering herself and Neve some vegan sausage rolls, taking the cue from Neve's oat milk note for her coffee that perhaps she preferred to stick with plant-based foods. Shell herself wasn't vegan or vegetarian: she starkly lacked the commitment to either, but was happy to order the newest addition to any standard menu, out of curiosity. But Shell decided against it, ordering just two oat flat whites and plucking a plastic carton of melon pieces from the fridge instead.

She hated that she worried she would incur some kind of judgement from Neve (slender, clear-skinned, had asked for just an apple) for eating pastries at seven in the morning, like a hungover college student—though the intensity of their dynamic in the back room had felt like those heady connections that felt so easy to forge back then. She picked up a croissant for each of them as well. That felt like a nice middle ground. Croissants had a slight touch more class to them than sausage rolls. An adult food.

The apple Shell chose for Neve was the pinkest in the row. Just ripe, firm, the natural arc of it folded down onto itself where the stem rose from the core, almost, if she held it just right, like the shape of a rounded heart. She'd considered the deep red apples beside the Pink Ladies but felt it would be a little too much—like handing someone an organ, scarlet and alive. The green ones felt impersonal to her, tart, generic, void of symbolism. The pink was just right for their first meal together. Shell, telling herself these stories about apples as she selected one, felt entirely insane, but it made for a nice change from feeling sad and sorry for herself. There was something playful about a pink apple, something easy—and that was how she was hoping the mood would continue with Neve.

That was the feel she wanted. A blushing.

In the very middle of these handheld planets, black seeds were hard and ready to grow, though they never would. They would end in the bottom of a bin, gone, never to take to soil. But something in Shell was taking already. Something was yielding.

When she got back to the shop, Neve had stood bunches of flowers in buckets out front, just as they had been when Shell stopped by the other day. Things looked just about open. She must have gotten a lot done in the fifteen minutes Shell was gone. From the doorway, Shell could see Neve was behind the counter, binding up a bouquet, and there was a man there. They were talking and laughing. Shell tried her best to bat back the jolted feeling she had at seeing a customer so early—leaning over the counter. Maybe a friend? A friend of Neve's had swung by, and he was telling her a story, and she was not only laughing but cracking up. Shell felt embarrassed, ducking into the shop, like she was intruding.

The man was tall and heavyset, and wore all black but for bright white sneakers. His jeans were tight and he wore a long knit cardigan over them, almost capelike. On closer inspection, it actually was a cape—it looked incredibly expensive, a fine Scandinavian cut on it. Under his arm he held a wide-brimmed hat. Shell could see his ears were full of piercings, and his long dark hair was tied into a low, neat braid that faded into a white bleach at the tail.

"Shell! This is Daniel!" Neve exclaimed, gesturing with her almost-complete bouquet. She was rotating it with one wrist and adding to it with the other hand. Where the shelves in the shop had been empty, they were now rammed with buckets full of lush, dense greenery. Ten minutes really had made all the difference, Shell thought, giving Daniel a wave as he turned to her. He was handsome, highly decorated—a septum ring with a jewel in it sat above his top lip, and he wore thick winged glasses. His neck was tattooed almost up to his chin with what looked to Shell from here like honeycomb, gold and black.

"Ahh, here she is," he said, giving her a warm wave. "Great to meet you, petal—now, first things first, will you do the rest of us a favour and make sure this dope doesn't work herself to death in here, please? Don't let her tell you your job is junior executive flower arranger or anything like it. I'm here to tell you your job is making sure we don't find Neve dead in the back room from exertion, right? It's on your shoulders now, but if you need any backup I'm upstairs in the salon, and free anytime to come down and reef some sense into her."

Shell laughed. "I'll do my best—" and Daniel gasped.

"Wait. Michelle Pine?" he said. "Michelle Pine from Mercy House? You were in—Jesus, was it the Debs? Are you for real?"

Shell blinked, flooded by dread for an instant before she recognized him, and was steadied slightly by relief.

He looked so different, but the same kindness was there beyond his slick eyeliner and cloud of cologne. He was still the tallest man she'd ever encountered, and though being six foot five and gay in school in 2003 hadn't been a joy for him, he was clearly thriving now.

"Daniel Kavanagh," she said, "of Madam. The best synth-rock five piece to make it out of the De LaSalle, 2005 legends of the wider Edenmore-Donaghmede demesne. I still listen to 'Night Kick' at least once a week." She didn't, but there was no harm in telling him she did. To make a fuss of him gave her a better chance of getting out of this interaction unmortified, unhumiliated in front of Neve. "Jesus, I'm so sorry I didn't clock you!" If she kept the conversation focused on Daniel, she wouldn't have to say much for herself.

"I'm on the other side of a glow-up, babe, I'm glad you didn't," he said. "You, though, haven't aged a day. How are the rest of the Debs? Haven't seen yous all together since we mopped the Woodbine Community Hall with you at the battle of the bands, summer after the Leaving Cert."

Shell blinked. How *were* the rest of the Debs? Their group chat lay mostly dormant except for the round robin of happy birthday messages—they'd grown apart, as most secondary school cliques of girls did, ten years into the rest of their lives. Shell had gone to college to study design. Wee Cara—lead guitar—

had gone to Galway to work in a pub and had both married and divorced a man twenty-five years older than her before the age of thirty herself. Aisling—on bass—had two kids and still lived somewhere around Donaghmede and as far as Instagram showed her, Tall Cara—the drummer—was managing an Irish bar in Portugal.

"They're good," she chirped instead. "We stay in touch, have a reunion brunch once a year!" They actually hadn't done so for the last four years, but they had attempted to make an annual reunion, for a while—Daniel didn't need to know that, though.

"Ah, god, you were a great bunch of goers, lovely pipes on you, Michelle, such a shame it's so hard to keep it together when everyone has jobs. Madam were going up until around three years ago—we'd a great run at it before everyone, well, got pregnant."

"Where are you working now?" Shell asked. "I'm—well, here with Neve as of today." She'd long taught herself not to add "We should get coffee" to the end of every statement, and she felt herself stop short of it, though as she passed Neve her flat white and apple and croissant she added, "I would have grabbed you a coffee if I'd known you were around!"

"Ah, you're a dote, but I can't have more than one cup a day or I'm bouncing off the walls. I'm lead stylist upstairs in Billie's—we're rushed off our feet nowadays, all the ladies of the wider Donaghmede expanse are sweating that we're shutting down. I truly think they're only there for the gossip about when we're closing and what they're building here, not for their perms and wet sets at all. You're to come up to me when you need your roots done, yeah?"

Shell said she would, and meant it. That was a nice compromise, a bridge to the old world.

Daniel gave her a warm smile and pointed firmly at Neve. "I swear to god you're to let her work, Neve. Lighten the load. I'll be keeping an eye on you. And please, Jesus, come up and let me fix your undercut—you're so shaggy, I can hardly look at you."

Neve raised her hands in surrender, the thin white scars pale against her palm—and, Shell noticed, no rings on her fingers today. "Daniel. I swear I will let Shell work and that I'll let you shave my head."

"Good. Now I'm going up to the Marys and Carmels and Dymphnas to do their perms and tell them they're great soldiers for putting up with all they put up with at home, and I'll see you tonight." Daniel gave Neve finger-guns and swirled out of the shop, Shell and Neve calling "Seeya, great to see you again" until it was just the two of them and me once more.

Shell fought the urge to ask Neve "What's tonight?" because, though she desperately wanted to know, it was absolutely none of her business, and the nice tension between them had to warm up again now that they'd been visited, their rhythm broken. Asking "What's tonight?" implies a caring, a curiosity. Shell felt both these things acutely about Neve—they had come on her like a fever—but betraying them so quickly wouldn't do. Shell wanted to invite herself into Neve's evening, or even have the imaginative line that would let her picture Neve's evening for herself. There was so much mystery, Shell realized, about this person to whom she was so attracted, so suddenly—and though she wanted to vacuum up all the answers to Neve's existence, she wouldn't.

To have a crush accelerate like this felt inhuman to Shell—and I would love to tell you that it was me spiralling through her, pushing her on, warming her blood. But it wasn't.

Isn't that delightful—that Shell felt this crazy all by herself? I didn't have to do anything, not crawl into the tiny muscles of her pupil and open her eyes wider to take in more of Neve's light, not elevate her heart rate. Nothing. The disaster was forming all by itself, and all I had to do, for now, was watch. Lucky me.

The hours darted by as Neve led further technical instruction and Shell took big, clear notes and drew diagrams in her little notepad. This study was just beginning.

Shell reluctantly signed out at midday. She offered to stay, but Neve shook her head—an eight-hour shift is an eight-hour shift, though the shop wouldn't close until nine when all the lights went out in the mall. Neve swore the rest of the day's work was mostly calm, and ushered her out the door just as the Crown was hitting its stride. The shop, by then, was almost sold out—she and Neve had darted and ducked from the back room to the shop front, taking orders, fulfilling orders, bunches and baskets and wreaths. She found the smell of them heartening. The lush, dense fragrance from the greenery and the flowers—it was good for her heart. It dragged her out of the concrete. It was a busy shop, though Shell had been sure busy shops didn't exist anymore, given that nobody really went to places like the Crown at all for anything other than supermarkets. When she remarked upon this, Neve laughed at her.

"People will always want flowers," she said. "People will always be born, age, and die. Flowers can say nothing at all, or everything. When things are coming together, or more often, when things are falling apart, people turn to flowers."

"Yes," said Shell, understanding that when she had fallen apart, she had done the very same.

Miracle.

That was what Neve had called me when I spoke to her first, before I was Baby.

And she was right, and she was one herself.

I had watched her for years. Marked her as a child, clutching magazines and sweet drinks at her mother's side, running her tiny hands along the glass of my sun room, my terrarium. My vines under her sneakers, teenaged, as she put on the apron for the first time, her aunt passing her the sharp scissors of the florist, saying Cold hands, bright flowers, warm heart. She did try to leave, a couple of times. But she didn't. She wouldn't.

She comes to me every night after the Crown closes, after all the shop fronts are shuttered and the fountain is off and the security guards tip invisible hats to her from their booth, jangling their heavy keys in a *bap-bap-bapbapbap* rhythm as a reminder to not be there too late, and she blows them kisses back against the scold, kiss-kiss-kisskisskiss. This was not how she would be with anyone else, not so playful. Only I get to see her softness now. The only other people left in the Crown are the staff of the radio station, but that is far enough from the terrarium, from me, that they don't notice her there at all. Their music plays down the narrow hallways, louder in the absence of shoppers. My Neve ghosts softly around the mall, apron off. The movement sensors sometimes set lights off, like the building is responding to her—this is how she makes me feel. Like a huge, ancient hallway alight, like the veins of me are flooded with gold, with good.

There is nothing good about me. Not a cell. But Neve makes me feel as though I could be. Golden. Good.

If only she'd give me her heart.

When she comes into my glass garden I feel every leaf in the place rise to her, salute, adoration. She unlocks the door with her key, and she locks it behind her. Behind us. It is just me and her and the insects now. They are not watching, though they have many eyes. I blind them when she is here, so it is just her two eyes and my one and we look at each other in silence for a long time.

She fills the small silver tin with water from the hose and pours it down over me into the earth where I meet the underneath of the world and where my network begins. I need her to feed me. It has to be her, it has to be Neve. I let her think it is the water that keeps me growing, but it was never the water, it is her voice and the things she tells me. She speaks about the people she has seen—though I have seen them, too—and she tells me about how she feels, turning the black ring on the chain around her neck with anxiety, always inward, always toward the heart. A delicious movement that ripples down into my roots and into the soil; her worry is as gorgeous as her delight. When I raise my vines, thin from the ground, to touch the ring she has hanging at her chest again, again, like I do every time, she pulls it off, and shucks it into a pocket, away from where I can access it. Sneaky.

She tells me about taking on Shell. She tells me she likes her. That she seems kind. That she seems like she could do with a job. Like she could be of use, she could help.

I use my voice to speak back to Neve and I say from my petal mouth, I love her already. We need her. I do not say why.

Day in, day out, three days a week for the following month, I watched and I watched. I watched keen and close as they worked, as Shell learned and Neve maintained her business, slowly allowing the pressure of keeping the shop open to be alleviated by Shell's fast composition of bouquets, her earnest interest in the care and maintenance of houseplants, her growing efficiency in conditioning and preparing the daily flowers.

She didn't make many mistakes, didn't lose Neve any money, kept her company.

Shell felt, showing up in the dark every morning, Hole or Metric or No Doubt blasting in her ears, that she would be a good investment for Neve's business. That, and her Instagram was starting to gain followers, leaving hearts and comments underneath the bright, Technicolor pictures she took of her bouquets every day. She felt rejuvenated, youthful almost, under Neve's command.

She hadn't felt this good in a year, maybe more. The Crown felt less and less like a bleak suburban fortress every day—it softened to her. Became almost gauzy. This might have been my work, my pollen in the air, or it might have been that Shell was so lonely, so desperate to belong that even the run-down brutalism of a desolate shopping mall could easily feel romantic to her. The romance might have begun with Neve, but it certainly began to extend to the Crown.

She was happy to go to work, got herself out of her bed and into her day with no hesitation. It was so nice to just do what Neve told her, in the cool back room of the shop.

Cut these; take the dead petals off the edges of these; she needed fifteen bouquets for a large bridal party by the end of the day so please don't damage a single one of these cream roses; yes, Neve, no, Neve; anything you say, Neve. Anything.

Shell's hands were cold from the work, but her heart was warm and her blood grew hotter every shift. Lovely to see. Delicious.

I watched the dozens and dozens of funeral wreaths the pair assembled before dawn, circle after circle brimming with lilies, dusky lavender roses, dark ferns that would hold their green for weeks on top of a freshly laid grave. I watched the pink rise in Shell's cheeks when Neve told her she'd done a good job, said things like Beautiful, beautiful job, and Oh, that's gorgeous, so impressed by her work, her effort, her skill. Shell would play the sound of Neve's voice back in her head when she was alone and chase the feeling it gave her like it was a wild rabbit under her skin.

All her emotion and desire, as pleasing as it was, was the background as I witnessed Shell gradually learn the route between what she knew about design and what she didn't know about floristry. Coloured petals that spoke to one another, textures of greenery that lay best behind different kinds of blooms. She ordered books from the internet on the subject. She sat at night with her mother at the kitchen table, poring over encyclopaedia-like volumes of instructional books, hardbound and white-covered, some illustrated with photographs of flowers taken long before she was even born. She discovered one of her sisters was allergic to lilies and so had to stop bringing them home—her father didn't like them, either, their saffron-golden pollen staining tablecloths and sideboard runners as it tumbled from the long, dragon-tongue antennae at their centres.

I watched her interest shift, deepen, and become sincere. Sooner than I'd anticipated, she took well to the soil. Cozied down there, germinating.

Her skin was dappled heavily with freckles, interconnected fair markings, all up and down her arms. She had a very soft laugh, and when Neve said something that took her off guard and she couldn't compose herself, the laughter fell silent and she would shake with it, which was so pleasing to see and to feel. Because of her attraction to Neve, every morning she would make an effort to brighten herself somehow. A tiny triangle of black at the corner of her eyelid; liner placed just past the edge of the natural redness of her lips, to make her mouth seem bigger. She showered every night, something she had never done, so that she always smelled like soap and togetherness, so that she could show Neve in these sensory details that she cared about herself. She largely saw nobody but Neve and the fleeting crowds through the centre, the ladies at the deli who had taken to warmly greeting her on her coffee run, but Neve's eyes on her were enough. Shell wanted to give off a glow that would silently tell the florist that she was good. She was soft, and she smelled nice, and the details of her were organized in order to please.

The constant rinse and chemicals and pliers and twine and wire of floristry took a toll on her hands, but she kept her nails filed and painted, and a small tube of hand cream in her apron pocket. This was not, she noted to herself one morning, applying a pink blush to the apples of her cheeks, how she would try to physically express her feelings if she were attracted to a man. It wouldn't be composed of so many details. With men it had always felt more like exertion than care—more like performance than tenderness. She had been with Gav for years, though, and the last time she had been single she was in her early twenties and buck insane with the newness of adulthood, so perhaps she wasn't adding up the score correctly.

She looked at her phone less, checked her group chats less. Ignored a new one that popped up, Kayla's Hen. It took Shell a second to work out who Kayla even was—a friend of Gav's, marrying another friend of Gav's. An acquaintance. A hen party full of partial strangers who only knew her as an ex, a person who would not be having a hen of her own—a potentially two-or three-day-long psychic torture session in an Airbnb somewhere in the Midlands, or worse, Lanzarote. They didn't need her there. She turned off notifications for the app, archived away that group chat with all the others, numbers of unread messages so high they lost meaning.

Her posts began to rack up almost a thousand little digital hearts, little likes. While her messages went unread, her Instagram broke ten thousand followers, ten thousand strangers. She got a little lift from it, but nothing compared to the validation it would have given her before the shop. It was nice that they were there. The number, the *10K* on her screen, felt like a victory—but she wasn't sure over what. Neve had laughed at her when she showed her in the back room, said she should have gotten the shop on Instagram sooner, might have helped business. Shell had put her phone away, a little ashamed. She'd hoped it would impress her.

That night, while her mother caramelized onions for a tart in the kitchen, she drank two large bottles of pear-and-strawberry cider and deleted every single photo before that first bouquet. Her mother said, "Good girl yourself. Fuck them," and Shell agreed, yeah. Fuck them. This was who she was now. She changed her account description to *Shell. Junior Florist in the Woodbine Crown Mall, Dublin 5*—and included the shop's phone number, too. There. Bouquet emoji, crown emoji, crescent emoji, sparkle emoji. She'd hand the following over to the shop. She wasn't who she'd been. Now she was a girl in a digital field of bouquets, crucifixes, wreaths. Who she had been before didn't matter. She ignored emails about freelance job offers, contracts, interviews. Let texts sit unread, including several from Gav. The path ahead of her was strewn with petals; the path behind rippled with flames.

She let the flowers, and Neve, pull her along. Neve gave away so little about her own life: her family went unmentioned. The ring remained on a chain around her neck, not on her hand. Shell and Neve talked only about what was around them in each moment. Flowers, music, a little of the news, the shopping centre. Daniel from the past—and from the salon—would pop in once or twice a week, but Shell found herself hiding from him with busywork. Not because she didn't like him, necessarily, more because she was sure he was talking to a past version of her, not a current one. He'd known her years ago, and she didn't want to find herself proving that she was different, acting something out. I hadn't thought she had the self-awareness to be capable of this choice, but it was a surprisingly wise one. Yes, it was informed by a cowardice of sorts, but also of a strange dignity, a refusal to be witnessed or judged. Just as she deleted herself from the internet, and replaced herself with flowers, she did so here in the shop, too. She liked pretending she had no responsibility to anyone but Neve.

She did always have something to do, something to build, anyway. The two women existed only to each other—until, three weeks and two days into Shell's time in the shop, Neve made her an invitation.

Shell was on her knees on the concrete floor, taping ripe bananas to a bucketful of tight, closed lilies they needed for a funeral the next day.

She had, as Neve had shown her on her first week, fashioned a sort of hood out of a black plastic bag, which she would sheath over the lilies, trapping them with the ethylene gas that the bananas, freckled and browning, would give off. This would speed up the decay of the lilies, opening them to their full, starry bloom, white and magenta and gold with pollen. As tasks went, it was gross, and surreal, but it worked. A sharp reminder that all of floristry was a dance around decay.

Neve walked into the storeroom and said, "Hey, Shell, what are you doing tonight?" and Shell's heart stuttered and her mouth went dry and time slowed to a pause as she considered how to answer. She was glad she had her back to Neve, so that Neve couldn't see the blush as it crept quick up her neck, pink and obvious. She had fantasized about this question from Neve a hundred times already, and I had witnessed every single fantasy; no dream was private from me. Was this an acknowledgement of the tension and warmth between them? Was she going to ask Shell over to her mysterious, anonymous home for dinner? Was she going to reveal that she did not, in fact, have a partner? Would she ask her to stay on for a later shift? Did she need her presence more around the shop? The power of this invitation was electric—it opened a portal between them, a hole in the fabric of the air in the back room. Yes, Shell was sure she felt something shift as she looked over her shoulder and replied honestly, "Same as usual. Drinking wine and watching YouTube with my mam." She meant, I will do whatever you want me to.

The answer was a statement of miserable fact, but Shell didn't feel self-conscious about it, not in the same way she might have before.

"Well, I—I've been thinking," began Neve, and Shell had been thinking, too, thinking constantly, and hope rose in her like a wild bird with wings the length of every wish she'd ever made in her sad, small life. "Me and the others—there are a handful of others who've been working here almost as long as me, Daniel and two others." Others, she kept saying, and Shell's flight of hope sank lower but did not hit the ground, rather coasted more realistically. "We have this silly thing—this kind of club, I suppose you could call it. We used to drink in the Woodbine Crown Inn next door twice a week, but since the whole . . . condemned thing, the atmosphere in there is just kind of off. So we drink, like, just us, up in the food court. I have an understanding with the night security, it's all good—we don't have to bump into any of the other staff from the Crown, we don't have to deal with customers outside of work hours. It's a sort of . . . biweekly party? A club. I know calling it a club makes it sound painfully uncool, but it is actually cool. And I asked the others if I could bring you, and they said yes, if you'd like to come up for a few cans. If you'd rather hang out with your mam or if you two have a standing thing going on, I totally understand, but I thought I'd ask."

Neve was nervous, asking her. I loved this, all of Neve's cool coming apart for just a moment, caught in the same risk as Shell, the same will-we-won't-we, what's-happening-here matrix of potential, of suggestion and rejection. Shell caught this nervousness and liked it, warmed to it, wanted to soothe it, said, "Oh my god, yes, sure," before she could consider that maybe drinking around Daniel would make her vulnerable to interrogation, before she could ask who the others were. She wanted to put her *yes* all over Neve, she wanted to wrap a yes around them both. She didn't care anymore that Daniel knew her from before, she cared that Neve had invited her into her life, a secret club—that her presence within this tiny structure meant that she was part of something, part of the Woodbine Crown. This was not invitation to a quiet dinner, just the two of them. It wasn't a suggestion that they go for a walk down by the coast. It wasn't intimate, but it was an opening—it was Neve pulling Shell into another tier of her life. It was Neve asking to see who Shell was socially; it was Neve showing Shell to her friends. How pleasing, how gorgeous to be called into someone's life, Shell thought, as they said, "Okay, okay, deadly, deadly," over each other and

Neve said to come back to the shop at closing time, which gave Shell a few hours at home to reassemble herself and trill in the excitement of having something to do.

When Neve went back out to the shop front and Shell went back to her bucket, her bananas, her tape, her lilies, her strange contraption, she smiled heady and hot-cheeked to herself with excitement.

Worrying about Daniel would come later, when she was at home, reapplying eyeliner and mascara, picking out a slightly different outfit, arguing with her mam about whether it was classy to drink a whole bottle of wine up there or whether she should stick to cans or even bring a gift for everyone as a thank-you-for-inviting-me—like snagging her cardigan on a door handle and pulling loose stitches from the wool, Shell realized it was Daniel's judgement she'd worry about. She worried, too, that Daniel would have given the others Neve had mentioned some kind of impression of her from her teens, which would outweigh Neve's good word for her. Shell felt her estate and teenage years rise hard against her then, as though she would somehow find herself in a loose, secret social club for the first time in her life and be denied a blank slate for the presence of a spectre of her younger self: singer in a shit band, talkative, messy, all wrong. No amount of expensive organic cotton handmade dungarees and coconut leave-in-conditioner could overshadow the fact that Daniel remembered her from her neediest, weakest years. The tattoos on her forearms and her elegant, clean makeup wouldn't hide the fact that her body was eighty pounds heavier than it had been back then. She was more beautiful now, for sure. But she was older. Though Daniel himself had playfully remarked upon his own transformation, so perhaps he would be empathetic to hers. He was kind, she had to remind herself. He always had been.

Of course, he hardly remembered a single thing about her, but Shell's own overwhelming sense of self-importance blew her image up in the mind of others and here again I wished to hiss to her through her headphones as she placed them into her ears to leave, Nobody thinks of you how you think of yourself, nobody thinks of you at all, but I didn't, I was not known to her yet, though I would be so soon. She was about to join Neve's little drinking club, but our secret society was yet to commence.

It was coming, though.

Neve was opening up her world to Shell, and at the centre of Neve's world is me, green and enormous and spooling, whether she likes it or not I am the seed at the centre of her selfhood. It would be any day now that she would show me to Shell, so my patience held firm—the wanting strengthened me, and my vines grew from the power of anticipation alone.

Bec, babes,

I know I said I'd write, but the nearest post office is literally a thirty-minute drive from the compound. Can you believe it? Anyway, look, due to the antique infrastructure in the locale of the outer Burren, email is going to have to do for now. Can we still be pen pals?

I'm typing this into an incognito window on my work laptop, in the lab. I look so busy and am functionally stealing government money by wasting their time and being a pen pal on the job. I feel like I'm owed the few minutes, given they didn't build the post office nearer the conservation center, right? It balances out. Over the top of my screen I can just about see Tall Lab Assistant Siobhan, and I'm not going to lie to you, I want to climb her like a tree. Is it too soon to say that? Is it too soon to feel that? Don't tell Neve there's a hot tall lab tech. I feel like she'd be angry or hurt if she knew you and I were talking, let alone if she knew I was reporting on the heat of the six-foot-one orchid specialist I work with. She's wearing really bitchy rectangular tortoiseshell glasses and basically doesn't say anything to me other than a spicy little "Good morning, doctor!" when I come in, and then "Have a good night, doctor!" when we're signing off in the evening. I'm no better than a man, Bec. Doctor. Imagine being called by your honorific. That'd be like you getting called Agent. I feel like Agent is cooler than Doctor.

To be honest I'd actually prefer if she was cool, rather than hot? They're all a bit stilted down here. You'd think between the remote lab and the garden and the Burren and all the pollen in the air that they'd be a little wilder or something. I feel like a crazy person, you know? I just need to blow off some steam, but they all just . . . go back to the compound after our shift, head off to their rooms and close their doors, and I don't see them again until the next day. There's a recreation center onsite, but it's just never used. Unless there's a secret after-hours bone-dancing situation going on that I'm not invited to because I'm new and an American. God, I'd be so mad if there was. I'm here months, and it's basically like being in a monastery. Even monks drink wine in Europe, right? I miss what we all had at the Crown, you know. That was all so easy. I promised myself I wasn't going to start talking about it, but I'm still so sorry I had to go the way I did. The breakup needed to be quick, you know? And I feel guilty, too, like I left for this new place, this new job, this clean slate, and Neve's life stayed the same. It's kind of easier to heal if you're dropped into a different world. I didn't have to adjust to our apartment, or, like, any empty chairs at the table.

Starting to worry that I'm a dick. Am I? Maybe I am. I'm mostly convinced that in the end of the thing itself, Neve was a dick, but possibly I'm also a dick. We're both dicks. Please tell me if I was a dick. But, like, gently. I'm sensitive.

Look, she wasn't well. I said that to you, didn't I? I don't want to sell her out fully because you know how cagey she is, but I feel like someone should be looking out for her and also selfishly, if I don't talk about this to someone I'm going to crack up. I'm not sure it'd make a great opener with Tall Lab Assistant Siobhan. Please, please tell me to fuck off if this isn't appropriate—the silence out here has made me weird. I thought I'd, like, graduated therapy after I left Donaghmede, but I think I might have jumped the gun.

Maybe I need to host a party in my quarters to break some of the ice out here. Strip poker and charcuterie. Mimosas and Twister. Never Have I Ever and big bricks of hash. Anything, Bec. Anything to get these people going.

Tell me how you are, oh my god. All the details. Spare nothing. Gossip would be deeply appreciated. How's Daniel getting on? Has he met anyone nice? Has Young Kiero (sorry, sorry, he's just so young it drives me insane) moved to London yet? How's the apartment coming along? Please send me all your interior design mood boards—this place is like an airport hotel, I just want to look at some wallpaper options. Let me decorate vicariously through you. I miss you, pal. I miss, like, everything.

The missing has only gotten worse over time. At first I didn't feel anything, because I was too busy and tired from the job, all distracted and kind of glamoured by the wilderness of it all. But now that I'm settled in, I've got time to wish I was able to have a few drinks with you and the boys. Neve, too. Even if me and her didn't work, being part of the Food Court Supper Club worked.

Write me back! I love you and I hope this whole email-instead-of-letters thing doesn't feel like administration! If it sucks I'll go to the post office, you're worth the journey!

Xoxoxo,
Dr. Jen

Jen pulled back from her laptop with a sigh, tugging the heavy cans of her headphones down around her neck where they sat like a collar over the soft little lapels of her lab coat. Trying to ask for Bec's help was going to be a nightmare.

Jen wasn't sure if her perky tone covered how guilty and ashamed she felt—she'd disappeared. She'd up and evaporated. She'd broken up with Neve and left two days later. She'd waited too long to instigate this contact. This friendly, normal, cheery contact. The Oh my goodness I've been so busy I've been meaning to reach out was bullshit and if she was lucky, Bec would see through it quickly and ask her what was really going on.

Bec would lean towards her and ask for a secret, surely—that was what Bec did at a certain point in all their nights out, all their parties up in the food court, shoulder to shoulder, perfume and coconut rum, Go on. Tell me a secret, and God forbid you refused, she'd insist, insist, I need secrets! They sustain me! You're keeping me alive! Have you ever stolen anything? You must have. Of course you have. What was it?

In starting to correspond with Bec, Jen was ready to hand over an answer to all those drunken queries. You want a secret, Bec? I've got one for you, but it's heavy and weird, and I don't know how the hell to give it to you. So let's start with small talk. Start soft. Pretend like no time has passed. Like a season hasn't evaporated. Like we just left off.

The lab was cold, and she hugged herself a bit. The other specialists were at their stations, heads down, almost invisible behind their screens, deaf to the room under their enormous soundproof headphones. What Jen wouldn't have given for a cigarette break with one of them, someone to lean against a wall with and say, I have to help someone that doesn't want help, by telling the darkest secret of their life. How do I do that? and even if they didn't have an answer, saying it aloud would at least feel like something.

Someone on this team would care. Someone who had witnessed a tragedy. Someone she could reach out to and meet in her strange pain. They'd all had lives before they took up roles down here, just them and the Burren and the samples. Their silence, their contentment and dedication to their work was maddening to Jen. It was so far-flung from what she'd had, back in Neve's life at the Crown. Everyone constantly gagging to be off work so they could sit around talking. It felt like being in college, though she was the only one of the group who had attended college: they had all just started work at the Crown instead. Work was only kindling for their lives, not the whole fire, not the only source of heat and light.

In some ways this colder monastic choice, this exodus to a professional hermitage across the country had been the right call. A total purge of Neve, the Crown, everything. A blank slate. The luxury of it, to just leave a bad situation and not look back. But when you leave at that speed, there are things you forget. A hard truth of this breakup was that Jen missed Neve's life more than she missed Neve. She'd tell Bec that. She wasn't afraid of that truth, not even a little.

Jen composed the email like it was a piece of music. It was the hardest thing she'd ever written, first in a series of terrible, hard things. If Bec leant towards her, hungry for secrets, for friendship, for intimacy just how she always was, then she would be given another verse of the song, a harder verse, an uglier verse, sung in Jen's bright, friendly tone.

After she hit send, she had to get up off her chair and walk around to shake off the dread. The air-conditioning in the lab was ramped up, whirring ambient pink noise. She'd kill it with the noise cancellation on her headphones, disappearing back into her screen once she had balanced herself. What she would have given for a single person in this room to talk to her, to really talk to her. Someone she could have maybe even practiced reading the email out to, asked, Hey, does this sound right? Does this sound pushy? Does this sound like I have an agenda? She did have an agenda, was the thing, and even if she was hiding it badly, she hoped she wouldn't be hiding it for long.

Walking to the Crown from home at nine in the evening was a different trip than the predawn voyages Shell had been taking for work. She had barely been out at nighttime proper since the breakup, which lent this trip a sense of almost-scandal. Her parents had laid her a gentle "Don't go overboard" when she told them she'd be drinking with some of Neve's friends from the mall. A casual warning. Shell couldn't really remember the last time she had gone out-out, sat with a group of people she didn't know. She was nervous meeting Neve in this context, outside of the clearly defined roles they had in the shop.

They still hadn't touched, not really, in a way that wasn't accidental or split-second, in the act of passing scissors or some tape or wire. Shell had no idea when the last time was that she'd touched someone outside of her home. Gav, maybe.

So she'd stay enough away from this social club. Keep a sensible distance, even though she craved contact. Besides, she was only a visitor. A guest. No use presuming she'd want to get close to them; either with her body or through conversation. She didn't have her earbuds in, or anything for this stretch across the estate and copse. She sometimes felt safer without them, like she could hear someone behind her if she was in danger. I found this shift in her concern for her safety funny—how some dark outsides felt worse than others. She was nervous: there was almost a nostalgia around the sense of insecurity she felt.

The urge to impress Neve's friends. The shyness around Daniel, observer and keeper of her past. She leant against the closed shutter of the Crown just like in the morning, but not at all like in the morning, and texted Neve.

hey! i'm here! Bouquet emoji.

Two blue ticks. Read.

Sound, on the way, replied Neve.

This speed gave the sense that she might have been waiting for Shell's contact—the instantaneous reaction was a kind of balm. Neve had, in fact, been waiting for Shell and was also very nervous, but for bigger and more tangled reasons than Shell could imagine. Any assumption, any curiosity that Shell had about Neve's private life was feeble in contrast to the depth of my best girl's inner landscape. Even her world outside me, outside us, before we were truly united and became as we are now. Neve was enormous, and I only made her bigger. I simply filled the palace of her with light, with green, with heat.

The wait for a head around the door to let her in felt excruciating to Shell. Longer than usual, longer than the duration of "Bathwater" from *Return of Saturn,* which she felt herself mouthing to match the time, the heavy slow funeral brass speeding up and up, and nobody was coming into the second verse. Shell stood in the car park night glow, so different from the morning. The McDonalds ran a drive-through even when it was closed. It was a strange location, forever open. She'd been taken there on Saturday afternoons in her childhood, and there it was. Still running somehow. She could kind of smell the oil and sweetness on the air. The parking lot was all gold and dark blue and speckled red taillights on the cars crawling around the side of the building. Shell watched and waited. The song ended.

It wasn't Neve who eventually opened the door, peeking her head out as usual—rather, a long, tattooed arm holding a wide-brimmed hat dipped out of the crack between the outside and the clandestine, locked mall. Daniel was Neve's emissary. Shell laughed warmly at the showmanship. She slipped in the door to him and Daniel said, "Willkommen, bienvenue, welcome," and the big central aisle that led towards the atrium was almost pitch-black, and my terrarium was a dark emerald but the central chamber was lit and the still escalators lit and the food court was lit, too, and waiting.

Daniel hurried Shell in and locked the heavy industrial staff door behind her with a fat set of keys just like Neve's. It gave a thick, faraway locking sound, and that was that. She was in. Shell reached into her tote and handed Daniel a small purple tin of passionfruit soda and gin, as well as removing one for herself. She had twelve more in the bag. Better to come overprepared than under-. Hard seltzer barely did any work on her, anyway. It was more for the gesture of drinking than for dealing any actual psychic damage.

"Walking can," said Shell, opening hers.

"A can for the walk—you're a lady of taste," replied Daniel, opening his, and they moved through the dead hallway towards the escalators. "I'm so glad Neve finally got her guts together to invite you, Shell. We've been asking her for weeks, but she wanted to keep you all to herself," he went on. "Such a typical Neve move, but now she's let you in we won't be letting you go!"

Shell was disarmed. "Oh, that's so lovely to hear," she started. "I've had such a weird, quiet year that I sort of forgot what it was like to be invited places."

"Ah, we're hardly *places* now, but we've been keeping each other going. This kip would put years on you; we needed a regular sesh for sanity. Such a pain in the hole, all of this, worrying about the closure, trying to keep going without knowing what's coming next. You just moved home, didn't you? I'd to do the same a few years ago myself."

As they moved towards the magazine kiosk, the first fountain, layered with coins and dead still, switched quiet for the night, Daniel began to ask questions in a buoyant, clever hairdresser's way. Shell liked him but gave simple answers, feeling her guard go back up.

"Had you a breakup?"

"Yeah, in winter."

"How long were you together?"

"Seven years."

"That's shite."

"It was, yeah."

Maybe it had been so long since anyone had really asked her anything about herself that Shell had accidentally become incredibly defensive—suspicious, even—about why anyone would want to know anything about her last relationship. The duration, the ending, the hopes she'd had for her life with Gav. Certainly the questions were buffered sensitively by Daniel's revelation that he'd moved home because he'd also broken up with his partner: "Jesus, I was sweating by the end of it with the pressure to get married, you're better off hun, you're still young, we're still young, all of us." He was right, but Shell could only nod and agree softly rather than offer any remarks about how deleting her Pinterest board full of engagement rings had felt, how she'd known she was an accessory in Gav's collection of ordinary things: ordinary mates, ordinary job, slice of cash, good house, new build. How the ordinary had begun to hurt her. How the big flat and his thin, high voice had felt like ruin. How it all came apart and she had to go home and maybe it was better, actually. Yeah. She'd say all of this to Daniel eventually, but she wasn't quite ready to throw her old life under the bus to a person she'd spoken to twice since she was a teenager.

The cadence of Daniel's chat was well rehearsed, a person who had to keep talking all day at close proximity to people's heads—so much so that he segued into the heavy in a way that Shell barely even noticed. "And, come here to me, did Neve tell you anything— Ah, she mustn't have. Look, I'll let her say it all to you herself, but it's been a hard year for her, harder than it was for most of us, but we've a good eye on her. Has she, though, said anything to you?"

And Shell absorbed the whiplash of information—Neve had something going on, but did she know the others—by tipping the sweetish, almost nothing-flavoured alcohol down her throat to buy a moment to reply, "Oh, no—we haven't really talked like that yet." She wasn't able yet to see what Daniel was doing here as a tremendous kindness. A laying of the land. Preparing her, giving her an advantage—a little context so that she did not humiliate herself. I enjoyed watching, and feeling her defences rise as she passed my terrarium on the escalators. I liked the sense of dread becoming a low, heavy tide under her ribcage. She was a little afraid, too, as they walked towards the food court, as though she were coming before some kind of jury, forced to stand witness to her own teenage years. Neve only knew Shell as her shopgirl. What if further than Daniel's memories of her, she had to fend off other people's? Prove herself different, accomplished, better.

Better than what, Shell? Than these people? This place?

"Look, I'll say little to nothing, but let's just say you and I aren't the only people who've had significant breakups recently. Neve hasn't really been the same since Jen left, but we all reckon that her taking you on in the shop is a good sign. She'll let that shop kill her, someday, but you being there kind of makes that . . . less likely, or something."

As Daniel said this, the flight instinct took Shell. That was a lot of pressure. A lot. She scrambled to find some boundaries, some sensible parameters to put around herself. If she didn't go up to meet Neve's people, nothing would change. She could remain in the soft, tense world that she and Neve had arranged themselves into. Nearby, there was soft music. The sound of pealing laughter from a woman who wasn't Neve (Neve's laugh was deep and filthy). Shell felt young suddenly. Not the good kind, the kind Daniel had been talking about, though Shell wasn't sure if there was such a thing as good young. Daniel was still talking, and she could hear him and was making the correct noises, but she was miles down inside the mines of herself now, and I liked her when she was down there, shaft upon shaft away from reality. It was there that she was capable of finding tiny, hard diamonds of self-awareness, forged in the crush of anxiety.

It is easy for me to tell you that Shell should have gone home. That she should have feigned dizziness, emergency, a text from her mother. She should have done a lot of things, if she'd wanted a life devoid of challenge. If she'd wanted to refuse the call, she could have ignored the sign in the florist's window. Shell felt the pull towards this next part of her life and was sick and afraid, and still she let it take her, instincts blasting and all.

Daniel was explaining who she was about to meet in further detail beyond the schools they had attended, gossiping softly.

"Well, you're going to meet Kiero up there, too. Jen used to give him real shit for being a bit younger, but if you're tempted, don't—like the kid really needs a break. His sister worked here, too; she was a dote and she died, and look, I won't talk about it until they all talk about it, it's his business more than ours. He lives at home, like you and me, but Bec got a mortgage when she was twenty-three. I know. I know. Can you imagine. Her aul lad owns the Maxol Garage on the coast road, gave her the deposit, but sure look that was when a deposit on a two-bed terrace in one of the empty estates was about eleven grand, so you wouldn't begrudge it to her, you know? She has it done gorgeous. You'd want it for her, she's an angel. She won't have to worry for work when the Crown closes, either, she's better set up than any of us."

Shell nodded, replied that it sounded like she'd fallen on her feet.

"She's true blue. She's been so good to Neve during all this, after Jen."

Neve had been trying, all this time, not to mention Jen. Shell felt this assumption clutch her. The ex-girlfriend. The former partner. The after.

"Neve actually hasn't even mentioned Jen at all," said Shell, tipping more aspartame-edged seltzer into herself.

He cut her off and said, "I said I'd let her tell you herself, but look, it might have taken you by surprise, so when she tells you, act like you don't know, but consider this a soft heads-up from me to you. Jen left, no contact since. Neve's kind of swallowed it, I think, but she was like a ghost for weeks and weeks. They were engaged, you know? And fair dues to Neve, she just put her head down and didn't make a fuss. Bec was very close with her, too. Jen up and moved, off to work in the Burren—gone, just like that. God, can you imagine?"

"I can't," said Shell, reeling. Reeling huge. Her own tiny problems slapped out of her hands. They'd both been engaged. They'd both almost been somebody's wife.

It was better that she heard like this. Daniel, a messenger, her escort through the lives of the people she was about to meet. These hard parts, a tour of what the last few years had carved out of them, delivered with the almost marvellous lightness of touch possessed exclusively, it seemed, by hairdressers, who could ask questions with as delicate an artistry as they removed and organized hair.

This skill was Daniel's gift, and in a sense it worked on Shell, who found herself asking then, "Is there anything else I should know about her?" A harmless enough question, really. Though

Daniel had immediately realized what was growing between Neve and Shell, he had the good sense and decency not to bring it up. What might have seemed like awkward-proofing the session ahead was a gesture of enormous kindness. Let this be the way you hear about the grieving so you do not stumble upon it. This was an act of love: Daniel was trying to be an ally to Shell, though she was not quite able to see it just yet.

I liked Daniel. I understood him to be good. I have listened to him and what the inside of him sounds like, and he meets the pain of others with love. The things he has overcome are not what he wears in his manner. It is a deep feat to move with grace when you have been granted little to none. I would never see Daniel hurt again in his life. At night, when Daniel prays, it is for love. And love I would grant him. I am not close to him in any way other than my leaves and vines and listening—I do not hold him the way I hold my Neve—but my vines are around him still. If Neve were not my favourite, my best one, it would perhaps be somebody like Daniel.

Before Daniel had time to tell her who Jen was, they were upon the tiny party and their conspiracy was over. Daniel gave Shell a look, though, as the earshot became point blank, that told her he was with her. In the private roller coaster Shell had been white-knuckling since she entered the mall only minutes before, she accepted this glance and returned one that she hoped implied a thanks. She will warm to him. She will. I will make sure of it.

Neve, Bec, and Kiero sat around two pushed-together food court tables, scattered wide. Neve smoked a cigarette and held a pint glass in her hand as though she were in a beer garden, not just between the shuttered hot counter at Keeva's Kitchen and the empty, lightless Subway concession. Shell took them in before they noticed her and Daniel and broke their rhythm for her, all but a stranger.

Bec was tall and slim and wore a tight navy blue dress suit with a neckerchief and was drinking from a box of wine. Shell clocked the tiny airplane button on her blazer, noticed that the yellow marbling her scarf and the bright blue of her hairclip matched the almost obsolete shop front of Cassidy Travel downstairs, with the clean oceans and clear skies rolling past on screens in their windows. Nobody wore uniforms this fussy to work, only travel agents. Shell was surprised—and delighted—that they still existed. Bec was very glamorous: Shell wasn't able to help noticing the heaviness of her top lip, the sharpness of her jaw, which were telltale of fillers. Her teeth, as she talked, were celebrity white. Shell hadn't seen someone so well put together in a long time, other than on Instagram. She felt scruffier suddenly.

Bec had that impact on people; I witnessed it again and again. She had that same frustrating smoothness that Jen did: a confidence that I could never quite break through. I understood why she and Jen liked each other. It must have been a relief for them to be in each other's company, so little insecurity between them. I preferred, myself, to ignore Bec. I did not enjoy her.

The third point at the table, Kiero. With a low mousy ponytail and a very slight beard, he leant back in his chair, also smoking, holding a can of Dutch Gold. He wore a grey hoodie, faded bootcut jeans with a rip in the knee, and the big sneakers that boys who skateboarded used to wear.

He was young, really young, but the clothes were old. Maybe hand-me-downs. He looked freshly laundered. His skin was good. He smiled at something Bec said and raised his eyebrows and suddenly, in this expression, was handsome. Neve was very fond of Kiero, and had on numerous occasions asked me to leave him alone, not to interfere with him. I had always told her I would spare him. I might, I might not. He was pliable, hopeful, stupid. Helpful qualities in a young man.

He noticed them across the food court first, waved his can, and gave an "Ahhh, howaya now!" to them.

Daniel said, "I found her! She's all in one piece!" and Shell gave an awkward little wave. Neve raised her pint glass and her other hand, holding a cigarette. Shell hadn't, for some reason, assumed she was a smoker. I do not like Neve smoking, and I tell her all the time. Sometimes, when she tries to take a small break, I snuff out the burning cherry as soon as she lights it to teach her a lesson. I like that she fights back against small parts of my will for her. I like that she has spirit. I let her have cigarettes that night because she was nervous, and I wanted her to enjoy herself.

Shell sat in with Daniel, and they made a fuss of her and ribbed Neve a little about keeping her from them, and Shell handed them tins of the hard seltzer, and Daniel suggested they all down them in one to get things rolling, and they did, more or less, except Kiero who spluttered with laughter halfway through and inhaled some of it into his sinuses and couldn't go on. Shell took a cigarette off Kiero when he offered, though she hadn't smoked for two years: less because she wanted one, more to belong—that teenage feeling again. Bec stopped the welcome procession then with a wave of her box wine in order to tell them the big *news* that she was saving: Chic Boutique next to the Smoothie Stop was closing down.

Another one bites the dust—another sign that they were nearing the very end of the Crown. Another sounding of the death knell. Collectively, the party gasped—even Shell, who had bought fake gold earrings there when she was fourteen. They had left green shadows all down her neck but were in the shape of two bright palm trees crossed into a heart. Chic Boutique had been selling cheap, high-femme party clothing for as long as Shell could remember. It was the kind of spot you'd save your pocket money for, to buy a skirt or a crop top or a packet of fishnets to rip up and use as arm warmers.

Bec gave a slow, wise nod at the reaction.

"Sickened. The market for the bits and pieces Sandra kept in stock plummeted, sure we're all getting our rig on the internet. She can't keep up. Can't see what next year is. Wanted out before the condemnation notice showed up. It's shuttering in, what did she say, I think it was a week—so get your final nostalgic selfies in the fitting rooms now before it gets turned into another temporary Vape Emporium or never opens again." On that, she produced a slim white vape from her blazer pocket and took a sip. It lit up bright blue at the contact of her breath.

"If you sit still for too long in this kip, you'll turn into a Vape Emporium," said Daniel, removing his own from his pocket. "There's what, three now?"

"Three and a kiosk," said Kiero, shaking his head. "I'd be worried they'd come for me, but people still need shit printed and don't want to deal with it at home. I'll be the last one standing in this place, I swear to god." His voice was surprisingly deep, and he spoke slowly.

Shell lifted her chin—yes, she'd seen Kiero in the top-floor Stationery Station, away up beside the nail bar and the lash salon and the library in the northernmost peak of the Crown. The whole shop front was glass, so you could see right into it from the escalators. She'd noticed him before, reading a fat, heavy book at the desk amidst the obelisks of photocopiers, stacks of paper, and huge boxes of pens and erasers and ink packs. How odd, she'd thought, to have a shop so open that everyone could see in at you all day. You wouldn't want to be on your phone, or even making an unattractive face. Reading at work was a kind of slacking, sure, but it was a slacking that made you look interesting. Kiero was in a glass house, and I was in a glass house, but mine was murked and stained and old. All of the Crown walked by me, and I saw them and they did not see me back. Kiero was on display. Mall rat, face deep in an old library Stephen King, wearing a tiny necklace made of shells.

Yeah, Shell decided then. He was younger, sure, but pretty hot. Not as hot as Neve, but hot. No one, she was convinced, would ever be as hot as Neve, for Shell. Even when the time came that she would wrap her body around Kiero like vines, she would think of Neve. Kiero was warm, but Neve was an inferno. Kiero had his place in all of this, too, but it was far from the scorching emerald heart of it.

"Why do you think that is?" asked Shell. "Are people just . . . falling out of routines with their local shops and getting really into vaping?"

Neve shook her head. "I have no idea what the deal is with Vape Emporium. I wish I knew. But I do know that one of the butchers is gone, Pat Kinsealy's, and I liked them because they'd give you a free bag of stuffing if you asked for it. And the little shop that sold Irish dancing shoes and costumes, the Reel Thing, they're gone, and I was fitted for mine in there when I was a kid. I'd imagine some of it is behind-the-scenes politics, as well as the market, you know? It's the people, not just the money."

Bec raised her hand. "You need to get into that sweet, sweet franchise security. No personal investment, no dreams, just take off the neck scarf when you go home and forget about it. Cassidy Travel isn't going anywhere. I'm not just selling cruises for two years' time: I'm selling hope. Hope keeps us going. Hope, and the glamour of not having to book your own flights."

"I feel like there's some black magic around how the fuck Cassidy is still going," said Daniel, "when barely anybody around here has the money to take a holiday abroad."

"Sacrificing goats out the back, are you, Bec?" said Kiero.

"Look, I can't talk about what they do in the head office, it's none of my business. They may do what they want as long as they keep paying me every two weeks."

"I think," said Shell, "people still want to come into shops, you know? There's a convenience thing in getting things delivered, but I think people still want to be together. Walk by each other. Touch things before they buy them. Look at boxes of cereal. That's important, you know? Just looking. I mean, my job went down in flames, but it was like . . . a modern job? An email job. Does that make sense? Shops are . . . old. Markets are old. People need the old."

There was a small silence, and Shell thought, oh, no.

"Neve. You never told us you hired a . . . philosopher," said Daniel, and the others laughed but not unkindly, and Daniel gave Shell an honest-to-god wink. Shell had no idea when the last time was that anybody had winked at her.

"Do you know what? I fucking love looking at boxes of cereal, she's not wrong," said Kiero, and Shell smiled at him, and there was a little click as they made eye contact, and Kiero's eyeteeth were set at angles, giving his smile a Cubist quality, an offness.

"I do miss touching things that aren't, like, plants," Neve said, and I rumbled under her and she thought, oh fuck off you know what I mean, and I did know what she meant but I still wanted her to know I was listening. "Like taking a long walk through the soft furnishings department of Dunnes and like. Giving expensive throws a little touch. I don't want to buy them. I don't need another throw. I just want to give them a little touch. I go nowhere that isn't the shop. Kind of limits your . . . touching opportunities." She laughed, the others laughed. Shell distinctly did not look at her when she said this, looked down at the tiny black opening of her tin of seltzer instead.

"I need to be touched, and thrown, myself. Cereal isn't going anywhere, but my best-looking years are blinking out around me," said Bec. "I'm expiring by the minute."

"No word from the Hot Doctor on the app, then, no?" asked Daniel.

"Silence. I'd say he's beating the young ones off him. Or up to his eyeballs on the ward, either or. I'll send him another message in . . . four days? Four days. Then that'll be it."

"Worth following it up, pal. I hear if you're cosy with a doctor they'll let you use the prescription pad for whatever you like," said Kiero. "Skip the line."

"Ah, but could you live with yourself," Daniel said. "I mean. I could, probably."

"Look, I'm either riding the text man for texts, or riding the prescription man for prescriptions," laughed Bec.

Daniel said, "Hear, hear," and Shell couldn't remember the last time she'd been around people who seemed as though they liked one another.

The stiffness of the last brunches with the girls and Gav's friends were stark against the softness of this, and Shell felt lucky, and she felt sad, too. A long, quiet year, and before it, things had been dying, and then they were dead, and she was in the dead, and here in the food court she felt, despite her reservations and neuroses, like she was coming back to life. Not just the life she felt in her wanting of Neve, her enjoyment of Neve. Beyond that, there was an ease here. I could feel her uncomfortable memories of the strained silences of the brunches, the relieved moment when the food arrived and everyone at the table—usually six, or eight—could eat their American-style waffles with fried chicken (twenty-one euros) or eggs Benedict (fourteen euros) or French toast covered in chocolate children's cereal (also fourteen euros) and not have to continue the conversation. She would leave the brunches with a creeping two-in-the-afternoon bottomless-mimosa (twenty-eight euros) headache, and she would say to Gav in the Uber home, "Can we . . . skip the next one?" and he, eyes locked on the football score on his phone, pint-heavy, would say, "Don't be a moan, Michelle, Jesus," and she would look out the window at Dublin's grey, expensive body and think, fuck. Fuck this.

And then, suddenly, it was two in the morning and Shell was starting to get a headache from the cigarettes and the aspartame of the seltzer, but she was laughing too hard to call it quits, to bail out on the now-raucous telling of Woodbine Crown myths the other four had sunk deep into. Nobody spoke of me. Rather, Bec and Kiero and Daniel performed for Shell the comings and goings of shops that had opened and shuttered, the two years when there were inexplicably five milkshake stations all around the premises, which then became Smoothie Stations, one of which remains. They talked about the corridors behind the shops and how all of the shops are, if you have the right keys and passcards, interlinked—Kiero had been collecting them for as long as he'd worked there and didn't even have half of them yet. He promised, valiantly, to take Shell on a tour of the rooms, and Neve didn't like that but didn't even change her expression when Shell said, "Oh my god? Yes? I'll bring my camera and take some cool pictures?" at the stage of drunk where she was so excitable that everything she said sounded like a question.

"Sick, sick, sick," said Kiero, and he was only going to get sicker yet, and Neve felt kind of sick at his excitement, and the night was over, really, now, just short of sour, so she stood up and stretched, her joints clicking, her shoulders and wrists making a soft undoing sound, and she said, "Right, that's me. I'm going to go downstairs and crash in the back until deliveries, you big bunch of rides."

Shell pictured Neve's slight, tall body curled up on the big old couch in the back room and wanted to say, Hey, I'll come down with you, but the courage wasn't that strong in her. It wasn't time for that yet. And one by one the others agreed, yes, sure, we're all up for more of it tomorrow, we'd better call it one, and Daniel offered to walk Shell back to her house and Shell said yes, as if she hadn't spent the former half of the evening distrustful of Daniel's kindness.

Kiero and Bec paired off as they always did for their walk back to their end of the estate down at Grange Abbey—they'd known each other well for a long time. Bec had been best, best friends with Kiero's sister, which was the only mention of death that had come up during the session.

"You're my brother now, Kiero, whether you like it or not." Bec had thrown her empty wine carton at him and he'd shielded himself and laughed. "I'll take it, I'll take it, she would have wanted it this way," and she said, "Well, someone has to stop you being such a fuckin' nerd," and they both laughed like that was how grief had to sound to them now in the surreal hell of life without her. They said Seeya, seeya, same shite later in the week yeah; drop up to the copy shop this week, Shell; come down to me in Cassidy's, Shell; Daniel, will you do my fringe for me, it's annoying me; great, look, I'll see yous tomorrow. The whole lot of them barrelled out through the empty, silent mall at speed—Shell picking into a loose, sloppy run just to see how it felt to sprint along the tiles and Daniel jogging after her, hat under his arm. It didn't take long for them to clear, and Neve was on her own then, leaning against the walls of my glass house.

I tapped the glass to her and she said, "All right, hold your horses," and I tapped again, softer. She took the key to my house out of her pocket, there on the chain with all the other keys, tiny and brass and anonymous. Nothing fancy, nothing that might make anybody ask any questions.

Nothing that spoke to the terrarium being, in fact, the nature of my growing place. This temple made of old glass and plastic, this sacred site amidst the busy and ordinary. Ordinary kept the door to me hidden, though I did not need to be made safe. I am outside of that. Neve, however, needs safety, in some regards. Though I am her guardian and protector and her bones and her breath, she still inhabits a world with other people who could hurt her. Neve needs the shop, needs the business, needs the Woodbine Crown, in order to meet me here. She needs a system, an architecture around us because she is not yet ready to join with me—she believes she never will, still, which is so silly of her. For her to come to me there needs to be ritual, cathedral, rite. That is where we are at this time, and I am turning the heat of it up so slowly she does not notice. When she does, sometimes, check her reality and take stock of her life and sees that I am all over every piece of it inside of her and outside of her, she does not wonder why. When she is afraid of me it is a good, rich feeling, but it does not arrive in her often. Mostly she just loves me, and she comes inside to the garden she has built around me and says, Hello, Baby, and I say, Hello, Neve, and she takes her sweater off over her head. It is very hot in here, though you would not know unless you touched the glass, and nobody ever touches the glass. In here with me are hundreds of plants that I am inside; there are poppies and there is fennel and there are posies and ferns. There were once tiles on the floor, but I have long grown over them, my vines tentacles. I am heady in the air, and I accelerate, clouding it a little, making all she sees green and she rubs her eyes then takes her glasses off.

I raise her veins to her skin so it looks as though she has black vines under the fair. She looks down at her body, takes off her vest, the tight camisole she wears to flatten her breasts. All over her body are deep black rivers, and she thinks for a moment that maybe this is what it would look like, joining with me. I laugh and every leaf in the place shakes and she says, "That's not fair. How am I supposed to imagine what it would look like? How am I supposed to know?" and I say, Neve, you can't know, but I will tell you that it won't look like this, though you do look so beautiful this way, and she shakes her head, kicking off her sneakers and stepping out of her corduroy slacks. She lets the heavy vines under the floor thud with life under her feet and walks on into the church of me, sweating now.

The part of me that is closest to corporeal is at the farthest end of the garden. I am in a white pot, a small bit of earth of my own, my long stem slight as a blade. My face is a perfect geometry, nine crisp white petals unfolded around my eye, yellow and bright, and Neve kneels before the little table where I am, for a second, before she lies down below me, closing her eyes, and I make my vines soft under her head so she is comfortable. I lean down and make my stem longer, longer, until my face is at her face and I rest my petals on her cheek. I use the tiny mouth I have to kiss her gently. I eat a freckle from her cheekbone near her eye, just taking the colour of it into me, then another. Neve loves how this feels, shivers against the suction. She says, "I love you, Baby" and I say, I love you, Neve, and love, love doesn't cover it. Love doesn't even come close. The things I have done to protect her stack tall. I purr into her ear that Shell looks so delicious. Shell looks like somebody I might like to eat up. Neve shakes her head softly, her body yielding to me. "Please, leave her out of this." I laugh. Too late, Neve. I ask her to consider, maybe, bringing Shell into this. She doesn't refuse, she just lets me take her, her body giving me the yes that I so love to hear.

You know, it took years after Carla for the hunger to come up in me again, to become unmanageable. I spoke to Neve about it, and for long hours she soothed me, assured me that I didn't need to kill anyone, nobody needed to die for the ache to ease in me, but she was wrong. She would tell me stories about her life, her day; she would encourage me to listen to the movement of the building, the people's stories out there, so that perhaps I might gain empathy for them and wish less to consume them because I could see them in the totality of their experience. This approach was well-meaning but a fundamental misunderstanding of what I am—though I never named my true self and true nature to her. I allowed her to continue calling me Baby, though I starved like I was grown.

She came to me in the morning and in the night almost every day. After the flashing circus around Carla, she sometimes slept in the Green Hall, before me, and I roamed her dreams like pollen in the air in summer. I told her again and again how hungry I was. I made her feel that hunger, too, said, Let me show you and put what I felt down into her body. She would fall to her knees with it, the hollowness—and though what she could feel in her human body was only ever an approximation, it was close; it was enough to bring her to my side, to understand that what I had done to Carla was not wrong, and what I would do again, and again, was not wrong, either—it was only natural.

Neve begged me to protect her, to keep her safe and clear. In exchange for her stewardship, to protect her, and I said I would.

In 2015 I chose him at random. A man, drunk, opened the wrong door from the bar at the side of the mall into the empty expanse after hours, looking for a bathroom, finding the end of the world. The instant the door closed behind him, I pulled him in his stupor by the ankles with one of my new vines, my grown vines, baby no more, across the atrium. To stop his screams I ran tiny creepers up into his nose, into his mouth, quickly silencing him in a muzzle, but keeping him alive long enough for me to eat what I needed from him. I pulled him down and across, dragged him through the atrium like a snared animal, and that trapping itself was part of the feeding, the thrill of it.

The hunt was effortless. He was at my disposal. I webbed him into the Green Hall, retracting my vines, my head fully awakened, grown, my mouth large and open and ready. He did not even know how he was dying, but amidst his stupor I read him, ate the love he withheld from his wife, ate the horror with which his daughters regarded him, ate the memory of a hit-and-run—a deer, a man in the road, he didn't stop—ate the feeling of his school tie on his neck, ate the dentist's hand and his sharp metal braces. I drank every pint he drank. Every sour bottle of wine. Every tiny bag of cocaine, I ate. He had been an electrician, and I ate the wires, the pliers, the gloves, the worst shock he ever got, worse than the feeling of me on his ankles—worse, that he never really registered that this was his end. Perhaps, had I read him and read something different from him, I might have let him go, might have just feasted a little and sent him away injured—he would not remember me, so drunk was he.

But not everyone deserves to live.

I did Neve a grace and did not leave anything of him on the floor of the Green Hall. I left no body. I did not believe that Neve could hide him, or should debase herself by deconstructing his form so she could carry him in pieces. I loved her by then, truly, and wanted to uphold the promise that I would simply never get her into trouble. I was the worst trouble; there should be no more. I could not help the bloodstains, though—I was a little passionate and could not help that he was slightly burst by the time I had truly consumed him, could not prevent some spillage. So Neve asked me no questions the next day, and though the smell made her gag, she did not hold me to task. Merely acquired some bleach and a mop for the tiles and an extra two bags of earth to lay down. All she said was, "You're full, then?" and I said, Oh yes, Neve. I am.

When the police were looking around for him, Kevin Letts, forty-eight years of age, missing—they didn't even step into the florist, staffed by a gaunt woman in her midtwenties, sure what would she know about it? How could she be involved? The detective did stop by at the end of the investigation for a bouquet of flowers for his wife, and Neve put it together with some extra baby's breath and lavender, to bring a little peace to his household. When she comes to lie with me at night, I think of how stoic she was in the face of suspicion. Her heart, immovable, delicious in her chest.

Agent Rebecca,

Literally bless you for writing back to me, and at such length. Reading your email brought a lift to my miserable little heart that I can't even describe: I'd suggest having a Zoom or FaceTime date, but honestly, I'm living for this correspondence and I don't want to puncture the novelty of having an in-the-flesh pen pal. Also, I'm not going to lie to you, the thought of drinking a bottle of wine alone in my quarters while talking to you over the phone and looking at your immaculate face is tempting, and I feel like we'd have a scream, but I don't think I can handle the moment the chats end and the screen goes dark and I'm alone again, you know? The comedown probably isn't worth the high. I also don't know if I can handle being hungover in the lab with all these excruciatingly quiet (but still hot) people. I still haven't managed to crack them, isn't that miserable? Me, the most charismatic person to have ever graced the National Conservation Centre, and I haven't had the opportunity to flex some of that charm for months. I may never get the chance to at this rate. A waste, Bec. A crying shame. Tall Siobhan is still both tall and silent. I can't get past formalities with her. I feel like if I tried to flirt it'd be inappropriate. More wasted potential!

Speaking of wasted potential, you really have to get Young Kiero to emigrate. I really thought he was on his way out the door. Like drive him to the airport and throw him over the security barriers. He kept talking about it! It was all I heard for years! He's gotta do it. I did it! If I can do it, a twentysomething-year-old boy can do it, and probably have a less traumatic time about it, too. They're more resilient at that age, right? Like, I will pay for his ticket. Make him go. Bring him home when he's thirty and less stupid looking, please. Sorry! Sorry, I mean that kindly. Like the vacant kind of stupid, not the malicious kind of stupid. The free kind of stupid, the lucky kind. Unburdened with the knowledge of adult life. Put that child on a plane, Rebecca.

Okay, I fully love you for giving me carte blanche to talk about the Neve situation. I know it's probably super awkward and I really, really, really don't want you to think I'm throwing her under the bus or anything. I'm not. I am probably going to say some demented things about her, but they aren't coming from a place of spite, or even of anger anymore, really. I've cooled off, I've accepted that we weren't meant to be. Now, though, what's left over is worry.

I think in, like, letting me in to the whole thing you guys have going at the Crown she took a big risk, right? I didn't know anyone when I moved here, and she came with this built-in social world for me to fall into. I don't take that for granted, you know? Making friends as an adult is brutal, and I feel that even more intensely sitting in this lab looking around at all these people for whom it isn't even a priority. Not worth the effort after a day staring down the hole of a microscope, or out in the field. I kind of don't blame them. Lots of them are only interns, here to do their time then move on somewhere else. Maybe they're all sitting in their quarters, staring into Zoom, talking to their real friends. Maybe they're all writing emails to faraway people from other chapters of their lives instead of filling in spreadsheets, too. So what I'm saying is I'm not out here trying to steal you away from Neve by telling you weird shit about her behavior at the end of our relationship. I think it's probably important for me to ask if you've noticed anything out of the ordinary, too. Like anything weird, or weirder than usual. Is she staying super late in the shop still? Does it sound demented for me to ask you to look at her hands, see if the red marks on them are still there, or fresh? I recognize this sounds like I'm asking you to spy on her. This isn't, like, jealous-ex spying. It's "hey, I'm worried about this person" spying. But yeah, it's still spying, so please tell me to piss off if that's too much.

I worry, because at the end I found her to be more obsessive than usual about work. Like we all know she's obsessive, right, so that even feels like the wrong way to put it, because I'm pretty sure it wasn't the shop she was obsessed with: it was the garden. Like fixated on it. The Green Hall. Bec, if I start talking about this, I'm pretty sure you're going to think I'm lying. So consider this your chance to bail on this conversation. If you do, I won't judge you, I won't even be a little bit mad. So this is your escape button. It's keeping me up at night, and, like, I don't want to keep you up at night with this, too.

To prove that I can talk about something other than Neve, can I just say I'm really rooting for your own doctor situation? He sounds great. Your screenshots of his messages are unreal. Love an illustrated report. Please feel free to continue to include them and any/all pictures he sends: it makes me feel like I am vicariously dating him and therefore alleviates some of the loneliness-related-insanity. I don't know, is his unreliability a red flag or is he unreliable because he's working in a hospital, pal? That's the biggest question the modern woman faces while dating a man. Have you considered dating someone who is not a man? Have I asked you that? Is that a thing I can ask you? Like you have very straight energy to me, I mean that with total respect, but I thought I should ask. Again, please feel free not to answer that. Abject loneliness is making me really good at being compassionate about other people's conversational needs and boundaries because at all costs I do not want to scare you off. This is the longest conversation I've had in weeks, and it's not even aloud.

Please tell Daniel I love him. Like, I adore him. Has he considered leaving the Crown and coming to do hair down here? My own is starting to grow out. Did you know he gave me a cut and color before I left? On the down low. It was very emotional—however, my roots have started to come in, so he should come down here and sort me out. I feel like the people of County Clare would be all over him, also my quality of life would be much improved by proximity to him and his capes. You should move here, too. You should all move down here. Except Neve. She can stay in the Crown. Or maybe the country air would be good for her.

Over and out, xoxooxoxo,
Dr. Jen

The worry really did keep Jen up at night.

The more she replayed that day Neve took her into the Green Hall, the more it felt like something bad had gotten into her head, and she couldn't get it out. A thought that burrowed like a hungry insect, all teeth and legs, down into her, and she couldn't tweeze it free. When she'd been planning out how to tell the story to Bec in the manner of a person Having an Extremely Normal One, rather than a person wracked with guilt and fear, she'd replayed the important details she wanted to confer to her friend, in the hopes that they might alarm her or spur her on to keep a closer eye on Neve. In the emotional tide of the breakup, some things had slipped Jen's mind, and now in the mapping, she was digging up a wave of bugs from the earth of herself. Most of them she could handle, if she didn't hold herself too much to account in overlooking what she had just put down as Neve's eccentricities. But one stood out bright and sick to her. She wished it would disappear into the soup of her memory again, but it didn't, it shone at the centre of her mind's eye and blinded her with worry.

It was the buckets, and the bottles, and the big heavy mop. There was too much brand-new cleaning solution sitting, just tucked away, almost out of sight. A stack of empty containers, too. If Jen hadn't been so deep in the garden, she wouldn't have seen them at all. If she hadn't been combing her memory so that when she told Bec the story it would all line up fact for fact, so that when the time came to land the horrible truth on her it wouldn't sound absolutely insane, she mightn't have recalled them at all. Or thought of them as anything more than standard heavy-duty retail cleaning supplies.

But the Green Hall wasn't clean. Nothing in it was clean. It was dense, overgrown. The windows were famously opaque with moss and grime. So why all this fluid? Why the huge plastic buckets? That horrible tiny insect inside Jen whispered to her, late, as it had every night since she left. Was this setup for her plant food? And if so, why did it make Jen feel so wrong inside? What was Neve using to feed them? What was she pouring into the ground? The heady plant smell all but covered it, notes of an unmistakable bleach that reminded Jen of a hospital. A surgery. Somewhere beyond that, it made her think of blood.

The first thing I felt was the hunger. No language, no names, no numbers, no wonder, just the simple knowledge that I had to eat. When I came up out of the earth, that slow unburying, and the slight and frail woman, Carla, was there, Neve—sixteen—by her aunt's side, the thing that would fill my starve became obvious, immediate. I opened and closed my new petals, a gesture of thirst. They found me sweet, treated me like a baby animal. Baby. Funny how when you name a thing that name turns over and over. Certainly I was new on their side of the earth, yes, I was small, but like a human child I was only ever going to grow, going to change, going to become.

Perhaps if they had recognized me as something other than sweet, things might have been different—but they wanted to care for me immediately. Carla came to feed me day after day, tended my soil, watered me, sang me gentle songs about a moon she assumed I would never see. Brought a heat lamp to stand over my tiny green body. Neve orbited her, a clumsy satellite, saying almost nothing, face dappled with acne, eyes glassy and already holding a secret bigger than her body. She was good at secrets. Perhaps this was what drew me towards her, the first thing I liked about her—she had a lot of space for me to grow. I would find more chambers in her for more secrets, over time, the girl a cathedral, a mall with an empty store for each bad thing she did for me, for each witnessing. She grew me for the span of her life over again; I was a hinge in the centre of her experience.

If she hadn't been devoted to me early, she would have killed me when I was small enough to kill, when I wasn't inside her yet. She had the chance when she was twenty-one, five slow-growing years after that first day. I had become too hungry to survive as I was; their feeding me mice and little packets of deli ham was mere pantomime, I was never satiated. Their voices soothed me, their love—that was something close to satisfaction, something to distract from the gnawing emptiness inside me, from what my mouth wanted.

I exerted some reserves of energy one night to grow large, temporarily—to imply to Carla and Neve that I was to be fed something more significant than the scraps they had brought me. Not a threat, exactly, more of a suggestion. I split the bed they had grown me in, allowed my flesh to expand heavy out into the floor of the Green Hall, allowed my teeth to grow long inside my mouth, blossomed desperately, thousands of white petals. I did not have the strength to sustain this form for long; I knew I would have to shrink again, disappear down again, maybe hide beneath the soil again if I wasn't fed. I did not expect Carla to become the object of my feasting. It was not as deliberate as my future feedings would become; there was no strategy to it. I was, after all, a baby. I found myself overcome by a need and, finally, large enough to feed myself if I was not to be fed appropriately. She was frightened when she saw me so large, when I opened my eye, when I showed her the huge, dark place beyond my mouth. The tone of my voice was no longer sweet, and it frightened her when I begged to be fed. The look on her face made her the meal: she knew she was prey in that moment and what was I to do but accept her as she was? Carla, benevolent florist, small business owner, unmarried, wedded only to her little shop. I extended my tongue and took her by the legs and swallowed her in a single breath.

For a moment, it was beautiful. Oh, to be full. Oh, to be at peace. Oh, her good heart, her clean soul. The gold in the lobes of her ears, the metal in her teeth, the peroxide in her hair. I ate the chemical mascara from her eyelashes, then I ate her eyelashes. The sheep wool of her sweater, the rubber in the white shoes she wore. The feel of the halo of communion wafer in her hands at five years old. The first, second, and third time she was kissed. The decade in which she touched nobody. The worst time she was hurt, the dark of an empty cinema, the horror of fourteen. Rosary beads between her fingers. The taste of milk. Fir trees covered in lights, paper in her hands. The first time she saw a flower and knew its name. Her blood was copper all for me, me, me, all of it, and yes, her heavy heart a gemstone, a black-red amulet, a soft ruby, mine, mine, mine.

I ate the entirety of her. The knowledge in her nerve endings, the secrets in her bones. I took all of it below the earth and then I spat the earthliness of her out, a husk, once I had consumed what I wanted. I kept her eyes. Her teeth. The nails in her fingers, her toes. Her rings. Her secrets. I shrank back down, an imitation flower, a clever mimic, satisfied for a while, full at last. When little Neve came looking for her, in the cold of dawn to get started on their daily work, I must admit I wished I had not left her in such a state—but Neve's horror was not total. She was pragmatic, standing there over Carla, Carla who had given her somewhere to go away from the violence of her household, the bigotry of her family. Carla was gone. Carla was part of me, assimilated into the green landscape of my body. It didn't take Neve long to understand this. I sang it to her soft, made no apologies, said only that I had been so hungry.

"I understand," Neve said to me. "But what do I do with . . . this?" She gestured her hand over flesh that remained.

"Nobody can know. You cannot ask for help," I said to her.

"I have never asked for help in my life," Neve replied, and it was true then.

The silence that took hold as she stood over Carla's remains was the one in which I became a part of her. I had merely admired her, crawled close to her until that moment, but in the quiet she became allied to me. I spored down into her skin. I filled up her lungs, her tear ducts. She could have taken a brick to me and done me terrible damage. She could have dug me up with her hands, or a spade, or poured bleach into the ground; I was young enough then, my roots spare and scant. Instead, she took the collection of skin and water and bone and organ that once had been her aunt, her family, and slung it up over her shoulder. Carla had been a fragile woman, and in her departure was easy to transport.

"Can you do something. To the cameras. There are cameras. So nobody sees me taking her," said Neve, clipped, grunting under the weight, face pale, eyes mercury.

And with the new strength I had from the feed, I focused and my eye did not grow large in my face but it did grow more seeing. I felt my roots get longer, far longer, spindle in width, plenty of them, each with the dexterity of a human hand. I moved myself like water through the brick and concrete and plywood and plaster of the building; all this new power made it easy to me. There were so few cameras in the building. It was 2004, wired things less intelligent, easier to corrupt, unplug, fry. The tapes in the empty security centre didn't run blank, but played over themselves, and over themselves, silent and static, and no teenager with a dead woman over her shoulder lurching through the empty mall would be recorded, tears streaming down her face but her heartbeat steady and unmoved. No evidence. None.

She was left in the car park, beside her tiny Ford Fiesta, slumped, for someone else to find. It was still dark out. Florists are the first to greet the day and thus, invisible. Neve would never have gotten caught. I would have wormed through the eyeballs of anyone who had seen her anyhow.

This act was her commitment to me: her siring. Such a circus erupted after Carla was found dead. Such sorrow poured by the locals, the news, down on young Neve—who left school that year, early, to keep the flower shop open in Carla's memory. There was never an instant of suspicion that the gaunt teenage girl had had anything to do with it. There was never a murmur of me. Brave, bold Neve, an empty beehive, how I would fill her with honey and sting and noise as the years turned onwards and onwards.

It took me some time to become truly hungry again, and I would never ask Neve to feed me anything that would leave blood on her hands, or fingerprints elsewhere. But I would ask her to take the skins, the husks, whatever I left behind. Eventually, I would begin to ask her to join me, join me in my hunger for real, and I think she knew it that day, all the cameras inside her shutting off, one by one. But she would say no. She would insist I could not have her heart. That she did not want to be like me. She said no with her mouth, but everything she did for me, with me, told me yes.

Shoot

Shell was, two days later, up a stepladder and hanging spring wreaths from a steel frame on the ceiling when Kiero threw his head around the door to the shop. Neve had been leaning on the counter, lazily directing her, watching the curve of her body as she stretched her slightly fleshy, tattooed arm to ensure the lengths of the twine that held the wreaths aloft were in appropriately ascending order so that when they all hung they'd look like an elegant pyramid—but Kiero's appearance made her sit up, surprised and, if I gauged the curve of her lip just right, a little annoyed. Kiero didn't make quite as frequent a habit of dropping by as Daniel did, because he was generally in the copy shop by himself. He must have had to close it to come down. Shell didn't know this, of course, and gave him a big "Ah, Jesus, it's himself!" and the wreaths swung, metronome from the ceiling. His ponytail was higher up on his head than usual. He wore a green plaid shirt and skinny jeans and carried a book under his arm. A packet of Amber Leaf peeked out of his shirt pocket.

Shell was thrilled to see him: she'd enjoyed him during the session the other night and had considered popping by his shop on her morning coffee run, but had chosen to not be too full-on with integrating herself into Neve's social group. When she was younger she might have, but not now. She found herself waiting for social direction from Neve.

"What's the story so?" Neve asked, and now she was definitely annoyed as Kiero extended a hand to Shell as she climbed down the ladder and Shell took it, even though she didn't need the help. Neve had watched her get up and down that ladder by herself three times.

"No story, no story. Dead up there. Tuesdays, you know yourself." And he was right, the Crown was very quiet today, the empty slump of early weekday mornings leaving the place spare and dull.

"It's chill right now, but we're keeping busy," said Shell, putting her hands on her hips. "I've got seven more wreaths to make. Two for doors, five for, erm, coffins." She gave a little smile. "They're different kinds of wreaths. All circles of flowers, just . . . different vibe."

Neve caught that she was flirting and didn't like it, and I didn't like it, either. None of this was going to work if Shell got distracted.

There was an old habit in Shell that liked the attention of a tall man, and Neve straightened up in her chair, all five foot eleven of her, aware of the tilt of Shell towards Kiero and how he was stooping slightly from the cavern of the shop towards her and they looked like a good fit, the two of them, and Neve felt a pull from me and a pull from her heart and I said, I'll stop it, and Neve thought, There's nothing there to stop, Kiero doesn't date, and I said, Are you sure you want to find out if that's still true? and she thought, It's nothing, I'm being paranoid, and I said, Are you sure, though? and she thought, Yes, Baby, this is ridiculous, and she said, "Yeah it's just filling orders at this stage, really, nobody's coming or going."

"Well, look, I won't keep you from your circles of flowers, I just wanted to drop this down. You asked about what I was reading." He handed her the book and said, "I think you'd like it."

Shell made a surprised gesture and said, "Huh!" and didn't say, I haven't read a book in two years and also I don't read books written by men, but instead added, "Thank you! I'll get stuck in and report back!" Shell didn't really remember much about the conversation she'd had with Kiero the other night about the book he was reading, or that she'd demanded he pitch it to her like a film, but Kiero remembered the soft tilt of her face, her drink-flushed cheeks, how her dungaree strap had fallen off her shoulder slightly while she listened to him.

"What book is it?" asked Neve.

"*Generation X*, another Coupland," he said, and Neve made a "pshhh" sound. "*Generation X*? Your parents were Gen X, Kiero. You're . . . Gen Z? Gross."

Twenty-two, Shell remembered, was not only a decade younger than her, but a full generation off. She cringed at the thought.

Kiero took it on the chin and said, "Well, I think it's good. I think it's really good, actually, and I think you'll like it. Just drop it up to me when you're done! And c'mere, we'll hit the back corridors this week if you're around, too, I haven't forgotten!" He was a little nervous but Shell was, unconsciously, standing on her tiptoes to talk to him, and he'd noticed and took a little encouragement from her excitement. Neve noticed, too. Neve was doing a lot of noticing. I, in turn, had a lot to notice as well.

"Oh yeah!" said Shell. "Sounds great!"

"See you upstairs on . . . Daniel said Thursday, yeah?" said Kiero to both of them then.

Neve, leaning back, said, "Ah yeah, we'll be there all right—come here before you go." He stepped over to the counter and Neve planted a freshly plucked and thorn-stripped pink rose behind his ear. "That one's on the house." And as she touched his hair she thought maybe she would kill him stone dead if he put a hand on Shell before she did, and the flower felt like placing a tiny curse on him, and I asked her if she wanted to curse him, and she thought, No, shut up, and I said that the offer was there for the taking, and she said, Stop it, and I said,

No, never, and you don't even want me to stop anyway you silly, jealous girl. Neve was seldom attracted to men but understood that Kiero was objectively attractive, even if she didn't feel it in a chemical way. He had the very specific clean quality of a person who showered briskly and efficiently once a day and used conditioner and conditioning treatments marketed towards women without concern about whether or not that would threaten his masculinity—Neve enjoyed the physical company of people who took care of themselves, given that her entire life was focused so intensely around fragrance and arrangement.

I will come clean: I did take his sister, but far and away from my usual approach. I poisoned her and took her in her bed. It took almost as much strength as my usual approach to do it, from just a few leaves in the unsold corsage Neve gave her without thinking one evening. The family thought she had gotten ill, had a seizure, something silent and fast. Neve didn't give me the chance to explain that I was just testing myself, just seeing what I could do— she told me to never do it to someone she knew again. Leave her little village of friends out of it. No Daniel, no Bec, no Kiero. They were not to be made meals of. She was angry that time. I do not like to think of it.

Kiero flashed Neve a white, crooked smile, and she smiled back and gave off none of her frustration at all, and he said, "See you soon," and she said, "See ya," and Shell said, "See ya!" and waved, before climbing back up the ladder again to continue adjusting her wreaths mobile.

Neve set her teeth and I wound my way into her mouth for a moment and she jolted in surprise at the feel of me between her jaw and she bit down and I held firm against her bite and she was comforted, strangely, by the resistance. Rather she bite against the illusion of a vine, against my energy, than strain herself or further grind down her teeth. Shell did not notice any of this, her head up in the ceiling. I will bring her down to the earth soon, down deep and low with me and Neve. With us.

And I was so surprised when Neve said, "Gotta hand it to him, giving you a book is a classy move, didn't think he had it in him," and brought the unsaid right up to said.

Shell looked for just a second as though she had been electrocuted before composing herself. "Do you think that was a move?" Both of the women knew it was a move and Shell was still making herself diminished in the shadow of the presence of a man who found her attractive. A boy, or something close to it.

"Ah, catch on with yourself now." Neve, blunt. "Clearly a move. Kiero's only a young fella, shy about that sort of stuff, so I'm surprised! Pleasantly surprised," she added then, and Shell clumsily dismounted the ladder to take the book out of her apron pocket and look at its hot pink cover again. She flipped it open. Kiero had written in his stout, even hand, his phone number on the title page and his name spelled right—*Give me a text about the corridors! Kieran*—and Shell didn't point this out to Neve, rather, flipped the book shut again. Right. That was a move, so.

"I don't actually think I'm going to date men again for a while," Shell said calmly. She tried to make this statement as flat as she could, this soft but sure-footed coming out, this deliberate distinction between "date" and "date men." She hadn't had to do it since she was in college. It felt like acknowledging a ridge in herself, and she looked Neve straight in the eye as she said it. Neve had gotten the feeling Shell was queer, obviously, like how down in the earth a beetle recognizes another beetle, but there had never been any talk of it directly. They hadn't been doing anything directly, other than arranging flowers. Shell felt, with the weight of the book in her apron, that it was enough now to be more direct. Not absolutely direct. Far from it. But clear, at least.

Neve heard it how she was meant to hear it and said, "Huh," affirmatively.

Shell said, "Yeah. That's the way the compass seems to be pointing, anyway."

That was a move, I say to Neve, and Neve thinks, Shut up, that wasn't a move, and I say, Grow up.

Shell waltzed behind the counter and out into the back room while Neve still sat there at the counter, reeling slightly. She'd clocked Shell, for sure, but she had somehow expected her to be more coy. She had read Shell as someone who was uncertain of herself, who was experiencing their attraction maybe without realizing what it really was. An unsure Shell was easier for Neve. If Shell wasn't sure of what exactly it was she wanted, or what was going on, or why it was they liked each other so much, or why they were so easy with each other, or why all the songs they played in the shop sounded so, so good, then that meant Neve wouldn't have to do anything and she could stay where she was, without Jen, with me, in that with-and-without with all these plants to keep her hands busy. It had been unfair of Neve to assume anything about Shell. Especially to assume that she was sexually naive somehow; that hadn't been fair, and Neve was slightly ashamed of herself. But it had been said, or something had been said, now. That compass Shell mentioned was indicating some kind of a direction, and Neve was, even as she sat trying not to clench her jaw at the shop counter, moving towards Shell's north.

In the back room, though, Shell was typing Kiero's number into her phone and dismissing a string of texts from rumbling group chats, a couple, weirdly, from Gav. Even if she didn't read the book, it would be nice to be polite and thank him. She hoped, too, putting the book in her bag, away from her, that Neve had picked up what she put out. She hoped that the slightly flinty look Neve had about her when she had remarked on Kiero's flirting was, actually, a tinge of jealousy because that was proof, then. Of something. Anything.

I could feel that Shell was considering Kiero, absorbing his gaze and letting it give her power, a more raw consumption of energy than the heady magnetism she got from Neve. One was good for one thing, one was good for another. There was a balance to it.

I had eyes on all points of the situation, and I had a suspicion what was to come down the line, but still sometimes Shell surprised me. How changeable she was. How she would agonize and live in the fleeting moment before the party then stick the party out until the very end of the night. How she was not interested in Kiero, not really, but took pleasure from his interest, albeit shallow pleasure, far from the deep water she had become accustomed to with Neve. How interesting to be able to enjoy the two kinds of desires in herself. How satisfying.

How good to be admired, to be a site of interest, and I felt this, and for second maybe Shell was closer to me in nature than she knew and I realized as I watched the gradient and roll of her emotions why it was exactly that I knew she was perfect, that I knew she was right, that despite all of her neuroses and inflated levels of grandeur and importance that she was, in fact, just like me and therefore just exactly the right instrument for the great crescendo of my unity with Neve.

She cannot be afraid of me—not all-the-way afraid. Not afraid in the way a person would be if a voice like mine manifested out of the walls without warning, if my leaves descended from where they hide to hold her body in place while I spoke—there can be no display of power here. No flex. I will arrive for her so that she, in some ways, expects me. She must find me agreeable: she has to agree to my terms. I have something to offer her, and I will unfurl a vine to her soon but not today, though today was useful to me. It felt good to see some of the makings of her desire, to watch her react, all chemical.

And my sweet kicking Neve, too, moving towards Shell's point on the compass, moving further towards where I need her so badly to be. Where she has refused to go, but she will eventually arrive. She changed the song on her playlist twice after Shell went into the back room, unpleased and unpleased until something with no words showed up in the shuffle. She didn't want any narration for a little bit, and she slipped her hand under her shirt to her breastbone where Jen's ring hung anew, a hanged man above her heart, and she slipped it half onto her finger, like an apology, and I didn't interfere. I have long since stopped telling her she has nothing to apologize for, or that Jen can't hear her. Only I can hear her, and that should be more than enough. In the back room, Shell bit into a peach, and it was delicious.

The rest of the work day ticked softly along, Shell bunching flowers then dropping them out front where they disappeared into someone's arms shortly after: today, mostly fat orbs of hydrangeas and long-tongued pink anthuriums with their waxy petals like the scales of a dragon. She built each bunch to look as though it were a comet, the core of it pink, delicate hydrangea and a long reed, and fuck it, sure, why not put in a few little feathery strands of pampas there to bump up the volume and the price—she took real pleasure in it. It was hard to think of anything else, really, with her hands full in this way, organizing the shape of things, with her nose full of pollen. The strain of wrapping her fingers around the fat, cold stems and extending her palms to accommodate the radius of the bunch ached, it felt like pressure on her wrists, but she fought against the frustration of her slim hands not being able to accommodate the work. She thought of Neve building bunch after bunch without even flinching, as she winced while binding one particularly heavy bouquet with string. Shell had no idea what Neve's hands had been through, what they had held. The white marble scars all along her palms still caught Shell's eye, and stuck in her, just as Jen's name had.

The bunches sold and sold even though they were meant to hold over until tomorrow, and every time they sold Neve would pop her head around the back room door and say, "Another one down!" and they would do a little cheer together. Shell took photos of four of the bouquets at varying angles and placed them, unfiltered, on her Instagram. Interaction pinged and pinged through the phone, the pleasure of it dispensed then dispersed, and there was a little more of that hunger satisfied, and a little more of her capacity to feed developed.

To see her in a state of organic pleasure was a marvel: she hadn't even really been rewarded in any way. Other than by the book, a hapless straight man's totem—by the public affirmation that her bouquets were pleasing. By being able to even slightly surprise Neve, and then surprise her again by production-lining out eight bouquets and selling them all on a quiet Tuesday as well as doing her funeral wreaths—now that made up the sum of a good day.

And it had been about to be a good day, a real good day, the likes of which Shell had almost forgotten, until, just towards the end of her shift, she and Neve received another visitor. Denim jacket and beanie hat and big, expensive, tortoiseshell glasses a little too round for her face, tote bag over her shoulder, Emily Smith popped her head into the florist, before the rest of her body, as though she were scoping out something terribly risky. Upon making eye contact with Shell, who had been in the middle of laughing at something Neve was saying—potentially about the perks of turning the florist into a Vape Emporium—Emily shrieked, "Shelly!" and Shell's stomach nearly fell out of her body with the horror.

No. Not Emily. An emissary from the long-ignored WhatsApp groups. A spectre of brunches past. Though here, Shell was the ghost—and she'd been caught in her hiding place.

"Oh my god, Emily," Shell said, trying to conjure enthusiasm but still falling a little flat. She was checking out, disassociating slightly to sidestep the panic of being found.

"Hi, Emily." Neve grinned, registering Shell's discomfort. "Welcome to our little operation."

Emily's body somewhat unwillingly followed her head into the shop, and she walked around with her arms slightly out from her torso, as though she were a toddler, or managing low gravity.

"This is where you've been! This place is so gorgeous. Pure salt of the earth."

This was a lie. Emily did not feel that the shop was gorgeous. She was being patronizing, and both Neve and Shell understood this.

"What brings you out this way? You're not from . . . Donaghmede, are you?" Shell was racking her memory to try to parse where Emily was from. Surely it was Dún Laoghaire. Surely she hadn't forgotten that much already.

Emily shook her head, "Oh no. Visiting an aunt. In Kilbarrack."

She was not visiting an aunt. She did not have any family in Kilbarrack. She was naming the train station she had disembarked at on her short trip from the city. Emily did not drive.

"Instagram threw your account up on my timeline and I realized I was near the shop, so I thought I'd pop in and say hello! Also! Me and the girls are having a dinner next Thursday, will you come? We're not sure if you're, like, using WhatsApp anymore, none of our messages seem to be going through, so I thought I'd deliver the invite in person if I saw you!"

Shell smiled wide and warm as though she were delighted by the entire situation. "That's so old-school, I love it. Yeah, not much time for the phone lately!" Her phone was in her hand as she spoke. "Just up to my eyes in here. But I'm sure the boss won't mind giving me the evening off to come and catch up with you guys, it's been forever. Can I get you some flowers? For your aunt? On me?"

Emily smiled back, but it didn't meet her eyes. "Oh my god, that is so good of you but I already saw her, so no worries! I won't trouble you! I'm going to split, but we're at Chloe's place on Thursday from, like, eight."

Such a polite, seamless no to the flowers. As though there were something wrong with them. Neve didn't like this. Shell pretended to ignore it. I, however, was disappointed. I would have liked to have gotten a close read on Emily. Follow her home.

"Sounds great. Chloe must be really far along by now, right?"

"Oh yeah. Just a few weeks left. Hey, you take care, don't work too hard!" Emily took Shell into a hug that only captured her shoulders, their bodies still apart. It was a quick one, perfunctory, broken sharply, as though in recoil. Emily Smith waved up at Neve on her ladder, said, "Oh my god, so, so good to meet you!" and backed out of the shop. "This place is so great! So great! Take care!" And she was gone. Her weird assault on the place finished.

Shell exhaled a deep whistle, and Neve said, a few moments later, to ensure Emily Smith was out of earshot, "What the fuck was that?"

Shell shook her head. "I don't know if that was an olive branch or—"

"A cattle prod?" Neve added. "Not sure about her now, not sure at all. Are you going to that party?"

Shell flipped open her WhatsApp, and scrolled down to the chat. She saw 286 unread messages; 400 unread messages in the one for Kayla's hen party, too. They should have filled her with dread, but she felt very far away from them.

"Yeah, I probably should. Just to check in."

I held her in a gauze of good feelings, there. Didn't want her to feel any nostalgia or shame. Just observed. She had a life of her own now. She didn't need or want these people. She wanted Neve. She wanted Kiero. She wanted her life at the Crown, for however long it was to last. And that state of want was exactly how I liked her.

She texted Kiero that evening. Sat down to do so, very deliberately, on the cool sheets of her bed, after a shower and with a fat glass of wine, her hair heaped and wet in a jersey cloth on top of her head, scented heavily from mousses and oil. She archived all her glaring unread messages, forty or so of them, so she had the sense of a fresh start. Shell was really getting into having a fresh start—as many of them as she could, in fact. She wrote, *hey pal, it's shell, when are we going out into the weird corridors of the crown?* and signed it off with a bouquet emoji. She thought, as the tart, cheap wine hit the roof of her mouth, that she'd like very much to text Neve instead, but it would be simply rude to leave Kiero hanging. Plus, Kiero felt like lower stakes to Shell. She would practice with him.

She filtered and cropped some pictures of bouquets while she waited for a reply—it took him about three minutes. Respectful, not too intense.

Hey! Yeah that sounds great. I can meet you tomorrow but I know it's your day off so no worries. Let me know what works, xx camera emoji.

Kisses, thought Shell. Confident, that. Like how a bright green shoot peeks out of the earth towards the light: something small making itself known, reaching towards the future. They talked a little then, a small back-and-forth of *What are you up to,* and it was easy. He seemed eager to talk to her, to ask her questions.

Shell wondered if Neve would be that eager if they didn't have the scaffolding of working together to ensure they stayed in their place. *What kind of camera do you use, can I see some of your photos?* Kiero was curious, and Shell, admittedly, hadn't picked up her camera in years. Nor had she really read. She had somewhat creatively plateaued, all the ambition of her own early twenties made quiet by work. She found herself admitting as much, but quickly following up with how excited she was to look around the corridors of the Crown, maybe it might inspire something in her. She felt inspired, all right, almost a little manic with Kiero's attention against the backdrop of the mystery of Neve.

It was more dopamine than her body had released in quite some time, and she felt, as she lay there in the smallness of her childhood bedroom, actually quite happy. I liked it, that feeling of happiness ballooning under her ribcage. All those blinking synapses, all that arousal. I hoped that feeling would take her from silly to stupid, and when stupid, she would be pliable, and when she was pliable I could move her to move Neve, and then, oh then I would get precisely what I wanted. Slow, warm domino girls.

The next afternoon she walked into the Woodbine Crown with her camera around her neck, lens thick and heavy and incredibly expensive and conspicuous over her pinafore. She had fallen asleep on top of her sheets, her hair still damp, lazily texting Kiero that she was passing out but that she was sending him a CMAT and John Grant song she wanted him to listen to, and when she woke up she saw that he had written *lol ok I will, can't wait for tomorrow xx*. She hadn't bullied a man into listening to music she liked since she first dated Gav. A mean little spark in her thought, as she put herself together, of Neve's spiky look thrown after Kiero had been in the shop and wondered if she would see it again.

Kiero met her at the Ticketmaster kiosk, now shuttered, still listing gigs on its whiteboard that had been cancelled eighteen months before. Neither of them could know how close to them I was, how their meeting was happening to me as well as them. Kiero's ponytail was shower-damp, and he was wearing little hoop earrings instead of studs.

He gaped at her camera and she was thrilled to explain it to him as he led her not, as she had expected, towards the flower shop, but instead up towards the copy shop, locked, lights on, with an A4 piece of foolscap taped to the door that read, in his sharp, boyish hand, OUT 4 LUNCH, BACK SOON, smiley face.

Beside the store front, there was a little patch of wall, a stitch in the architecture before the next unit—Jessica's Nails—began. Slim and unobtrusive, a door stood there, about three-quarters the width of your standard household doorway. Shell never would have noticed it, but she supposed that was the point. She hadn't been working in the mall long enough to have her eyes peeled for these kinds of things, to understand that there were chambers and passages not meant for the public sitting everywhere. She supposed she was still just a shopper, really, as Kiero pulled a heavy ring of keys, brass and metal, from his pocket—they were attached to his belt loop with a chain.

He didn't even have to fumble to check which one was the first key; it came to his hand easily. He unlocked the door then with a heavy machine noise, let them in, and quickly closed the door behind them.

The air quality was different back there, which was the first thing Shell noticed. Dusty. Not dirty, necessarily, but inhospitable. The light was yellow, and the corridor ahead of them was long, with a junction a couple hundred feet ahead.

"Jesus," said Shell. "It's not small back here."

"It isn't," said Kiero.

Next, Shell noticed the difference in the sound. The people and the soft drone of pop from the Crown's radio station evaporated and was replaced by the vibrating, deep tones of halogen lighting, and something else that she couldn't quite place. If Shell had known how I sound she would have noticed that my breath was there, too.

The corridor pulled back almost into darkness: somewhere

down the line the white, buzzing lights were off. The carpet was beige, laid in tiles. The walls were, or had been, painted white but had aged into a near yellow. It was notably cold, and Shell felt her nose turn pink against the change. She felt like she had stepped into somewhere winter, somewhere distant. She loved it.

It was also Kiero's kingdom. He raised his slim, muscular arms above his head, knit his fingers, and stretched, allowing all of his bones to click, then, daring, outstretched a hand to Shell to lead her into the strange labyrinth.

"Hold yourself right there," she said, instead of taking it, holding her camera up to her eye, then pulling it away to catch the shape of the shot. The flat light gave the picture an eerie, other-time look. Kiero was half smiling over crooked white teeth, his hand outstretched to the camera. He looked, against Shell's better judgement, very handsome.

"You look great," she said, and he let his hand fall, gesturing to her to follow him.

"You'll have to send it to me," he said, then the pair of them walked into the depths of the mall, their footsteps eaten by the carpet and the hum, neutralized so they were almost completely soundless, numbed into the system of corridors, like ghosts.

Dear Secret Agent Rebecca,

Are you actually serious? Are you being serious with me? She took on an assistant? A woman? An honest-to-god living human being who she's paying to work with her every day? She's letting her in the shop? In the back room? Has she let her in the garden yet? Pal, I'm going to need a robust breakdown of what their day-to-day looks like, and no, not because I'm jealous—because I'm worried. I literally beg of you to not mistake this interest for jealousy. So now that I've stated clearly and with no caveats that I am not jealous, I'm going to ask you a question that will probably undermine that statement, but I literally need to know.

Is she hot? I know, I know, but I require this information because I have to know what kind of breakdown Neve is going through. If it's a sex breakdown, fine! Fine, we all have needs, I respect it and I myself am on the cusp of similar. Like, do you think it's a romantically motivated hire? Or do you think Neve is genuinely inviting someone to work in the shop with her to like . . . alleviate how much she's needed in the florist? Has she been spending more time in the Green Hall? I feel like such a freak asking you these questions.

My heart is genuinely racing. Okay. Look, is it weird that I've built a little minibar in my quarters? (By *quarters,* I mean my compound apartment. By *built,* I mean I'm using a shelf in my tiny fridge exclusively for locally distilled whiskeys and gins. I'm supporting a cottage industry, also I have nobody to drink them with so they're kind of just sitting there, waiting for either Tall Siobhan to come and visit me or a personal crisis of this exact nature.) Is it inappropriate to hop out of the lab now and have a little morning drink to settle my nerves? I'm not handling any serious equipment or specimens today. Okay, wow. Wow. An assistant. A woman.

Okay, okay. I'm calming down. Okay. Like, this is important because she might be in trouble. Not because Neve is going to do anything to her—I promise that's not it—but because, well. Right. This is where I'm going to start sounding, like, fully wild. Off the rails. So you agreed to let me talk about it, thank god, because now talking about it or telling you about it is absolutely critical for that girl. Has Neve let her go in the Green Hall? Has she brought her in, or anything? Bec, she's growing something fucked up in there. I mean really fucked up. I think it's making her act really weird, and engage in ritualistic self-harm, or she's, like, feeding bits of herself to something in there, or bits of something else. I know how that sounds. I know. It's either her having delusions, or something much worse, and I might be a coward but the second she started to try to pull me into it I ran like lightning. After three years, like. She scared the shit out of me, and I'm still scared.

In a way, I'd sort of rationalized it all down, like, look, the girl has experienced enough grief in her lifetime, and if this is how she's letting out her stress then fine, I'm not with her anymore, her life is her own. People do worse shit to themselves from a place of pain. But if Neve is dragging somebody else into it, I feel like I have a responsibility to let the girl know, or do something. Like, she wasn't a difficult person to be with, not more than anybody else would be. I'm not saying that. I really didn't realize there was anything wrong until it was much, much too late, which I guess is testament to how opaque she is and how committed to keeping her secrets absolutely secret. It's not like we didn't talk; it feels like we did nothing but talk for the first few years. It was when the talking stopped that I knew it was over: you have to learn to love somebody in the quiet of themselves, as well as the noise, the chatter. I'm not sure she loved me quiet, either; it doesn't feel like an imbalanced falling out of love, more like a mutual drift, then the last few threads just snapped when she tried to bring me in on her Green Hall stuff. Maybe if we'd still been close I would have enabled her, or followed her into her fantasy, but we just weren't in love by then. Maybe she knew that, and showing me what was growing in there, in her, was an attempt to reconnect us. It didn't work, obviously.

I feel like I'm really selling Neve out here, but if she's involving somebody else in that, like she tried to involve me, I can't just sit here in my stupid lab across the country and not say anything. I feel like I'll be able to explain properly once I calm down. I am absolutely not calm at this moment. Please send me back any and all details, urgently, or, like, alternatively, never talk to me again because I just said some really deranged shit about your friend's personal life to you that sounds so surreal that if it was a lie, it would be kind of a reach. Thing is, it's not a lie. Neve's into something bad with the Green Hall, Bec. Really, really bad.

Hit me back up, and hey, this email will self-destruct in . . . I don't know, whenever you hit the delete button, which you probably should at some point. Like, please delete this. After you've replied, of course.

For real, though, please reply ASAP, I'm losing my mind.

xoxxxox,
Dr. Jen

Jen had taken up smoking again. Starting the new job, she'd wanted to come in with a clean slate. All that boozing and vaping and smoking and the little bumps of coke with Daniel and Bec, gone from her life now. She'd taken the fresh start so seriously at first, and in some ways had been enabled in this purity by the total lack of company. Drinking alone was grim. She did it, but it didn't feel good. Her rationed stash of weed gummies had run out in the first month. She didn't want to smoke in front of the team because she was afraid they wouldn't see it as a social invitation—which it was—and rather would see it as a performance of intensity or darkness or some other bullshit. She missed when socializing didn't feel like a set of matrixes and rules. She missed when it was just her and Neve and the others. Easy.

It was talking to Bec that drove her back to the cigarettes. She'd gone out to the gas station—a fifteen-minute drive from the labs—especially for them. So now, when she needed to think, or try to get to the bottom of the worry that was crawling under her skin and into her gut, she'd step outside and stand in a corner of the courtyard at an angle that made her hard to see from the enormous windows that looked out from the office. She'd have preferred to go and sit in her car, or smoke out of her apartment window like a teenager, but she'd have to check out with her badge before that, and it just wasn't worth the hassle, being held accountable for four or five little nips back across the campus a day. She didn't want them counting. They were nice, but this wasn't collegiate. She had hours to track, focus to keep. So the sacrifice of just standing in the courtyard where she could be seen and judged was better than her check-in logs being witnessed and judged. Either way, they'd know something was going on. And how was she to say that to them? I'm having a rebound case of heartbreak after a breakup? I'm increasingly worried that my ex-girlfriend was doing something at best deeply unethical and at worst, illegal, but either way incredibly fucked up with a plant in the shopping centre where she works? Absolutely not.

Jen was grateful that she had been outside in the courtyard when she got the email wherein Bec mentioned that Neve had employed someone. Jen had gasped aloud at the paragraph where Shell was introduced to her. Her place at the table filled. A staff member at the flower shop. A girl in the mouth of a Venus flytrap. She stood in the quiet shade of the courtyard and stared at the email while her stomach turned, her cigarette burning into a pillar of ash between her fingers as she read it over and over, mouth open. It was critical that in her reply she didn't sound as awful as she felt. That she addressed and therefore punctured the presence of jealousy. That she let Bec know there was a serious problem without frightening her off with the depth and degree of the dark.

When Jen first met Neve, she'd written her a set of emails, too. She'd told the story of her day-to-day to the Irish girl in the flower shop, which progressed to the telling of her history. Neve's emails were funny, smart, immediately attractive. Jen found a way to match that charisma in their correspondence. Neve had reached out first, finding Jen's field of study a funny link between them. Hey, you like plants? I've got loads over here. I grow them, I sell them, they're practically my whole life. You should come and check them out sometime.

"Sometime" turned out to be just six months later. "Checking them out" turned out to be packing her world up and relocating to an island more than five thousand miles away. "Practically Neve's whole life" turned out to be very much the truth. The emails became endless conversations: Neve's voice elemental, everywhere. Their life had been good, until it wasn't. Until it had come down to this. Jen hadn't deleted those first scores of emails yet. She probably wouldn't look at them again, but she wouldn't get rid of them, either. She was shocked to find herself begging Bec to leave no digital paper trail of their conversations—but as she wrote back, fevered, she found the truth of things bubbling up into the text that appeared onscreen, felt the power of an accusation she couldn't take back gather, like electricity in a storm.

Shell and Kiero softly explored the deep and unattended corridors and back rooms of the Crown, taking in the rising heat of their bodies despite the chill of rooms that had fallen long dormant. Shell was, to her own surprise, a little scared. It was an old feeling: that of trespassing. Shell had never really broken many rules, and here she was, using bargained and stolen keys to roam places she frankly should not be in at all.

Sometimes, without apparent reason or function, the carpet would change, as though it had simply run out. The new carpet was taped in at the seams with fat grey ribbons of industrial tape. It wasn't unclean, per se, but it was neglected. Unattended.

Outside some of the storeroom doors, little coils of wires sat, tangled and filthy with dust. Their use was impossible to tell. The occasional stray folding chair leant against the walls, cast out into the non-space of the corridors to save room in the limited, cramped real estate of the mall's concessions and shop fronts. The florist didn't have one of these corridors attached to it that Shell knew of: it just opened right onto the car park where the Dutch men in their vans would drop off the deliveries every morning.

Shell examined the walls as they walked—they held a kind of grime that could only have come purely from age, not from human contact. Something, she thought, like decay. Even with no people busying the hallways they still went bad, like fruit unattended, but with a slower and more gradual rot. It was just as she was trying to articulate this feeling to Kiero—how she felt like she was walking through a dead place—that I decided I would show her something really alive.

I became tired of observing them, so I decided to be bold. I was sure and I was hungry, so I dropped a single vine, coquettish almost, from the ceiling. Just a few feet ahead of them. Quiet but not soundless. The sight of it froze them. They startled at the disturbance, then they could not move for a moment, trapped in the realization that they were not alone. Oh, they have never at all been alone under this roof, or in their own thoughts, not in the garden of my surveillance, but what a horrible little shock for them nonetheless.

Kiero instinctually reached out to grab Shell, as though to protect her. He stepped out in front of her, and moved her behind him sharply. Heroic, all of a sudden. He called, without a tremor in his voice, "Who's this?" like he was receiving bad, strange phone calls rather than witnessing a young god unfurl himself. Myself.

You cannot protect her from the bullet of me, I will go through you like plain air—how I would love to have said this to him. To say, Sweet boy, it is me, and something in him would know me though he would not be able to name from where. I would have loved to greet them, to watch them calcify entirely, but instead, I just hung there, swaying softly in the just-about-unfeelable air conditioning, old and dusty breath from beneath the vents. I am a shock of pulse in the dead veins of these corridors. An unexpected organ, still beating.

Shell moved out from behind Kiero's guard then, pushed his protective arm away, not unkindly but with a determination. Afraid but curious: I had entered the stage, one leg appearing in the spotlight from behind the red curtain—but Shell had the eyes of a woman for whom the tease was not enough. A pleasing quality.

She marched, emboldened suddenly, up the corridor. The old carpet swallowed the noise of her footfalls, her lips pursed, her fists clenched. Kiero stayed rooted to his spot, his brief role as her bodyguard over.

Shell stood in front of my offering for a few moments, staring at me. That funny feeling, that sense of knowing came up through her as she inspected me, curly blond head tilting this way and that. The thick cord of green woven over rough with slim bright vines, almost, she thought, like wire. A handful of thorns dappled the curve of me as it hung in a curl from a sly hole in the ceiling tile. Not so many thorns that she would immediately believe me to be dangerous: no tiny white prickles that might leave her with a sting. I was a richer green than anything that grew from pots in Neve's shop, anything that came in from Holland. I was reflecting back all the dead halogen light into something that made the girl say, without thinking, "Gorgeous," and lift her hand to connect her skin to me.

This was how it started. The tips of her fingers, then her palm against my flesh, the tiny fibres of me fusing with the pink-white of her. Human skin has so many holes, so small that their own eyes can't see them—but I can see them. Passages towards their insides. Open doors all over their body. I plugged the tiny threads of me to the pores of her and in an instant we were locked together. I was truly with her. With her. So, when I did choose to speak, I would already be swimming inside of her so she would know for sure who I was. There would be no mistake.

I was warm and she was surprised. She thought she could feel a pulse. She took her hand away after what I made into an eternity, and, with a flourish, I withdrew like a sharp breath.

Up into the ceiling hole, slithering every trace of my form away from where they could see, should they have gone looking.

But they didn't. Shell let her hand follow my ascent, a reach that was little more than a gesture, no want for any further contact from her. Not just yet. After I was gone they stood in silence for a minute or two, too unsettled to speak.

Kiero broke what had crystallized in the air first, saying, "I'd better head back to the shop, Shell," though Shell had expected him to remark on the vine that had come from the ceiling at least, or maybe acknowledge the audacity of putting himself in front of her as though she were a damsel, but he didn't. So she didn't, either.

They skirted awkwardly back the way they'd come, all their flirtation and nervous energy muted. They saw each other off at the copy shop, said, "Pints this week?" Said, "We'll text, yeah?" Said, "Thanks, can't wait to see the photos." Almost past Shell's perception, almost past what her body knew how to tell her yet, as she walked away her palms began to itch.

I had been bold to do it, so clearly, so cleanly. I never act outside the dark. Only once did I feed in raw daylight, and Neve was so angry after that meal that she did not visit me for a week. I did not intend her to find out about this one, to be frank, as there are some things I can privilege above her. I do not wish my feedings to hurt her feelings; that is not what they are for. You could say the meal was a child, certainly. A lost child. Strayed from his mother. You could call it that. You could note the reams of press that followed his exit, attention from journalists, more police, far more than when I took on the grown man. Neve didn't have to help me clean up when I ate the child. No chemicals, no earth, no shovel. No dragging of bodies, blacking out cameras. He was small. Five, good, honest, silly. Easy. Fulfilling.

The aftermath rocked the country. A child evaporated. Not a trace. Walked behind a shelf in the supermarket, never to be seen again. Nobody noticed him, but he lives on in me. Neve never asked about it, though she knew. She never brought it to me. Never waved the newspapers in my face, as she had the man, as she had Carla. No screams, as there were for Caoimhe. Perhaps by articulating it, she would have made it too real, too frightening. I worried, I admit, that our collusion would sour because of this, and elected not to eat a child again. I wouldn't need to feed in that way for some years to come, so I had time to ingratiate myself with her once more. To remind her that I, too, was a young thing. A baby.

Shell's palms itched in the shower, and only briefly when she ran the water cold did the feeling subside. They itched as she sat at the dinner table, drowning in the noise of her sisters bickering over the drone of RTÉ News listing immovable housing crisis statistics on the screen, the housing minister bumbling his way through vague non-strategies for new builds and ensuring the interests and investments of landlords were protected, as it truly was a hard time for *everyone.* Shell clenched her short, painted nails into the heel of her palm for relief against both the reaction in her skin and the frustration boiling in her blood. Her old apartment with Gav had been largely a silent place—a state of the air that she had grown used to. But her family home was always pulsing with noise. With videos from multiple phones, tablets, ambient radio, television, cutlery, plates, voices, breathing. Every fifteen minutes a train would rumble by the back of the garden, a soundscape Shell had always found comforting until lately. The house and her palms throbbed the same.

A spot under her left eye began to itch, then, too, and she rubbed it with her palm hoping the feeling would cancel itself out, but I do not cancel myself out. I only multiply. Her mother gave her a sympathetic glance across the table and topped up her glass of wine. Things had become incredibly European in her house since she'd moved home. Wine with dinner, regardless of the day of the week. She appreciated it. When she was done and had loaded up the dishwasher, Shell evaporated from the noisy kitchen-dining-open-plan hell and closed her little bedroom door behind her with a deep sigh. Closed doors were a blessing in a busy house, thrumming with adults and opinions, too full of broadcast. Her room was quiet enough. She lay on top of her sheets to rest.

She placed her palms down on the cool cotton of the bed and turned her face into her pillow, and the relief was so brief that it almost made the rising return of the itch feel worse. So Shell took out her phone to distract herself. A silent, busy world to look at. She soaked up some of the warmth from compliments on her most recent arrangements and considered dropping one of the many work selfies she'd taken in the workshop.

Instead, she reached for her camera and began a Wi-Fi transfer of her photos of the back corridors from the memory card there to her laptop, open beside her as she lay on the bed, softly illuminated by the blue glow of the screen. One by one the images popped up. They weren't bad. Kiero was a really easy model: probably due to his age, she thought. His skin was good. He was lean, long-limbed, unselfconscious. She picked out a few to send him, taking photos of her laptop screen with her phone and attaching them to a text that read, *unedited, unfiltered, organic*.

In one image, Kiero was leaning against the grim white-yellow wall and tilting his head towards the camera, a small smile on his face, his hands in his pockets, his own camera slung around his neck like an amulet. He'd taken her direction well. Behind him, the corridor went on for what looked like forever, an almost maddening distance of rot and stale light. Kiero looked too good in his heart for the place. For a second, a little unkindly, Shell wondered if he was a virgin. He had that about him.

She waited for his response and mulled this over. She scratched under her eye, worried at her palms, slightly pink and rashy now from agitation. She rummaged in her bedside locker for antihistamines, took two, and prepared to shoulder the dry mouth for potential relief. No relief was coming, but she didn't know that yet.

Kiero's reply took a few minutes, though the notification on Shell's message and pictures switched to Read immediately. When the message came, it was a simple *Wow, that's me all right*, followed quickly by *Here's you!* attached to three pictures of her in that very same corridor, through the gaze of his lens. One was in black and white. Shell bat back the instinct to assess herself critically in some brutal side-by-side with her younger and smaller self and listened instead to the quiet surprise that flashed inside her: she looked nice. Like herself. Kiero hadn't made a fuss of posing her the way she had demanded of him: one image was her inspecting a doorway, her profile soft, her eyes curious, looking out of frame. In one she walked ahead of him, looking a little over her shoulder, her hips round, her hair half over her shoulder, her own camera in her hand, strap hanging from her wrist. The last one was farther in the distance, inspecting the hanging vine that had interrupted them. My guest-starring role in their afternoon. The expression of marvel clear on her face, her mouth open a little.

Shell hammered some exclamation points into the keyboard by way of a gasp. *thank you! these are gorgeous! you have a great eye!* Exclamation points, unguarded, earnest.

It doesn't hurt when you have a compelling subject. Winky emoji, he said.

Shell smiled. *you're pretty compelling yourself!* So many exclamation points, she could be shouting. Her tone seemed, upon a quick scan back through the texts, slightly demented, but at least not fawning or seductive. Best keep it chirpy for now, she decided; she could shift the tone as needed if the time came. Kiero took a moment to reply here, and Shell held her breath, wondering where he would take her compliment, but instead of escalating, he turned instead back to the picture: a zoomed-in crop of herself and my hanging vine appeared on the screen.

What do you think that thing was?

i have no idea, to be honest, said Shell. *but maybe it was a stupid idea to touch it. my hands won't stop itching, and i must have touched my eye because that's annoying me now, too.*

Send me a pic? He was very quick with that request. Shell raised her itchy palm, facing out, to the cheekbone near the inflamed stripe under her eye and angled the camera so that it was clear she was lying in bed. Might as well tell a little story with it.

The skin on her palm and cheek where I had left myself on her was pink and slightly risen. Her flesh, soil to me now, though she just assumed it was some kind of slight allergy. An unpleasant reaction, a little hay fever, a sting. It didn't look terrible, she decided, regarding herself in the screen and filtering the image slightly to make herself look a little warmer, less tired, but not so much that Kiero would be able to tell, necessarily. She sent it with no matching text.

Doesn't look too bad, he replied. *Not that I'm a doctor. Might be worth showing it to Neve tomorrow, though, I'd say she's seen it all. Might have some plant-allergy-specific cream she can give you.*

Neve. Yes. Shell closed her eyes a second, and in the eyelid dark, she thought of the ring. The anchor Neve sometimes wore on her hand, sometimes on her neck, black and thick, and Daniel's remarks about Jen, the ex, the recent ex and all these things were stark signals that had to override the connection she felt to the other woman. A boundary as clear as day. Neve clearly had been quite irritated by Kiero's persistence at the shop, by Shell's delight in it—that much was clear. So was it even appropriate to text her and say, *hey, i was having an adventure in the shopping centre's secret corridors with your young friend kiero and a strange thing happened and now i have a rash, please help?* Of course it wasn't.

Shell was immediately bored by her own neurosis. She hated

having to worry like this. Her life had been simpler, emptier before. Void of social complexity and emotional etiquette. When she'd been with Gav, her social role helpfully began and ended at Gav's Girlfriend. She didn't have to make choices with her feelings all the time. It was almost impossible for her to actually hurt anybody because she effectively didn't exist outside the scope of her relationship: there was no other intimacy in her life. It had all been so casual. All this felt so uncasual, and she hadn't even kissed anybody yet. There was so much to overthink. She wouldn't text Neve. Her little flare of jealousy had been pleasing, but Shell wasn't really a sadist, or at least Neve didn't bring that colour out in her. She was spooked and uncomfortable, and she didn't want to stoke any drama. Aside from the physical annoyance of the reaction, she was two full glasses of boxed Chardonnay deep and in bed, feeling suddenly sad about how tricky things could become if she thought about them too much, or didn't think about them enough.

good idea, she typed. *neve is wise. our plant queen.* Pink flower emoji. Small growing sprout emoji.

We'll have cans tomorrow night anyway, he replied quickly as speech. *That way the full medical team can have a look.*

thanks. see you then! Shell replied, happy at least to be invited so easily. Assumed, included. All but adopted. She ended the conversation on another exclamation point, knowing she could have walked down any number of paths during their chat. His suggestion of a picture, his quickness to reply, and his enthusiasm. But her head was wrecked now; the wine was starting to make her maudlin, combined with the persistent discomfort in her hands and on her face. She wanted to dig her skeleton out of her flesh to give herself a break from it, scoop a spoonful of cheek and skin and freckle off her face. Instead, she dragged herself from the bed and trundled downstairs, unobserved by her family lost in their own wall of sound, and removed a bag of peas and a bag of raspberries from the freezer, shouting across the noise to her mother that they would be replaced.

In bed, she placed the berries over her eye socket and clenched the bag of peas in her hands. She pressed her palms flat for maximum surface exposure to the ice, almost like she was performing a prayer for relief over a cold rosary—and you know, her desperation was so theatrical, I did ease off for a moment. Shell was a miserable heap, annoyed at everything, at herself for touching my vine in the first place, at Kiero and Neve and everything being complicated. At Gav. At the rumbling noise of everyone else who lived in her family home—her family, she supposed.

She had no choice about them, or about Gav anymore. Or about the vine, not really—she hadn't ever had any choice in that. If she had not lifted her hand to touch me, I would have summoned it, but Shell really did have a quiet drive towards places that weren't very good for her. That was something I liked so much about her, even if it wasn't something she particularly liked about herself. Eventually, she began to get sleepy, the voices on the podcast she had flicked on to drown out the family sounds becoming a drone, white noise as she slipped away, and while she slept I began my work inside of her, building a garden.

When she woke up to her 7:37 a.m. alarm (the shop's opening shift alarm, much later than the delivery shift alarm), I had dissolved the itch from her skin entirely, so Shell had a few moments of relief, lying there in the damp of her pillow—the raspberries had melted into a deep red mush in their plastic bag. The peas, now body temperature, had migrated somewhere under her duvet. Both had burst open during the night. Disgusting. When she brought her hands up to her bleary eyes, though, her relief curdled and breath left her body like she'd been plunged from her bed into a winter lake: her lungs forgot to work and her heart became a fist, pounding adrenaline through her.

Her right hand had quieted. Her left palm, though, where the bad feeling had been, had changed, become textured. Not risen or inflamed or bulbous or scabbed, but soft. Green and white protrusions came from her palm, tiny buds. And she recognized them quickly as buds, too, knew intrinsically that they were the family of what she had touched in the corridor. She knew something was different now, that I—though she had no name for me—had been roaming her as she slept, dreamless. That I'd been walking the fertile landscape of her form and pushing shoots through the earth of her skin as dawn turned to a soft light down on her. Not a lot of growth. Just a little. Just enough to show her that she had gone somewhere new. Somewhere she would not be returning from.

Magic was not something that occurred to her, though, as she scrambled from the sheets and to her dresser, holding her face close to the mirror to inspect the trickle of buds, not yet bloomed, that led from her eye down to her cheek. Disease was what she thought. Madness. Cancer. Both. Worse. Magic never even crossed her mind, such is the tragedy of adulthood.

She snatched her phone from her sheets, full now of stray peas and the scarlet stain of defrosted berries, and held its camera to her face, turned towards herself. The camera was a more specific, intelligent mirror. Using her finger and thumb she zoomed in on her cheek, trying to work out what was happening.

As she stared at herself, mouth dry, sick, I began then to bloom each tiny bud as she watched, as she made eye contact with herself through the screen, magnified. It didn't hurt her, rather gave her the same sensation as being very softly kissed. Was that not what she had wished for? And what places to be kissed! Her palm, her cheek! My tenderness knows no bounds; this was all but an act of worship!

She grazed her thumb over the red spot on her screen that marked record, as if capturing my display would make it stop, or prove it to be a hallucination. It did neither. I was as real, unfolding white crescents of petals, tiny scallops in a flourish on her skin, as I was in the expensive pixellation of her device. Her palm, too, was made a tiny orchid grove, as she shook from bone to hair at the sight of this becoming.

Dearest beloved spy, most Secret of Agents, Rebecca,

Right. I've slept on it. Well, half slept. Mostly I've lain awake on my hard bed staring at the stipple on the apartment ceiling, feeling my heart race in my chest—but, then, around four, I took a Xanax, which sorted out the heart-racing problem but didn't help much with everything else. I'd been saving those for a rainy day, and here we are. So while I'm not well slept, I'm at least kind of benzo-hungover, which is . . . worse, but a more interesting place to talk from. Vulnerable. The right state of mind for an unhinged confession about the end of your recent long-term relationship. The lab crew can't tell I'm coming down, either. Not that they'd care! I can feel myself starting to turn on them. They're too quiet!

Look, honestly, it's good to know that the thing with the new assistant seems a little romantic. The hope is that if Neve feels something for this girl, then she might be less likely to throw her headfirst into whatever she has going on in the Green Hall. Keep in mind it took her like three years to show me what was going on in there. So we've got time. Or she's got time, we've got . . . nothing to do with it, I suppose. Shell is a nice name. A nice, normal name.

It's super funny that Kiero fancies her, though. She'd be better off with him, even if he is, like, a man—or a boy, I suppose.

Is that unkind? That's unkind. But I also sort of don't care if it is, and I also sort of mean it.

I'm glad you noticed the marks on her. They're not from the work she does, which is really tough on the hands for sure with how cold the stems always are and how much clipping and stripping and chemical handling she does. Like, they're not just on her hands. If they were I'd have just assumed they were from the labor. They're in weird places, and they change all the time. So at first I thought they were self-inflicted, but that's not necessarily right, it doesn't fit how they look, if that makes sense. They're, like, rash marks? So in terms of them being self-inflicted, it's like she's deliberately invoking an allergic reaction in order to forge a sense of closeness to the plants—or a single plant—in the Green Hall. Like the plants get a bit of her, and give her something back. Like a parasite, but worse. I know how that sounds—I mean, I was looking it all dead in the eye for a long time and wasn't able to comprehend it. I'm a plant person, Bec. I literally have a PhD in plants? It took me three years and being brought into the Green Hall to see what was going on to realize that what was happening with Neve was coming up out of the ground.

Like, it is, from what I can tell, one plant in there. She only brought me in once, and I didn't stick around, or take any pictures—and I should have, like I really regret not thinking of it, but I was so frightened in that moment that I was hardly going to start waving my phone around. The thing I think is the problem, the one plant, looks kind of like a pretty generic boat orchid. You mightn't even notice it unless you were shown it; it certainly wouldn't have leapt out at me. When you look closely, it has a kind of mutation that's given it a kind of triskele effect, so there's, like, three "faces" instead of one, if that makes sense? I've seen that mutation before, it's not uncommon—you get it in roses regularly enough. I think maybe if the plant is something dangerous, then the power it has is one of camouflage. Especially if it is a parasitic thing, disguise would work in its favor. I honestly haven't been able to find any parasitic orchid strains in my studies, but I'll keep looking.

That one morning, Neve was kneeling there on the floor of the Green Hall in front of this weird little orchid and talking to it, like it was a person. It was just standing there, like any other flower, but she got so frustrated when it wouldn't talk back, it was like she was hallucinating something, or realizing her own delusions weren't connecting with reality, or getting angry that I wasn't playing into them—look, I don't even really know what happened that day, but I knew immediately that I had to get out of there. She was almost feral, or something. Our relationship was pretty much over by that stage, so it wasn't like that was what put us under or anything. But I didn't love her by then, so I wasn't going to stay to either play into her fantasy or help her get up out of it. Neve doesn't accept help, anyway. Or, I mean, she didn't. I guess she just hired help. So that's something—but I don't know if it's something good or something bad just yet. Either way, it's just not like her, and a change is something to take note of. Like a creep. Like a creep who's writing long emails about her ex-girlfriend who has been secretly having some kind of nervous breakdown.

I mean, here's a real question. Did you know any of this? Am I just totally shortsighted? Has it been super obvious all along that Neve was into something dark, or is what I'm saying the worst and strangest kind of news to get? I am aware, I swear to god, every sentence I write I am aware of how unhinged this all sounds. Like, Bec. I know. Parasitic orchids. Neve letting the plant infect her skin, for some reason that we can't know. Even the thought of it makes me feel sick, the worst kind of sick. The kind where I feel like I left her there to die.

Even typing that out feels fucked. Like, you walk away from a person you can't help, you don't want to help, you don't love, and you leave them there in your old life with all their problems and their sorrow, and you're risking the version of reality where you could have fixed them. I can't fix anybody. I've got my own shit, we all do. Every time you leave someone's life you risk being the worst thing that's ever happened to them, or the last thing to ever happen to them, don't you? Thing is, I'm not even a little bit the worst thing that's ever happened to Neve. I have a suspicion that that's still happening to her, in the Green Hall, and that she's about to make it that poor Shell girl's problem.

I physically beg of you to delete this message, and to not say anything about all this to Neve. Talking about her like this is such a betrayal, and I've got the guilt of that added to the fear. What a nausea cocktail. God, if a single one of these lab coat freaks would talk to me outside of basic monosyllabic exchanges I could at least be distracted for fifteen minutes, but I've got nothing. Just all this in my head, and now worry for this poor girl I don't even know. Like, really, consider giving Young Kiero a little encouragement. I mean, if he's still in the country that is, which I feel like realistically he's going to be for some time.

I have no idea how to sign off other than: please don't hate me for saying all this, and also please reply soon. My downer stash won't last that long, and I could do with a morsel of peace. A shred. A grain. A microdose of peace, please, Bec.

xoxoXO,
Dr. Jen

The rest of the house was mercifully silent as Shell crept into the world. She briefly considered asking her mother for help, but her mother was out. Everyone was out, in fact, and if Shell hadn't been so propelled by horror she would have savoured the hush of the place over a long cup of milky instant coffee and three slices of batch toast with butter and crunchy brown sugar. But there was no time. No time for anything. She didn't want to touch anything with her new hands, least of all food, for fear she was a contaminant herself. She balled her fists in her jacket and placed sunglasses over her eyes, big ones that just about obscured the new flourish on her cheek. She put in her earbuds for a distraction and to keep her walking pace high and took off towards Neve in the Crown. Instinctively, she knew Neve would be able to help her. All confused emotions about their non-situation were dissolved immediately by this urgency, and she thought of the scarring on the other woman's hands as she felt the alien, grotesque softness of the petals coming from her skin. The clever girl then realized that they must have this, or something like it—me—in common.

Shell tore through the estate, paranoia flicking through her. What if somebody saw, what if somebody blamed her, what if she made someone else sick—the judgement, or perceived judgement, nauseated her, and she ended up all but running towards the shopping centre, just to feel like she was pushing back against what was happening to her body. Shell was not in control of this, no, I was, and some wordless suspicion inside her already knew that. The green body she had touched chose this for her. My green body.

The Crown was quiet, too. Sparse. Only a handful of people on their Wednesday morning grocery run, their quick nip to the bookie, their walk with the baby to the Juice Stand, their drop-off run to the library. Shell slowed to a determined walk when she got inside, so as not to draw attention to her rush, and zeroed in on the florist, her florist, where Neve was standing outside, lining up succulents on a little table. Her apron was tied in a bow just at the small of her back, and Shell was struck by the spot where her little navy crewneck was slightly caught in the tie, revealing a pale band of skin above the waistband of her corduroys. Shell closed her eyes in a long blink and descended on Neve then, grabbing her wrist, and said, "Something happened, and I don't know what to do."

At the feel of her palm, Neve's face fell from surprise to flashing shock, then to concern. She took Shell's arm and ushered her inside, closing and locking the door behind them, flipping the sign hanging in the window to CLOSED FOR LUNCH, LADIES.

"Show me." Neve demanded, standing back from Shell as she hesitantly took off her sunglasses, no deliberate and elegant makeup today, just her eyes made small from crying, her cheeks puffy and pink.

Neve's mouth hardened into a line at the sight of the arc of tiny orchids—unmistakably me—on Shell's face. How destabilizing for her to see my work on someone else, despite the lengths she had gone to in order to keep me and my blooms all to herself for so long, only ever once risking inviting someone else to touch me before (someone who had, sensibly, refused). Shell raised her hand, too, and Neve, not letting the revelation linger, said, "Okay. Let me sort you out," as though she were addressing a cut knee or a finger sliced open by a thorn. She walked towards the back room calmly, and Shell followed her, comforted by Neve's practical reaction. She said, "Oh, thank you, thank god," but Neve looked over her shoulder and said, "Thank me later," with such a flat tone that Shell's relief was coloured differently, with just the faintest stripe of shame.

In the back room, they sat up on the high backless stools at the work table, and Neve produced the most-used tools of her trade from her apron. Her yellow-handled scissors, her tape, some stray wires and elastic bands: she was clearing out her pockets, looking for something—oh. There it was. A pair of tweezers and then a tiny plastic disc full of assorted sewing needles.

"The first-aid case is on the shelf above the rolls of paper and cellophane; grab it for me, would you?" Neve pointed over Shell's shoulder, and she did as she was told as Neve kept rummaging in her pocket, producing two small white tubes, unlabelled, like the ones used to contain toothpaste but with the text and patterns removed. They were squeezed already, but not empty; one was demarked from the other with a piece of blue tape.

Shell reached up for the heavy red tin and brought it back to Neve's makeshift operating table. Neve herself was washing her hands at the industrial steel sink that she usually just used for filling buckets with water for the flowers. The unmistakable smell of antiseptic wafted through the air—it reminded Shell of her childhood, one or the other of her and her sisters taking a fall and having a graze doused, stinging, and the hospital reek of Dettol. It gave her a safe and cared-for feeling.

She placed the first-aid box on the table with a thunk as Neve came back over to her with two glasses filled from the tap, one in each hand. She opened the red tin and removed two sets of effervescent painkillers marked MAX—the kind you could only get in England, usually reserved for period pain, exceptional hangovers, or comedowns. Neve prepared the two glasses ceremonially, and when the fizzing tablets finally dissolved into a potent seltzer, she drank hers in a single gulp, gesturing at Shell to do the same.

"Is . . . this going to hurt?" she asked, hesitating at the glass, which was emitting a radio static sound from the fierce little bubbles containing the opposite of pain.

"Yes," replied Neve, ripping open a sachet and using the alcohol wipe within to clean her tweezers and a small scissors from the kit.

"Why did you take one?" Shell pressed, gesturing to her own painkiller before drinking it quickly.

Neve said, "Because this is going to hurt me, too. Put your hand on the table. We'll start with that so you can see what I'm doing, before I do your face."

Shell placed her hand, palm facing upwards, outstretched on the table. Neve stood up then and chose the white tube with the blue tape first. She opened the lid and squeezed a pea-sized quantity onto her finger, transferring it to Shell's hand and in a shocking crescent moon under her eye and rubbing it in with her own thumb. It felt hot and astringent and Shell hissed at the sensation.

"It would feel worse if I plucked them out while they were still alive," Neve said, picking up her tweezers, and yes, I felt it, and yes, it hurt me, but this is a small wound for what I would gain.

The blooms went from snowy white with bright green stems and leaves all scalloped so prettily to brown and wet, poisoned quickly to rot, and Shell felt a stab of disgust so acute that she retched and then apologized, and Neve said, "Don't worry about it, I know the feeling."

She then set about extracting the bed of ruined flowers, one by one, with her tweezers. She pinched the heads and pulled, pulling roots like floss woven down beneath Shell's skin. It hurt like each strand was tethered to the bones of her skeleton, though I was holding on to something much harder to name. I let each strand go, but only because I knew the land of her would be more fertile after this reaping.

One by one, Neve harvested the spoiled crop, and Shell, by the end, was only flinching at the pain that broke through the chemical gauze of the effervescent Neve had handed her, the disgust somehow manageable now. Neve told her she was taking it like a champ, and Shell almost laughed. Where each shoot left her, there was a tiny red laceration, and Neve spritzed those sites with a bottle of alcohol, which stung but felt clean to Shell, too. This procedure felt impossibly intimate, Neve performing a kind of surgery on her, holding her hand open and healing her.

"In a minute, I'll move on to your face. Are you ready for that? Or do you need a break?" Neve didn't look Shell in the eye, instead meticulously weeding out the last of me from her palm then dousing her again in clear, stinging alcohol. Sweat beaded her hairline. This did, in fact, hurt her, too. I made sure of it.

"Can I have a moment, actually?" Shell's voice was papery, her skin pale.

"Do you need a drink?" Neve replied. "Because I'm going to have one."

Neve had lost colour in her face, too, trembling slightly from containing the screams I shot through her nerve endings, kind of like a strike for every extraction she made. Nothing too bad. Just some light electrocution. Just a reminder that I was going nowhere, that I was alive in the room, their third at the table, a second in each of their bodies. Shell just took it as concentration, exertion, but it wasn't. She would come to know the shine of sweat like this on Neve's skin, in time.

Shell said, "It's not even nine in the morning."

Neve replied, "That's not a no," and went to the little closed cabinet where she normally kept her leftover sauce from the food court parties. She leant down—the small of her back in Shell's eyeline again—and clanked around abandoned half-full bottles until she found an American bourbon. She stuck it under her arm, grabbed then drenched the two painkiller glasses quickly with a roar from the highly pressurized work sink, and filled them halfway while they were still wet from their rinse.

Neve slid one to Shell, who was quaking, staring at the tiny puncture wounds in her hand. She downed her glass in one without prompt. If only the cocktail of codeine and neat whiskey had ever worked for Neve before, during the times when she had to perform this kind of operation on herself. It wouldn't work on Shell, either. Lay waste to yourself all you like, I will grow in your ruin.

"You won't feel it," Neve said through a gasp from the heat of her own shot.

"What, this?" Shell gestured to her cheek. "I think I will, actually,"

"No, I meant it's fine to have the whiskey. It'll be neutralized by everything else. The adrenaline and that. You won't be too drunk to work later." Neve began to pour them another shot each.

"Work?" exclaimed Shell, waving her hand, now prickling with blood. "I can't work! I don't even know what happened to me! What the fuck is this, Neve? How do you know how to deal with this?" She was becoming a little pitchy now, her calm and collected veneer starting to crack.

"Drink first," Neve commanded, and Shell did. The bourbon was warm and spicy but good, and there was a little too much of it, so she needed to swallow twice, trickles of it escaping the corners of her mouth.

Neve took up the tweezers and said quietly, "I'm going to

need you to let me come very close to you now. The nearer I am, the less risk there is of me hurting you by accident."

Shell nodded, mute, as Neve came around the table to her and stood between her knees. She took Shell's chin in her hand and said, "You might want to close your eyes," so Shell did, almost relieved that she wouldn't have to experience Neve's face at what was, effectively, kissing proximity. She could smell her hair, the mint and whiskey on her breath, and worse than all this, feel the warmth of her. Their legs were touching.

The sheer intensity of it would, Shell prayed, get her through the pain. Her fingernails dug into her unwounded palm to release pressure, and her jaw was locked shut with anticipation. The pain was undeniably part of it, the bowstring between them.

"This is hard, so I'm going to tell you why this happened while I'm doing it, so you don't lose the run of yourself and get all shrill again." Neve began to work, and Shell didn't make a sound, just listened to her voice, now soft, and took in as much of their closeness as she could handle.

"Don't move a muscle," Neve ordered, soft, and Shell obeyed.

"Good. Now. This happened—the itching, the rash, the growing—because of a plant that grows here in the Crown. I've been working on it—well, with it—for years. It leaves traces of itself when you touch it, like an infection, kind of. I don't really understand it, but I've been caring for it. It, well—him. Him. You probably had a brush with him, probably in the back room. I've never heard of him showing himself to anybody else but me, so he must like you. Or be interested in you. I don't know."

Good. That's how you tell her.

She took a breath. "He's big. Bigger than you can imagine, really. But he's clever. Good at hiding and watching. Knowing things. He wouldn't have let you touch him by accident. He'll leave marks on your body, but they won't be as visible as mine. It's more, well, him getting into your head I'd be concerned about.

Though I should stop. It's rude to talk about someone who's listening. There. You're done. On your break you might want to go over to the supermarket and get one of those big kitchen cartons of table salt. Rub it into the places that the shoots grew, and they shouldn't come back. I mean. I say shouldn't. But who knows."

I don't like salt. She did have one on me there. The salt of sweat is tolerable to me. The salt of tears. The salt of the body. But the white crystals are rough. Unpleasant.

Neve daubed an alcohol wipe under Shell's now-streaming eyes, wiping clean the site of the removal and then, on her other cheek, sweeping away Shell's tears with her thumb.

"What the fuck, Neve," Shell whispered, not opening her eyes, afraid.

"I know, I know." Neve stroked the side of Shell's face, setting in close to her for a moment. "I wish I could explain better. I've never had to explain before—not like this. I've gone to some serious lengths not to have to explain. But here we are. He was going to crawl out at some time or another."

They stayed there a moment in a haze. Shell scared out of her mind and rolling on adrenaline, Neve in a kind of mourning, having spoken of me aloud. Our secret was out, or, well. Our secret was beginning to emerge. She had been reserved. Said very little of the truth, as was her habit, only enough to give an outline. Less than she had told Jen.

"I'll have to show him to you," Neve finally said, stepping away from Shell and out of the sphere of tension, which had blown like glass around them.

Shell opened her eyes then, released from the spell. Not, though, from the desire—that was still there—but at least the temptation was broken. She could have closed the space between them at any time, stopped the sparse horror story Neve was telling her, and in doing so, ruined everything.

Her will was iron. The only reason she didn't do it, all things considered—the surgical weeding of her face, the profound strangeness of what Neve had just said to her—was that she didn't want to hazard what they had. Not yet, anyway. Being rejected in this instance was about the only thing that could have made it worse. At least not kissing Neve felt potent and heavy, and could be preserved exactly as it was inside Shell's head. She had also not been with a woman since she was twenty-four. A world ago. Barely into adulthood. Shell wasn't sure she'd have any idea what to do with Neve, but that was part of the call—Neve would show her. Neve would give her clear instruction.

"Now, I'm going to open up before I miss any more sales. You get yourself together, then there's sixteen wild bouquets to wrap. I've more eucalyptus than I know what to do with, so feature it heavily." And Neve was gone out front again, all of her tools still laid out, and that was that: Shell dizzied, still sitting. Too much, all of this. Too much. Two feelings meeting in a wild place, and she was all alone in the workroom with the fear and the . . . well, lust, she supposed it was. Not love. Not that.

". . . Neve? Can we talk?" Shell called after her, her voice feeling very far away.

"Later, I promise" came Neve's reply, accompanied by the little ringing wind chime of the shop door being opened. Back to business, as if nothing had gone on between them at all.

Later, then, Shell mouthed to herself, looking down at her hand and touching the wounded spot on her cheek with the other.

After a few minutes, as though on autopilot, she packed away the first-aid setup, rinsed the glasses, and put the whiskey back in the cabinet. Neve had taken the tweezers with her, though, and the two unmarked tubes.

The rest of the day tottered along slowly, on uneven legs, Neve staying out front and Shell only really engaging with her to mechanically pass over bouquets and wreaths. Her hands stung. Her head spun. She tried to focus on listening to soft Americans on the radio, their voices disappearing in the air, becoming a drone.

Neve would sometimes call back requests and Shell would obey quietly, like a cook working alone in a kitchen answering orders for eggs Benedict or French toast. She was in a daze, not really able to figure out what Neve had done to her, what she had said. That wasn't even the whole truth, was it? The breadth and depth of Neve's secrets might have cracked the girl open, but Shell held it together—didn't lean in for the kiss, kept the kiss to herself for now, allowed a kind of surgery on her body in the back room, hated herself for being so aroused by it. That was a more helpful line of focus than Neve confessing my existence to her, than any mention of a creature.

Shell dithered over going and demanding information from Neve with every bunch she assembled, her hands aching at their weight, stinging at the open pinprick sores left behind under a pair of gloves she had found tucked onto a shelf. She wanted to storm to the front of the shop and demand details, cause a scene, raise her voice.

Shell couldn't remember the last time she'd caused a scene.

Spectacle wasn't really for her: this was both her power and her curse. She'd let anything happen and stand there, internalizing, not acting. A perfect little coward in the face of conflict or change. There hadn't even been any scenes when she broke up with Gav. Sure, she told herself she wanted to usher out any shop customers, shouting that they were closed for the foreseeable, and lock the door behind them. Certainly, she wanted to get very close to Neve again, maybe hold her by the shoulders and say into her face, Tell me what is going on. Maybe instead of speaking, Neve would kiss her. Shell would do neither of these things. Instead, she simmered, doing her job. She felt she would likely make a scene of some kind soon; it was rolling up inside her, like thunder.

It was easy now for Shell to conjure up an image of what that kind of tense intimacy with Neve was like: it had her sort of ruined, focusing on the wrong thing, all Neve when she should have been wondering more about me. All she had to do was think and breathe, and she could conjure up the feeling of Neve that close to her, just as she had been. What a terrible gift she had been given. That at least got her through her workday, including the lunch break when she did, in fact, dart out to Dunnes supermarket to buy a fat tub of salt to apply to herself, as advised.

As they quietly locked up for the day and migrated through the quiet, closing mall towards the food court for drinks, still, as though nothing had happened, Neve hesitated at the bottom of the escalators, by the Green Hall. She and Shell took a moment before stepping onto the still-locked metal staircase. I writhed my vines behind the glass, and Neve noticed me but Shell did not. Neve's gaze darkened as she took Shell's arm—so at ease touching her now—and led her quietly to the door. I was thrilled by this, by Neve's tone as she said, "I don't want to bring you to him yet. I'm not ready, and you're not ready, but—he's in here. And everywhere else. But . . . mostly in here." As she stood in front of the murky door, almost unidentifiable from another pane of glass but for a metal strip with a keyhole punctured into it, an email landed in her inbox. Shell's, too. Neither looked at their phones, their alerts firmly switched off.

"We're not going to... say anything to the others about what happened earlier?" Shell asked softly, as they trudged up the steep, toothy escalator.

"No. We're not. There's absolutely no need for any of them to know. In fact, them knowing would be very bad, and very dangerous for me, do you understand?" Neve stopped suddenly on the steep step above Shell and loomed down at her for a second, like she had never said anything as serious in her entire life.

Shell nodded, mute.

"Good," said Neve, like a threat, and continued her climb.

By the time they got across the stretch of mall to the food court, Bec and Daniel were sitting at a table, staring at their phones in silence. Bec was chewing her vape nervously, and Daniel had a hand over his mouth. It was a sombre vignette.

"Did you see?" Daniel asked, through his hand, barely looking up as Shell and Neve sat down. "Did you see?"

"There hasn't been—" Neve started.

Bec said, "Nobody's dead this time, no more missing people. No." She wasn't looking at Neve, or Daniel, or Shell, just down at her phone.

"Did you not read the email?" Daniel said then, scowling slightly. "Do you ever check your email?"

The atmosphere was flinty. Both Daniel and Bec sounded as though they were about to burst into tears. Shell flipped open her email—the account linked to the shop's Instagram—and there it was. She and Neve saw the message at the same split second and both gasped, breath gone out of them.

The subject line read **URGENT: WOODBINE CROWN PERMANENT CLOSURE**

This was the second time in the span of a single day that Shell would have had every right to cause a scene but instead froze still, looking over the email that laid out the impossible. I felt it all, too, the caving in of the world we had built, me and Neve, who whispered deep, No no no no *no* as much to address me as to show her horror to the group.

The message was short and blunt: the kind of instrument that can cause the most shocking wounds when delivered with enough force.

> **For the immediate attention of all vendors and staff of the Woodbine Crown:**
>
> Due to the increasing instability of the architecture of the Woodbine Crown and the risk of harm this poses to the public, the board have elected to name the closing date of the building and all interior businesses and public services—radio, health centre, and library included—as one week from today, Wednesday the 7th of August. Please vacate the property by then.
>
> Sincerely and with thanks,
>
> Brendan Corrigan, Sandra McIvor, and the Board of the Woodbine Crown

It took me a moment to parse what was going to happen through Neve's eyes, her heart rate rising. I was aware suddenly that something was about to change, and that if I wanted to act, I must do it quickly.

I must not panic. I must not be afraid. I must simply act. I will not starve. I will not disappear. I will not simply wither back to where I came from. I still hunger. I still have so much to eat.

At the table, Bec was typing something violently into her phone with her thumb while absently chewing her vape.

"Are you replying to them?" Daniel asked. "Because if you are, I'm going to."

"Nah. No point," Bec said. "I'm . . . forwarding it on to my regional manager. I think . . . I think they can move me to the head office. Look, I'll feel less sick if I send this. Just give me a second."

"Solid problem-solving, babe." Daniel leant over and put his hand on her knee, a comfort. "Ask if they'll move me to the head office, too, yeah?"

"I fuckin' will," she replied, looking over the edge of her phone sadly.

Shell was still spinning and Neve was frozen and neither of them were aware of the state of the other, so huge was the realization that their world was crashing down around them, around us.

"But I just got here," Shell mumbled, still staring at the email, as though if she looked at it hard enough her want would change the text, change the reality.

"Could be worse, you could have been here since you were sixteen, like me," Daniel said. "I've been working up at Billie's for more than half my life."

Shell thought, Jesus, that's miserable, but she didn't say it.

"Well . . . maybe you can go freelance?" she said hopefully. "You know? Go to old ladies, instead of them coming to you?"

"I'm going to have to," Daniel said. "It'll be fine, I'm sure, but . . . just . . ."

But, just. But, just, the almost empty temple of linoleum and tile that his life was built around was being shuttered, then floored. But, just, this was his life. My life, too.

Neve didn't speak. I ran myself through her body, looking for the truth of what she was feeling, and I did not like what I found. I found, for the very first time, betrayal where I thought I would find her fear, her horror at losing me.

Beneath her silence and her empty gaze at the email, she felt sorrow, and uncertainty. But underneath that again, where I know her best, she felt what I least expected. Relief.

She wasn't even trying to hide it from me. The audacity of her made me furious, and I squeezed the bones in her forearms to let her know I was paying attention, and she winced but would not engage with my presence, and in the channels inside her head where I normally sang and spoke, I said, How dare you, and she did not reply to me in the private landscape of her mind, but she heard me. The sensation of relief is like a heavy, hard thing inside the body dissolving, returning to blood. I am that heavy thing, and she cannot loosen herself of me but she still felt lightness. I said, You will never be free of me, and she said, loud, through the chambers of her body, Yes, I will.

And I withdrew from her insides then. I would not hear this insolence from her. I would not permit her to push me. I would not lose my temper. Though temper is pleasurable, at this juncture it was not going to help me get what I wanted, within the approaching chaos of what I would not be able to control. The fact of it was impossible. All my power, the vast expanse of my vines, the reach of my tendrils both inside the bodies I choose and out, out into the world. I need a greenhouse to grow in and I need a gardener to tend me, to feed me. I would have them both but here, this cold threat, this dull and heavy reality, reminded me suddenly that there were things outside my control.

Not for long. Not for long.

Kiero tottered up the escalators, weighed heavy with wine bottles, the news already down on him, his eyes tell-tale puffy, sniffling. Shell's heartstrings whined softly for him in her chest as he approached.

"Well, it's all fucked, so," he said, clunking the plastic bags of bottles up onto the table. "I'm going to have to get my shit together, but not tonight."

"Hear, hear," said Shell, giving his shoulder a tender rub, and he leant into her touch, the warmth of it genuinely comforting him.

"No cups. Going to have to neck them," he said, unloading

what became quickly apparent as four bottles of cheap prosecco. "Might as well celebrate. End of an era."

"End of an everything," Daniel said, and Bec hummed, still tapping her phone. "Almost done. Almost."

"What are you thinking, pal?" Daniel asked Neve, releasing the cork on his bottle.

Neve looked at him for a second. "I'm . . . working out how I can make this work for me. Shell, how many followers did you say you have on that Instagram account?"

Shell, without a blink, answered, "Twenty-four thousand, should hit twenty-five this week."

"Do you think we could just start . . . using it as a shop? Like, I can move the studio stuff home to my house, and we can work there, and do deliveries?"

Shell nodded, relief washing up over her. "Yes. Yes, I get messages about deliveries every single day but I always have to say no."

"Well, we can find a driver and—"

"I can be your driver," Kiero said. "Easy."

Neve clapped her hands together then, a single slap. "Right. Right. This is going to be fine, so. Not a bother on us. Fine. Absolutely fine. Jesus, we'll have to sage the place before we go, won't we?"

Her nerve. Her absolute nerve at saying that out loud, with her mouth, her full chest, her guts. She meant it, knowing full well I could hear, knowing what it would do to me, how hurt I would be. Perhaps she was trying to hurt me, as if that hurt might deter me in my love of her, my need for her. She was trying to pretend she didn't need me, shutting down the part of herself that had so closely been my attendant for as long as I have been this side of earth. As if there weren't blood on her hands, too, oh, finding her exit, finding her sweet second life after me. There is no life after me, Neve. There is nothing after me, only us.

This is where, staring down at them as their mourning turns to a strange, sad celebration of the lives ahead of them, I realize I have a challenge ahead. I had imagined Neve and I would have a longer life together in the manner in which we had been dancing, before that courtship would come to an end and we would at last come together. The hunger that was gnawing at me grew in the light of Neve's betrayal, the space in me I had been cultivating for her so fertile that it had its own pulse. I had been working on her too slowly, assuming the luxury of time, of the permanence of the Woodbine Crown. No mall's roots go that deep. Nothing put up can't be torn down again, I know that now, and watching them drink I began to build out my plan, careful and slight—it was time for Shell to enter her new role, sweet leading lady, oh new gardener of mine.

"We're nothing if not incredibly practical," said Daniel. "To be fair to us. But we'll have to find somewhere else to drink, some other excuse to not . . . you know. Drift."

Shell nodded. "Like, it would be just the worst if we turned into another weird, stilted WhatsApp group. I don't know if I could handle that."

"I do not need another awkward WhatsApp group," said Bec, exhaling a sigh, her fevered emailing done now, her phone disappearing into the breast pocket on her work blazer. "Like, can we just not do that? Can we just pick somewhere to have a drink twice a week and do that, the way, like . . . old people do?"

"Old. Speak for yourself. We'll all see each other, obviously," Kiero said, gesturing at Neve and Shell, "since I'm going to be driving for them. Daniel will be cutting our hair as per usual. You'll be the one working corporate, so you'll have to make sure not to forget us off in the glamourous Cassidy Travel Headquarters Compound, right?"

"Well, that is if they take me on. If they lay me off, I'll work it out. I'll find some way to pay me mortgage, marry a doctor or something." Bec opened her own bottle and waved a cheers to the table. "To getting out of this kip," she said, playful, but full of sorrow, too. The cheers, the sláinte that came around the table held that same note of conflicted emotion. They would be fine, certainly, but they would never be the same. They each knew the building was rotten to the core, even those of them who did not know about me growing in the rot. They loved the Crown anyway: they had come of age here, found each other here. Their lives had played out over the linoleum and under the halogen, the back-and-forth with their customers, the reek of the supermarket deli and the food court, the rotating seasonal decorations, day after day, year after year, the place getting more worn and them just living through it. Thriving against it, in some ways burning all the brighter for the decay. They would be fine, after. Better than fine.

"You're whip-smart for starting that Instagram, Shell," Neve said, looking at the other woman with a slight smile, with all that had gone on between them, all poison and salt and me temporarily diffused in this news. "That'll save us. That'll be the ticket now. You just keep me off camera, right? Make a gentle announcement that we'll be . . . shutting up shop?"

"No, no, no—we'll be transitioning to deliveries only due to circumstances outside our control. We're devastated," began Shell, in a clipped mockery of a professional voice, "that due to the long-planned and now final closure of the beloved Woodbine Crown, we, like many other businesses across the world, will be turning remote for the foreseeable. The good news is"—she stood up for this, addressing the circle, seven-euro prosecco astringent in her throat but good for her head—"that we'll be able to deliver a wide range of arrangements, houseplants, and more to your homes—We're so excited about this next chapter in our journey!"

A ripple of applause rolled back to her as she took a silly little bow, prosecco bottle held out from her body, the perfect prop.

"You sure you don't want to try and steal a job up in corporate?" Bec asked. "Because that's some professional-level bullshit right there, admirable stuff."

"I worked for a design agency for years—it's like a second language," Shell smugged. "Glad to be putting it to good use."

"I'll do my own announcement of exodus, I think," Daniel said. "I somehow doubt the Bridies and Fidelmas are going to be following me on social media to keep up with all I'm doing. I'll have to tell them all in person, use a little black book. Ring them on the third of every month to remind them to come in for their wet set perms and violet rinses, Jesus wept."

"Look, you'll be in no shortage of work. You can go to their homes, make it a more personalized service," said Bec.

"But where else can they even go all day, like? Eighty years old and you're just sitting in your house, staring at the shite news all day? If you survived the last few years you want to get out and about to get your rinse done. You don't want everything brought to you. You want to go out," Daniel said.

"I want a violet rinse," said Kiero, giving his hair a swish. "I think it'd suit me."

"You're sixty years too young," teased Shell, but the *too young* felt sour in her mouth.

His eyes caught hers for a split second, and in that fraction of a moment he looked a little hurt, before plastering on a grin. "Exactly! If I'm to be a delivery executive for your floristry services, customers will take me more seriously if I present as a mature gentleman. Plus, I'll be twenty-three in September."

"Twenty-three," laughed Neve. "Christ, I forget that all the time."

"You should! Especially when I'm on staff. I expect to be treated as an equal in age—I can do anything a person in their thirties can do, only probably with more energy, because I'm full of, like, the vitality of youth."

"Vitality of youth is a very fancy way of saying you're too stupid to pace yourself, and I don't want to hire you—I want you to leave the country, and so does everyone else!" Neve jabbed, picking up the bottle on the table in front of Kiero, which he had too enthusiastically downed as though it were just a sour sparkling water.

Shell wanted to disappear into the floor, considering suddenly how working in close quarters with both Neve and Kiero would require a lot of very firm boundaries and control. If Kiero was to deliver for the flower shop and she was to be working more closely with him, as well as Neve, she would have to cease all flirtation with both of them until further notice. Especially Kiero—well, mostly Kiero, because she wasn't sure that what she was doing with Neve, after today, was even flirting anymore, anyway.

Oh, it wasn't flirting. What a small, silly word, flirting—the implication being that she could simply tip the edge of something, or be tipped back, with little to no consequence, or commitment. A flirtation is the edge of a petal, not even the yellow of pollen. A flirtation is a dance you can walk away from, or a walk you can dance away from. Neve was neither dance, walk, nor flower. And up in the food court as they drowned their sorrows and summoned celebration for what would come after the Woodbine Crown fell, Shell was in the last nights of a life she could never return to again. So I let her drink up and drunk up and become sodden and disappear into herself: have a blackout, her first in years. As a treat, you know? Before her fate was unveiled to her, a little gift: such rich, well-deserved unknowing. It was Daniel who carried her to her front door.

Bec, no. Like, no way. My gut says no. Okay, my gut and my whole body are saying no, but I'm going to have to think through it, because maybe yes is the right answer and I'm just scared out of my mind, so my gut is all I have to go by.

First of all, okay, before we get into the absurdity of what you just asked me, they're actually going to close the Crown? Isn't there, like, a full library and supermarket in there? They can't just . . . close it, can they? I know they'd been threatening to, I know it was on the cards, but it was all talk, right? They'll hardly go through with it. Like, I absolutely refuse to believe they'll go through with it. There's miles and miles and miles of suburbs around the Crown, and basically no other food stores. There's a McDonald's in the parking lot! There's a whole sports bar! Are you telling me they're going to level the whole thing to build apartments? I mean, a part of me would believe it given the desolate vibes of the Crown (no offense, truly no offense) and how much the land would go for. Like, think of what they're doing to the city center, you know? Last time I was there was a hot minute ago, but even then you could see blocks upon blocks getting shut down and emptied out, and the skyline was full of these huge, sinister cranes—in a way it makes sense for someone to flatten it and build up housing. It comes down to money, you know? It's not like it's publicly owned land.

If I was Mr. Johnny Woodbine Crown himself (I assume this is his name and that he is a real person) and my legacy was a two-thirds empty shopping center that hasn't been renovated in fifty years, honestly? Gun to my head? I'd want it off my hands, too. Like, before the wrong ceiling tile falls down, or someone gets electrocuted from standing underneath a particularly violent light fixture. I can't believe I'm empathizing with not only a landowner but also a property developer, but here we are. And look, I only say this because I'm fully not worried about your job—you can do that remotely, right? Daniel could freelance. Kiero should, like. Go leave the country. Neve, though—Neve. I can see why she's freaking out.

Like, I can't believe she cried at the end of the night. She must have been fucked up to let it all out like that. When have you ever known Neve to be anything other than totally stoic? She doesn't cry. I was with the woman for three years, she's not a crier. She didn't cry when I left, you know that? I mean, maybe she cried in front of you guys and she was just playing hard in front of me, what do I know.

Okay, you can't tell, but I got up and walked away from the computer to do some research before I chose that particular inconsistency as a hill to die on, and unfortunately, apparently conservation can, in some cases, be a cause to slow if not cease land development. By research, though, I mean I used this question as an excuse to talk to some of the lab techs, and they did in fact have answers and also we had a little machine-coffee about it! It was a proper social moment, I'm very proud of myself. Anyway, yeah, the conservation thing tracks. It doesn't happen often. Like, there would need to be something really, really special growing in there and only there. Nowhere else in the area, nowhere else in the county. Preferably nowhere else in Ireland, and you guys have a pretty diverse range of flora so that might be a tricky call, but that boat orchid with the mutation might be the ticket.

Now, I recognize that this requires me to come up to Dublin, investigate the situation, take samples, drive back out here, test the samples, and run them against the database of national and then local records. It's not that big a job, and I can write off the hours as part of my usual reports—that's not what I'm worried about. I'm worried about going in there with Neve again, I'm worried about seeing her and whether she's deteriorated. But looking more closely at the plant might give me some clarity about what's happened to her. I'll be able to test it and see if there are parasitic qualities to it, you know? I'll be able to run studies on the pollen. That might give me a bit of peace: like if the plant is making Neve sick, and I can prove that—I can tell her, and show her, and use proper scientific data to back up my point. That might hurt her, sure, but in the long term it'll save her. I can't believe I'm still trying to save Neve, Bec. Jesus. I left that job, that life. I didn't want it anymore, and look at me talking myself back into it.

If it saves Neve, it'll save the other girl, too. And like, god knows who else. If there's something sick growing in there, it might not just be affecting Neve. Like, I've seen the back room of the flower shop and some of the corridors down behind the other retail units; there's vines coming in from the ceiling—you've seen them, haven't you? I know they're sort of part of the run-down charm of the place, but what if they're putting something unhealthy into the air? I mean, Neve is obviously impacted the worst, but I'd imagine that even ambient exposure is probably not so great for you. Sorry, I'm aware this is probably paranoia-inducing stuff here. But basically, I know I said no to helping, but I'm going to say yes, and I'm not going to go up and delete the first paragraph of this email where I said no because I want to be clear that I have had to talk myself into it and I'm not racing down, heart in my mouth, to rescue Neve from gradual poisoning and, ultimately, herself. That's not what's happening here. I'm looking for an answer to a question, and look, potentially could have a hand in keeping the Crown where it is, too.

I know the place means a lot to you. It meant a lot to me, too. Though realistically, between the Crown Inn, the library, the radio station, and the enormous international burger chain in the parking lot, I think there'll probably be enough backlash to demolishing the place without my help, but I'll pitch in, anyway. Might help me get some sleep.

Let me know when I'm needed.

Xoxoxoox,
Dr. Jen

Blossom

Shell woke up from a blank sleep with her mouth dry and her head sore. Last night, pissed and exhausted, she had left herself the gift of a pint of water and two different kinds of painkiller as well as a sachet of the kind of electrolyte powder used to treat dehydration that her mother swore was a cure for anything from a sick stomach to a broken heart. Shell had both.

She was looted by the whole day before. The flowers. Her skin. Neve's frightening disclosures. The mall closing down, a new approach to the business. But not a thought of the Green Hall. Not a moment of consideration for the fact that something special lived there, something she herself had encountered. The earth I grew from was important. The place where I began. The soft spot in the earth where I slipped into existence was, to Neve, as holy as me. I would show her soon. I would not allow myself to be an afterthought ever again. I would be the only blossoming thing at the centre of the garden in Shell's mind.

She built herself a foggy healing cocktail with the various sachets she had left for herself and downed it in two nauseating gulps, then flipped her pillow and hid her aching head on the cool side. After a few minutes, the balming effect began to rush over her and she felt able to reach for her phone to check the time and her notifications. She didn't have a shift today, so eight in the morning meant a long, silent lie-in. She had two messages from Kiero, though, both from the night before. *Get home safe*, read one, and the second, *Let me know when you're in?*

She didn't really remember getting in. The spectre of her drunk body might have been considerate enough to lay out a partial cure to the drink (had she been in better wits she might have left a can of Coke or some salty crisps for herself), but she had not managed to summon the decency to reply to poor, invested Kiero.

omg i'm sorry i'm such a dick! i passed out when i got in! i'm dying. how's your head? she typed out.

And, in a move so audacious that Shell let out a gasp, Kiero immediately, barely ten seconds later, replied, *Never had any complaints, if you're asking* with an honest-to-god emoji wearing sunglasses.

Shell paused upon her reply. The nerve. She hadn't thought he had it in him—but it was first thing in the morning, which in her experience was when straight men were most sexually courageous. She felt the threshold of her flirtation with Kiero shift as she replied.

She typed, *well if that's the hunger talking, we should go and get breakfast. that'll cure our hangovers.* There. Not too hardcore.

Shell hadn't had sex in more than a year.

Yeah, I'm starving, Kiero replied almost instantly. *Where do we go then? I'll drive us. Consider it my interview for future flower shop delivery boy.*

i just kind of want to sit outside, get a decent coffee, Shell said, feeling the charge go out of the conversation immediately.

If you're up for an adventure, I can spin us up the coast. Howth has a few nice spots, outdoorsy, and it has the sea.

Shell laughed. God, Howth. At least she wouldn't bump into anyone she knew there. The small seaside town just past a crest of coastal suburbs was mostly a tourist spot in her mind; she hadn't gone there in years, despite it being less than a twenty-minute drive from her family home. It felt like a place for people who were on holidays, or people with dogs and children, or people her parents' age who loved a nice pub lunch by the ocean, staring at the liquid parking lot full of rich people's sailboats, dreaming of a more opulent life. But in her current fragile state, and desperate for a break from the claustrophobic warren of Donaghmede—which she had barely left at all since moving home in the spring—it felt good to her. Though the estate was anchored near enough to the sea that on summer days you could catch an edge of salt in the breeze, Shell thought that maybe seeing the ocean itself, the dark blue body of it, might cure some of her stress. Unwind her a little.

She had been operating on rails between her home and the mall, which had been in some ways quite pleasant, a surrender to rote and routine under Neve's eye, but perhaps going somewhere different would help her shake off some of the madness, the bad feeling she was starting to get under her skin, or the sick sensation she got when she recalled the hour in the back room with Neve yesterday. Her palm had healed over. She glanced at her face using the front camera of her phone—still a crest of pink above her cheek, though. She'd cover it. Covering was easy.

Going to Howth with Kiero was a good idea. If you could see the ocean you could see the whole world. Plus, they did have nice places to eat, even if they were for old people and tourists. Shelly hadn't eaten anywhere outside her mother's house and the Crown in what now felt like an untrackable length of time. Outdoors would also proof their tension—seeing Kiero in a different landscape than the dark intimacy of the mall would be a good test of the authenticity of her attraction to him. Daylight did something to people's faces. People were different outdoors, their skin in the sun, their eyes in the light. How they were in their bodies around the public, in the unexpected. Even sitting outside a café having coffee was so different than having a coffee in the food court, or sitting in front of the florist. How did Kiero's hair move in the breeze? What did his laugh sound like, undampened by the low ceilings? The elements would make a better gauge than the closed world of the Crown.

Perhaps, though, this would pose a good opportunity for Shell to let him down gently, she thought. Absolve any tension in a good heart-to-heart chat. A hey, I like you, you're sweet, but you're going to work with me and Neve so no more flirty morning texts, let's all be grownups here shape of a chat. Very mature. Great choice. Yes, she decided. She would look at him in broad daylight, examine the feel of it all, and make a healthy and open statement to him wherein boundaries would be laid and henceforth upheld. So Shell said yes to Kiero's invitation to adventure.

yeah sure, when can you pick me up?

And he said, *An hour?* And the violence of her hangover was tempered then by the structure of having an hour to assemble herself.

She took a short, hostile shower, letting the water run too hot to invoke the sensation of being lightly seared: the crawling feeling of my infection in her palm and cheek echoed, and she wanted it gone. She wondered should she burn some sage, but her sisters would lose their minds if they thought she was burning any kind of incense in the bathroom: she wasn't interested in the "Shell's been smoking drugs and trying to cover for it again" conversation at her big age. She felt like she was moving through a busy hotel. She hadn't the time or energy to wash her hair for Kiero, and her curls were holding well, so the noise of the water on the plastic shower cap almost, very almost, drowned out her thoughts. As she dried her body with a towel she knew had lived in this house since she was a child, she hoped the starched fibres of it would exfoliate any traces of bad plant, of me, from her. She thought about how every pore on her body was a potential site for growth, for seed. She didn't stop to consider how I had taken root inside her bones, wrapped myself around her nerve endings, made great green swathes of the red inside her. Still, she scrubbed. At the sink, she salted her face, her hands, and it stung me, but I was embedded inside her still. I was growing there, listening to her, close. Letting her go about her life without interference for now.

Shell dressed comfortably. A soft athletic outfit, though she herself was not athletic in the slightest. Leggings and a large hoodie, blessedly left clean by her mother. White socks, white sneakers. A big neon green scarf. Less expensive than the clothes she would wear for Neve, or for work, she corrected herself, as she looked at her soft body in the mirror. This was an untrying. The presentation of authenticity to Kiero. She wanted her look to proclaim, You must stop fancying me immediately, and if you continue fancying me you must keep it to yourself. I am ten years your senior and you are lucky to be in my company at all!

She tucked her loose ATM card and phone into the pocket of her hoodie. No handbag. While she was applying a tasteful depth to her eyebrows, Kiero texted to ask her address so he could pick her up. She blinked at the messages: how strange to be showing this guy—this boy—her mother's home. She dropped him a pin and wrote, *no climbing up on the porch to my bedroom window please. it's all plywood and plaster, my parents won the extension in a raffle, you'll take the whole house down.*

Kiero simply replied with *Look, I'm light as a feather, I won't make a dent in it* and that sunglasses emoji again. She shot him the same symbol back, and they passed the cool little guy back and forth between them in lieu of conversation. It was silly. Silly felt good.

Outside the day was fine, August just starting to surrender, the sun low in the sky, kind of dull and muggy. Shell wore enormous skiing sunglasses from a trip with Gav because they were the nearest ones to her hand, which diffused the light to an amber colour. She thought they'd make a cute nod to the rows of cool dudes they'd sent to each other: Shell wasn't above being cute. Her eyes were also still falling out of her head from the night before, so they made the daytime a little less aggressive in the pulses of her hangover. She leant against the wall at the front of the house, looking at the identical rows and rows of homes all around her, the roof of the Woodbine Crown visible in the near distance. Closed in. Donaghmede was a labyrinth without magic, and here, her red ribbon came around the corner in a scarlet Ford Fiesta that was years older than its driver. Kiero wore fancy Ray-Bans, and his hair was wet, rolled into a bun on top of his head.

The car smelled of pine air freshener and weed and clean man. It was spotless, which was a relief, and when she planted herself in the passenger seat, Kiero gave her a half hug, and a tiny shock of a kiss on the cheek. He was listening to some rumbling, unfamiliar music on the radio. It had no lyrics.

"Absolutely dying today," Kiero began as they pulled off. "My ma made me check if I was still over the limit to drive before I came out."

"I'm not far behind you, I'd some day yesterday. At least the drinks rounded the edge off." Shell rolled down the passenger window to keep the air moving, keep it from getting too warm, too close. It would keep any hangover-related nausea at bay, too.

"Sure, didn't we all. The poor Woodbine. Neve was in bits at the end of last night, but you were six sheets to the wind—she was crying, like." Kiero was a calm, easy driver and the old, paternal-feeling car pulled out of the estate and onto the main road softly, belying its age.

Shell paused at the mention of Neve, fidgeting with her keys. I listened keenly to the frequencies inside her, and she was hurting and it was a sad, delicious shade. She didn't bother to conceal her hurt but instead gave it a different shape.

"Can we not talk about . . . all that, if that's okay?" Risk it all, Shell. "I kind of feel like Neve's sidekick in there, you know?

Her handmaiden in the rose garden. Out here, I don't have to worry about some gross dirty greenhouse, and the weird shopping centre I apparently have spent a bunch of this year working in now. They're knocking it, we're starting over—can we . . . pretend all that isn't going on?"

Kiero furrowed his brow. "I mean . . . I've worked in the Crown since I was fifteen. I don't think it's weird there. All my friends work there—Daniel and Bec have worked there forever. My sister worked there. So on one hand, yeah, sure, let's pretend we're not . . . I don't know, tied to it, but also, let's not pretend to be . . . better than it?"

His tone was a little tinny. Shit. Shell had thought—she had assumed—well, she had assumed totally wrong.

"Oh, I—I didn't mean it like that!" she stammered. "More just, well, onwards and upwards and all that?"

Kiero nodded, still a little stiff. "Ah, yeah. Upwards."

Shell didn't say anything for a few moments, as they turned on to the coast road and the low blue of the ride split onto the landscape like a ream of fabric, banded loose under the dishwater sky. The air pouring in the window became colder, fresher, and Shell closed her eyes and sighed into it, that deep familiar salt.

She didn't see it, but Kiero smiled at her as she relaxed at the mere proximity of the sea, the dopey expression of a person who was too far gone for his own good.

"I can't believe I live, like, five minutes away from here and I just ignore it," she said, eyes still closed.

"Well, it's a longer walk to the sea than that, but I'm happy to drive you down here at high tide whenever you need, to get your fix and all that." Kiero was earnest, and Shelly laughed to puncture the promise.

"Ocean delivery boy," she said. "A part-time gig, on the side of your flower runs."

"Sounds pretty good to me. What's the hourly like?"

"No cash. Just my company. A privilege."

She couldn't stop herself. She was trying to, but she couldn't.

And they were warm to each other again then, the crystals of ice that Shell's gaffe about the mall had caused melting into nothing at all. The coast curved slightly and the road was empty and they listened to the music that wasn't really music coming from Kiero's stereo until Shell asked if she could put on a song and Kiero said, "Oh, of course," and she flipped out her phone to pull something she could Bluetooth into the hodgepodge makeshift radio system that had been hacked into a car that antedated any sort of streaming technology at all. She bit the bullet and put on a roaring club banger from the end of the nineties, "Sandstorm," and the sound of it alone made Keiro laugh.

"Wow," he said.

"Wow yourself," she replied, pleased. "I can't get a hold of this hangover so I'm going to put on music that makes me feel like it's two in the morning and I'm dancing, instead of ten in the morning and I'm dehydrated."

"Yeah, two in the morning at fuckin' . . . Creamfields or something." He laughed again.

"Hey, who's the snob now? God, what I wouldn't do for a festival." Shell moaned.

"Hate to tell you, pal . . . but I get the impression you're what, thirty-two?"

"On the button."

"Well, mate, if you're anything like Bec and the others, you'd hate it at festivals now. We tried to go to one a few years ago with Caoimhe, and those two got sleepy and gave up and went home. My sister's back half went out. They couldn't stick it. No stamina."

He hadn't really mentioned Caoimhe to Shell. She treaded

softly at the conjuring of his sister's ghost. She almost said she had lost her last festival years to her relationship breakdown, but that wasn't right. She'd lost some things, sure, but nothing so dark and huge as a sister. She thought of the pair she had herself, knocking around the house, permanent fixtures. Their four lungs. Maybe I will show her, someday, what I did to Caoimhe. I wonder would she like it.

"The worst thing is they were right to go home and all. That would probably be me, too. Maybe festivals are a kids' game, but look, look let me pretend I'm still able for the hangover and standing up for twenty hours. I can't hack the truth right now." Shell exhaled.

They swooped up the hill towards the seaside town, the houses getting measurably larger and impossibly expensive around them. The music beat along with their pace, at a dissonance to their surroundings.

"Pretend away," Kiero said, and Shell did, leaning her head against the window frame and letting the breeze stream in, softening her.

They took coffee and little cream cheesecakes not much bigger than two-euro coins from a kiosk and walked along the pier of the humming little seaside town. In the bay, the sailboats bobbed in the slight breeze. The houses up on the hill at the very edge of Ireland were blanched and tall, only a few deceptive miles away from the burnished and grey suburbs. They were palatial in contrast, looking out over the ocean towards England. The salt air felt so good to Shell that it was almost cleansing. She was looking for a cleanness that she wouldn't find.

Howth was not a place Shell had ever really given much thought to, but after a claustrophobic season and the intensity of the day before it felt so nice to be away. It felt abroad to her, and she raised her little coffee cup to Kiero's in a cheers, then took some photos on her phone of the morning skyline, beginning to clear. Stripes of blue-and-grey emptiness on her screen. Souvenirs.

"Feels almost like being on holiday, doesn't it," Kiero said, seeming to read her mind—though never as well as I could. He looked out over the blue expanse with one hand over his brow and the other on his hip, like a sailor in a plaid shirt and ripped jeans.

"As far as I'm concerned, I am on holiday," Shell told him, turning her phone camera towards them both, Kiero standing over her shoulder in his pose and Shell giving a small pout under her sunglasses. A photograph of a couple. She could easily have been in this frame with Gav, if he were fifteen years younger.

"Should have brought the real cameras," Kiero said. "What a shame."

"No." Shell walked on, and he beside her. "Too hungover to look for beautiful shots. No art today. No work today. Holidays."

And how short-lived that sentiment was, as after they walked the high pier out to the red pillar of the lighthouse and reached the village again, their coffee cups drained, while they paused to consider whether they were too fragile for bags of chips, Shell was distracted suddenly. A tiny florist nested in the row of shops—she had somehow not seen it when they pulled into the village. She peeled her sunglasses up into her nest of hair and prowled over the street to take a closer look. She hadn't been in another flower shop since she started working with Neve, not in real life. Spending hours and hours peering into international flower shops and studios and wholesalers online didn't count. This was the real thing.

Outside Seaside Blooms stood a shelf full of hall-door wreaths. They were fat with eucalyptus, a crescent of lavender on some, a small few sprigs of baby's breath on others, a couple simply made from pampas grass. They were gorgeous. Expensive, and expensive looking, and Shell snapped a picture, including one of the signage—hand-grown lavender, hand-dried! Eucalyptus from Carol's Garden! Facts declared in pleasing, neat cursive. Somewhere inside her, she wanted a shop like this. Out on a main street, not hidden in the guts of a mouldering shopping centre. Maybe after a little time doing remote work, they could find somewhere like this, somewhere in a posh little village to open up together, her and Neve. It was nice to have a target, a sense of something for the future. She wandered back to Kiero, who was now holding a brown paper bag, hot with golden chips.

He offered her one, which she took from his fingers then placed into her mouth, without flinching at the burn.

They perched together on a wall by the sailboats, sharing their snack, salty and doused with vinegar. Shell knew this was the time to say it to him, to offer down a tender boundary, to note that this all felt a lot like a date and she was sorry for flirting but they had to get their shit together now. If they were all to work together, there weren't to be any shenanigans of the heart or the body. Once she said it, it would take all the sizzle out of things with Kiero—but it was proving harder to just lay down the line than she'd hoped it would be.

"Strange how much everything is just . . . going to change," she said, preparing herself, finding the words, getting them ready.

"You worried?" Kiero was playful, an elbow literally in her ribs.

"What—" she began. "What would I be worried about?"

Kiero hummed. "Ah, I don't know. That taking the shop out of the Crown won't work. That things might get weird with you and Neve if you go into business together proper."

Shell was surprised by how copped on he seemed, a few steps ahead of her.

"I don't . . . think so," Shell lied. "But I mean, it's Neve's show, it's Neve's shop. I'm in the background."

Kiero seemed satisfied with that, a successful parry. "I don't think you're in the background. You're my favourite, anyway."

And that word elicited something in Shell, a little spark. It couldn't snuff me out, just like the seawater couldn't drown me out and the salt air couldn't scrub me, but it was new. Small but warm. I couldn't let it continue much longer, but I wouldn't stamp it down just yet. So when Kiero put his hand on her arm and boldly took her sunglasses right off her face before leaning in to kiss her, Shell let him, yielded to the tension, not violin-string taut or white hot in the way that not kissing Neve had felt, but it was good, a tightrope she was confident she could walk along. It was good to be kissed. She had not been kissed in a really long time, and yes, good, it was good, and the world shrank down to the size of their mouths for a minute or so, before she broke away laughing, pleased. She was laughing a lot today. Both of them were. This was absolutely not what she had intended to happen. The opposite, in fact.

"Well," she said. "Wow."

And his pupils were stupid and open from desire, his cheeks flushed and he said, "Wow," too.

He drove her home then, and they talked and listened to more songs that Shell chose, and he kissed her again when they were parked outside her house, and she said, "Now now, slow down," and he replied that he didn't really want to slow down but he'd do anything she said, she could take control and he'd listen, a heat in his gaze that she liked quite a lot. A bud, opening, petals satin and bold. A terrible idea. A bloom.

"I'll remember that," she said. "Thanks for today." And she got out of the car and went back into the house feeling lighter. More normal. She only felt this way because I permitted it, and I only permitted it again because when the time came that I would I crack her world open I wanted it to feel seismic and scorching. So let her have her date, her young man. My vines were in her bones and Neve was waiting for her in the flower shop. Her friends from her old life were waiting for her in the city, too, and she would have to go and see them that night. Until that trial, she was on holiday.

Bec, my love, most special agent,

That sounds great. I'll drive up later, swing by the Crown, do a flying visit and crash at yours, then turn back the morning after. Keep all contact extremely minimal, for everyone concerned. I can't wait to see your house, I physically dream of it. Maybe Daniel can sneak over and do my roots for me? Young Kiero can come if he brings a few spliffs. Oh my god, I'm not throwing a party in your lovely house, I swear, I swear, I just miss everyone so much? Okay, I take it back about Kiero. Just Daniel then? Ask him, but tell him not to tell Neve. It's purely a professional visit, and nothing to do with the fact that I love every fiber of him and want to make him tell me every shred of gossip from the old ladies in the salon for hours. All that aside, my hair's been growing like a weed. Maybe if he works his magic on me, when I get back here Tall Siobhan will be like, oh my god, Doctor Jennifer, you are so attractive and charismatic, can I come and drink in your dorm? She'll ask me, I won't ask her, because that would be potentially inappropriate. But I'll say, yes, Siobhan. Yes, you absolutely can. And I'll pour us big drinks and we'll sit out on my little balcony and look out over the Burren and we'll have a lovely normal conversation in low tones, and I can start, finally, to move on with my life. I'm manifesting, Rebecca. Setting good things into motion.

Hey, I'll see you soon, sweet friend. I'll text you when I'm on the road.

Xoxoxo,
Dr. Jen

Shell kept her eyes closed for the majority of the taxi ride to the party. She wanted to stave off the feeling of oh-back-then that she would get at the sight of the tight redbrick estates that Chloe lived in. Emily lived just a short walk from Chloe, and Lorna lived on the other side of Dolphin's Barn. Shell and Gav had planned to buy a home nearby. A two-up-two-down former council house would easily be half a million euros, but they wanted to be nearer their friends. In a community. A neighbourhood. Raise their own kids, maybe, with the others. How all those hopes had dissolved in the acid of her and Gav's breakup. How she'd forgotten to want the small red house, the friends-from-college, the all-our-kids-running-around-together. How all of it came back like a sickness as she opened her eyes to the Dublin evening out the window of the cab. The other life. The one Gav had wanted for them. She couldn't summon the details of his face properly, as she sat there, waiting for the curves in the road to tell her she was in the city and out of the suburbs. He had all but disappeared.

His world wasn't for her now, and she was going to go into Chloe's house and behave normally throughout the dinner and maybe try to find her way back towards warmth with these girls. It would, after all, be sad to think that Gav had just inherited them, and all the memories they'd had together would just belong to him and not her in the future. There had been some good times, after all. They had laughed. It had been fifteen years—of course there had been laughter, somewhere back there. Shell just couldn't quite access it.

It was nice that they'd invited her. Called her in. They didn't have to. She knew she shouldn't be so anxious, that she should be excited to roll up to Chloe's freshly renovated house, see her in the flush of her pregnancy, present her with a lush bouquet—white hydrangeas, peach roses, baby's breath, eucalyptus, palm, a flourish of pampas grass, and me—as well as a fancy bottle of botanical non-alcoholic spirits, safe to drink during the baby's gestation period, and, as if that weren't enough, a soft navy blue bunny rabbit for the forthcoming infant. It had tiny silver stars in its ears, plus, navy blue was gender neutral. Her card (a thick letterpress one, from a Dublin designer), read WELCOME TO PLANET EARTH, LITTLE ONE! and also, for theme, featured a bunny. Navy and peach were friends on the colour wheel, too. Everything matched. Everything looked good, looked considered. Shell herself felt neither good nor like she was being considered, at all.

Shell was good at gifts, always had been. She'd had to become good at them because Gav wasn't, and because their social life was constructed of birthdays and weddings and her own gnawing sense of what she would reluctantly admit was competition. A master of the Secret Santa, able to turn a twenty-five-euro budget into a gift so thoughtful it would elicit a big gasp, a soft Oh, Shell! You're too good! She would be thoughtful, and chic, and generous. She'd be consistent. That way, if these women truly thought she was a mess, or a massive bitch, or something worse, they at least couldn't say she was tight. The gifts were in some ways an artillery. They also made a good disguise for her unease with and even dislike of some of the wider group. The effort itself was part of the weapon that the gifts became.

The taxi stopped outside the end-of-terrace house that Shell knew so well. That she'd raised glasses on New Years' in. She'd opened that very front door to let the old year out and the new year in, just nine months ago, and the January before. Two Januaries ago they'd all been in Galway. Shell's old life folded out in front of her as she disembarked, murmuring a thanks to the driver, and traipsed up the newly tiled path, decked out black-and-white Moroccan style, outrageously tasteful. The front door was new, sage green, with a brass knocker, with a summer wreath that Shell knew by the look of it cost about two hundred euros from one of the posh city-centre atelier florists. She knocked, her knuckles on the wood, instead of using the knocker, which was brass and shaped like a cherub, aiming his bow down towards the ground—so when you pulled it up, the point of the loaded arrow was aiming directly at you.

Music and warmth emanated from inside, and through the little portal of stained glass, Chloe's figure emerged and flung the door open wide, her arms even wider, and embraced Shell with a squeal, squashing the flowers a little. When Chloe stepped back, she gestured to her convex belly and said, "Welcome to our home!" as if Shell had not stumbled drunkenly in and out of that doorframe countless times in the last six, seven years that Chloe and Damien had lived there. She said it like she was greeting a documentarian, not an old friend.

Shell said, "Oh my god, you're so pregnant! You're glowing!" and her jaw was tight and her stomach leaden. She needed a drink. Two drinks.

The house felt to her impossibly more expensive than it had been the last time she was there. It had the distinct scent of a place that had been recently painted, but a fancy candle or three had been lit to just about mask the chemical-wash smell. The front of the house was mostly as Shell had remembered it, the little living room to the left of the hallway, the steep staircase she had had many nights sitting on, talking to Lorna or Chloe herself or one of the lads while a party hummed on around them. She'd burnt a hole in the former carpet with a spliff once.

The real renovation had happened beyond the staircase, in the kitchen, and the long yard that had once been home to a stack of bikes and a colony of feral city cats. The bikes were gone, the cats were gone, and now all that remained was a tiny courtyard in the far-left corner of an enormous concrete, glass-walled kitchen. Somehow they had not only had the house extended backwards, but also upwards. It had the feel of a cold atrium in a boutique hotel: there was a moneyed hostility to the architecture. Something dark to it, despite all the light.

Shell felt ridiculous, trailing Chloe, who announced her arrival as though she were rolling into a pantomime from stage left: "Girls, look who we've got here!" and the players in Shell's old life all erupted into a welcoming chorus of her name, Great to see you, You look gorgeous, Oh those flowers, Look at you, You look great. Shell echoed back their greetings, heart high in her chest. Why were all three of them there before her? Lorna and Emily both had near-empty wine glasses, already clouded from their mouths. A little bowl of olive pits and a dish of oil sat in front of them. They'd been there a while. Shell wasn't late: she had just been invited at a different time.

"Can I pour you a glass? Oh, wait, let me get a fresh one," Chloe said, picking up the bottle of pinot grigio and realizing that it was empty, then swanning over to the fridge to replace it.

Chloe passed the double-door Smeg refrigerator in a tasteful cream and went to what Shell hadn't noticed: a slim wine fridge, installed in the wall. Shell winced slightly but sat down on the empty side of the bench that faced Lorna and Emily, placing her bouquet beside her, and her bag of gifts, neither of which had been acknowledged in the cascade of greetings. Chloe materialized next to her, dispensed a fat glass of wine, poured two more for the others, and removed the flowers, all in one go, while the What lipstick are you wearing? Your earrings are stunning! God, you look amazing part of the conversation was still folding out, by rote. Emily always loved whatever earrings Shell was wearing, and Shell had long suspected that Emily simply hadn't any idea of what else to say to her.

Here, already wide-eyed with drink, Emily was singing that old song again with real passion. She loved those earrings. The colour. Were they clay? Beautiful. So sustainable.

I, in my greenery amongst the blossoms, was placed in the sink, and Chloe cooed over me across the acres of kitchen.

Shell correctly interpreted that Lorna had probably had three glasses of wine, and Emily had had two: Lorna was drunk, and that became apparent even from the way she was holding herself across the table, limbs soft, mascara rubbed a little under her eyes in smudged half-moons, vape in one hand, the fourth glass of wine in the other. The look she was giving Shell was one of a curious regard, like she was looking at a funny little animal that had trotted into the room instead of somebody she had known since she was just out of school.

"Okay, Shell. What's the deal," Lorna said suddenly, across Emily remarking that she knew a gorgeous clay jewellery artist based in either Ennistymon or Ennis—immediately souring the air in the room even further, like bad milk poured into burnt coffee.

Mouth dry, Shell said, "What's the deal?" back to her.

From across the kitchen where Chloe was removing a loaf of bread from one of the ovens, she called softly, "Oh, Lorna, we were going to wait until after dinner!"

"Yeah, well, we've waited long enough, I personally feel. It's disingenuous to sit through a fucking... charcuterie doing small talk at a time like this, and I won't tolerate it." Lorna was operating a laser beam through the blur of her drunkenness. Emily sighed deeply and took a big sip from her own glass. When she surfaced, she said, "Lorna's right. It's weirder to sit here eating."

Shell's stomach had solidified and her ears rang with tinnitus—her body was entering a panic state. She semi-ascended from the shock, left her body at the table, and entered a quiet quadrant at the back of her skull so she could watch what was happening here, more than feel it. It was something Gav used to give out to her about: he called it checking out. He never understood how useful it was. The little paper gift bag with the rabbit and card was close beside her.

"Look, if we're going to do it now, we need to just get it all clear before the lads get here. I just think it would have had more impact if they were involved, too." Chloe sounded tired of the conversation, as though she had seen too many rehearsals, and this was not how the performance was meant to go. Half the cast were missing, apparently, but Lorna hardly waited a beat to begin.

"Shell, we need to talk."

"Okay?" a voice said from Shell's mouth, while she watched, a hundred metres back, in the cheap seats of her own head.

"We're worried about you," Emily said, high and false, reaching her hands across the table where they would have met Shell's, if hers hadn't been limp in her lap. Playing dead.

"Worried?" the voice said again.

"So, so worried," Emily continued. "I was just so freaked out when I saw where you were working that I just knew we had to, like, intervene. That place is really rough, Shell. Like, all your pictures on Instagram make it look like the flowers are so fancy, if you're into that kind of thing, very traditional, very nineties— but that shopping centre is honestly so grim. I think it's dangerous, you know? I just got the feeling, and when I get feelings, they're never wrong."

Chloe called over from the kitchen, now emerging from the Smeg with a fat paper packet of what would quickly be revealed to be large shrimp, still in their shells, whiskered and fresh, "Emily's feelings are literally never wrong. She knew I was pregnant before I did."

Emily nodded sagely, as did Lorna, even if she looked like she was barely agreeing, biding her time, mouth closed tight as if to contain hornets or bile. Clearly, Emily going first had been part of the choreography.

"I just worry there's, like, a chasm between what you think you're doing and what you're actually doing, or what's happening to you. That shop is so bleak, you're so skilled, it just freaked me out to see you taking such a dive from Fox & Moone. Nobody wants to see that happen to their friends."

They're calling you deluded, I transmitted to Shell, as she curled up in the dark of the back row of her head. I found her there, shocked and tiny, and from the sink I said, They think you're unwell. Lying to yourself. They think you can't possibly be happy, but we know different, don't we?

Shell said, "It freaked you out?" No new language would come to her, just shards of what they were saying echoed back. All she could do was seek elaboration. Explore what was happening. She couldn't react properly. She was the one who was freaked out.

Emily nodded. "It did. I was—am—scared for you. Ever since you and Gav broke up, you've just been off the map. We're all worried. You basically blanked Kayla's hen, that was so unfair of you—you know her dad died this year? She thinks you hate her now, we've been trying to reassure her, but honestly—it's like you basically do hate all of us now. It's like you just disappeared, dispatching these weird Instagram posts, changing your account, and I go to check on you because, like, of course I do—and I discover that's where you've been? Shell, I saw a ceiling tile fall down outside a vape shop. There are, actually, five vape shops in that shopping centre. Come on."

"Hey," said Lorna, leaning towards Emily, fist full of her bright pink grapefruit-flavoured Lost Mary, "don't be classist."

Emily took a deep breath in her nose and said on the exhale, "You know I'm not being classist. I'm literally not."

"I know." Lorna's hard mouth softened to a smile, as though impressed by Emily's empathy, and Emily hummed, ready for her final bars.

"We just want what's best for you. Gav does, too. When he gets here he'll tell you himself."

Shell felt her body slouch forward slightly, as though she had been administered a blow to the stomach. Even from the back row, she felt sick. She hadn't seen Gav all year—had hardly thought of him—and he was coming?

Lorna leant in for her verse. "I'm going to deliver you some home truths, Shell. You might not like it, but your actions have been hurting all of us, and frankly, I'm surprised we had the energy to take the time to talk this through with you. This disappearing-act thing is selfish and weird. You've been blanking the group chat. Also, you haven't listened to a single one of poor Gav's voice notes, and I know this because he sent me the screenshots. Unlistened to, Christ, how could you do this to him? You were together for years. You were meant to be getting married. I had a dress bought for your wedding—did you know that? I bought it in Brazil and literally carried it across the world, to wear to your wedding. The one that isn't happening, to the person you're ignoring."

Shell's mouth was dry now, and something was happening to her. The acute shot of shame that had gone through her had turned into another thing, and she recognized it immediately as anger.

Lorna took another drink. "If you think you're better than

us now, on this weird sabbatical with this weird job and all these random people we don't know—that's fucked, Shell. Like, there's something wrong with us?"

Shell started to answer her, but Lorna raised her hand to cut her off. It worked.

"No, don't talk. I'm not finished, we're not finished," Lorna said, taking a hit from her vape. "You're not allowed to just interrupt when I'm making the effort to tell you my truth. This has been so hard for me, for all of us."

Shell shrugged, still kind of limp, and took her drink off the table. Emily looked, concerned, over at her then at Chloe, giving her a cue, as she sizzled the enormous prawns in a stainless steel wok. "We really worked hard to make sure to keep all this helpful and civil, Shell," Chloe said. "We just needed to let you know where we are with all this. We're worried, but we're hurt, too. Consider this a bit like an editorial at work, you know? It's not you, intrinsically, the person . . . it's just . . . the situation. The behaviour."

"Everyone needs one of these every now and then, you know?" Emily chimed in. "It's healthy. We're calling you in."

"I mean, we're calling her out, Emily," Lorna said. "We're calling her out. But just, in here."

"Either way, we're calling," Chloe said warmly, her pan emanating garlic and parsley and the ocean. "And we just hope you pick up."

They'd definitely practiced that. They let the silence ring out, and Shell assumed she was supposed to say something. Her voice soft, the anger still somewhere within her away from where her mouth was, she said, "I'm kind of confused. I'm not sure I really deserve this," which felt moderate, considering. Moderate responses, she felt, would be the best way through here—so she could parse further exactly what had brought all of this on.

"Okay. If you don't think you 'deserve it,' then you're not actually engaging with this meaningfully, Shell." Emily's tone was tinny now. "We need you to actually hear us, and not go on the defensive. Like if that's your position, we actually can't make meaningful progress here."

"Also," Lorna added, "you framing this like something you 'deserve' or not is super manipulative, so I'm just going to have to stop you. Gav's basically ten minutes away, so we really need you to be present in an authentic way for this, because we know he'd like to talk to you himself. We're really confident you can meet us where we're at, Shell. This is conflict, not harm. Harm is when you drop all your friends for a frankly inexplicable new life. Harm is when you ice out your former fiancé when he wants to heal with you. That's harm, Shell, so let's not get into who 'deserves' what. Come on now."

"Harm," repeated Shell. "Right. Harm."

What do they know of harm? What do they know of the world crumbling around you, the chill of realizing you are alone in your relationship, your most treasured sanctuary, what do they know of the slip of an engagement ring off your hand, of loss, of conceding defeat, of surrender, of sleeping in your childhood bedroom when you should be striding off into your adult life? What the fuck do they know about minimum wage? They were the ones who went silent first, they retreated first; they long had let Shell know she was not like them; she was somehow all wrong, crass, less educated, funny in accent, funny like different, funny like wrong. There are no olive branches in this grove, only nightshade and lantana, and every breath Shell took was poison in her lungs. Harm. The harm was old, and any Shell had administered was merely a catalyst for her escape. But here she sat, distinctly unescaped. She had walked right back to them, after all that work to get away. How, exactly, could she burn this bridge so badly that they would never reconstruct it, that no architect and no engineer could pull the smoking pieces back together?

I decided I'd help her. I'd give her a little nudge. Hadn't she wanted to cause a scene? Hadn't she longed for it?

Shell stood up, then, and said, "Harm," again. She kept her wine glass in her hand and left the little bag with the blue rabbit and the expensive non-alcoholic botanicals and her card on the bench, and walked silently over to the kitchen, where Chloe was plating the shrimp in their garlic and parsley bath of butter onto a serving dish that looked as though it were a gigantic cabbage leaf. Shell took the bouquet out of the sink, walked past Chloe again back towards the hallway out, but on her way, took a downward swipe at the just-full serving dish, knocking it away from Chloe and her bump, and onto the kitchen floor, where it shattered into an oily, expensive mess. Some shrimp became airborne, their hot butter a storm around them. Shell did not stop to see where they landed. She was, though, aware that Chloe took a leap back and gasped, and Lorna and Emily leapt to their feet and were shouting something, but she could not hear them. She made a beeline for the front door, her phone precariously in her free hand, ordering a taxi for two streets away, her wine glass in the other, me under her armpit in the bouquet. At the threshold, she stopped and opened her mouth wide, drinking the rest of the wine in a single gulp. When it was gone, she threw the glass on the ground, its shatter high and bitchy, prompting more gasps from the girls who were not following her, not pursuing her, not trying to get her to stay.

Hold me fucking accountable now, you freaks, Shell thought, leaving the door wide open behind her, not giving them the benefit of the slam, rather leaving them with the draft that would come in, the inconvenience and indignity of having to close the door themselves. I am sorry she did not leave me, or throw the bouquet on the ground. I wish I could have heard what they had to say in her desperate, furious wake.

She'd only been in there half an hour but the night felt rich to her now, as she strode down Reuben Street, aiming for her pickup point around a couple of twists of the labyrinth. A man walked by her on the other side of the street and said her name and she said absolutely nothing, because she had absolutely nothing to say to Gav; she didn't even want to look at him. She didn't want to tell him that he was walking into a kitchen full of spilt shellfish butter and "harm." She kept moving, and he didn't follow her.

By the time Shell was in the cab, barrelling back towards Donaghmede, rain had broken, sudden and summer and temperamental. She still felt far away from herself, and her phone was alight, messages from Gav, missed calls from each of the girls mounting up, texts from them, too, and she didn't even open a single one. One by one, she calmly blocked each of their numbers, and blocked them on Instagram, too. She blocked liberally, with abandon. Blocked Gav's sister, blocked Emily's sister and mother, actually, too. She blocked all their husbands, with their almost empty accounts sitting there, faint gestures at participation in their partners' lives. She searched for the little private account Chloe had made for her unborn child, in which she had been posting daily updates about her journey—she blocked the unborn child. She exited group chats without reading the new messages, she exited the long-abandoned historical ones, silently, without leaving a stamp on the scroll of old conversation, including and most especially the one for Kayla's hen night. She deleted the groups once she had left, so she would have no echoey memory of them taking up space on her phone, taking up space in her head.

Her heart was beating hard as she did it, sure, but not from fear. From excitement, or something like it. The quiet admin of the dramatic exit was oddly pleasing to her. Bye, so long, peace out, blocked, blocked, blocked. She felt like an animal, running mouth open into a field, the barn burning behind her, paws wet with gasoline.

It was all done by the time she had hit the coast road, so she flipped open her texts to Neve, and her texts to Kiero, and sent them an identical query. *few cans at the crown? rollover sesh?* It was only eight p.m., so it was likely everyone would still be in, she'd catch them just in time. I was green and full in her lap, delighted. Come home to your friends. Come sit in the glow of my glass hall. Drink until you are sore in the jaw from laughing. Fall soft. Show your belly. Do as I say. Her phone chimed a *Sounds good* from Neve and a *Didn't you have plans?* from Kiero.

Shell replied, *plans change!*

At work the next morning, in the fuzzy and desaturated world of five a.m., Shell and Neve manhandled bushels of greenery bigger than their upper bodies up onto the work island. Neve peered over her boughs of fir and said, "After we're closed, I've decided you should probably come in and see. The plant. The orchid. That, erm, gave you the rash. You should meet him, I think, now that, well. Now that we're leaving this place." Nervous, fractured, looking for the right words in the right order. She wore a cropped linen shirt under her apron and loose cotton pants that obscured the shape of her almost entirely, almost pyjama, almost skirt. She'd put black flicks in the corners of her eyelids, something Shell had only seen her do twice or three times before. Her ring on a chain sat high on her chest and above her apron, a talisman, placed as though a boundary in itself.

Shell's phone weighed her apron pocket down, so dense was it from messages from Kiero last night. She felt like she was hiding it from Neve deliberately, caught in the grey murk of Well, you haven't made a move, and you wear that horrible ring on you all the time like you're trying to send me a signal. There was a brattishness to it, to the Well, why shouldn't I, followed eventually by Well, I kind of like him, actually, even though he's younger, and no, it's still not as much as I like you, but he's very easy and I can still do what I want. Her inner monologue was a roaring argument with someone who could not hear her.

Shell was all right at concealing mess, at containing it inside her body, her whole body a mall, all corridor and shutter and locked door and storage room and loose wire and crates to store bad behaviour and selfish choices in, just out of sight of the customer she was trying to impress or extract capital from.

She didn't like it, having to transfer any ease and heat she'd had with Neve away, having to tamp down her curiosity about the Green Hall, about me, dismissing the deep feelings of suspicion and wonder as weird vibes about an old place. She assumed this kind of rationale was for her own good. Better entangled with someone a decade younger than her who would be fully into her than a person she really liked who had all of . . . well. Whatever Neve had going on. Me, that is. So in some regard this was a sane choice, maybe some innate self-preservation deep inside Shell. A fair effort. Useless, but fair nonetheless.

I was on the cusp of closing something around her and around Neve, and I was going to receive my feed.

Here in the workshop, though, Shell's guilty little "Yeah, after work sounds good," spoken over the buzz of her phone, a good-morning message from the already ruined boy driving himself slightly mad with lust for her. Shell ignored the text so as not to draw attention to it. I told Neve, in her ear I said, Kiero wants to fuck Shell and he might, and I sickened her softly with that and she batted me away. This shit is why I want to leave you, leave this place, thought Neve, and what they're doing is none of my business, though truly Shell stood within the walls of her business, and she had made herself Neve's business, and weren't they all going off to start the business anew, and I was there between them, weaving, serpent, storm.

Shell did not check her phone until Neve had gone out front, an hour later, to place some of their sweeping bouquets around the shop's front room. Kiero's message said that he had woken up early, and maybe could catch her around lunch. *I'll drop into the shop to say hello!*

She shook her head at the phone, thinking and almost saying that he should get a grip, in fact that they should both get a grip, but texted him *aw that would be so nice,* and then flicked the signal button on her phone to off, airplane mode, as if she were going anywhere near the sky as opposed to being pulled down to the cold wet earth.

The quiet of the oncoming morning shift was broken by not only a visit from Daniel, but Bec, too, before Kiero's inevitable and eager arrival at lunch. Daniel swept in not long after opening, wielding a large paper bag of soft, still-warm croissants and Danish from the supermarket and a tray made of cardboard, stacked full with iced lattes.

"It's a cope breakfast," he announced. "Because if I can't cope with the current state of affairs, I'd say neither can you. Not many mornings like this left, might as well make the best of them!"

He didn't of course say this to Shell, who was out back, scowling with frustration at a wreath that she had overstuffed and unbalanced on one side, but his voice met her ears all the same. She wasn't sure she was invited, or even if she wanted to be invited to the breakfast summit, so she flicked on a podcast and allowed herself to diffuse softly into the audio of friendly, inane voices. This balm lasted a few minutes before Neve threw her head, tousled, lovely, around the door and said, "Fair play to Daniel, we've a French spread out here. Come out or you'll waste away. The sugar is good for your spirit."

So Shell joined them, feeling distant from their patter, tamping down acidic guilt over Kiero as well as what amounted to fear about the Green Hall, about what Neve was going to show her. She didn't say anything, just watched them, realizing that it wasn't going to be long before they wouldn't have this, these tender little mornings in the rhythm of the mall.

After Daniel left, the shop fell into a pedestrian rhythm and Shell resumed her methodical production line for two hours. Eleven thirty chimed, and with it, Bec, who flipped the sign on the door to CLOSED as she came in, also holding sustenance. More coffees, more offerings. Sushi, this time, in little plastic trays. She'd had them delivered from a pan-Asian takeaway in a neighbouring estate. She had also picked up the fancier bottles of water at the supermarket that inexplicably cost three euros each. Shell was adjusting rolls of ribbon on the back wall and gave her a quick wave before refocusing on the fiddly task of getting all the ribbon ends to line up in a way that looked pleasing.

Bec immediately assumed the same seat as Daniel had, perched on the shop counter, unpacking her little plastic bag full of snack accoutrement: napkins, disposable chopsticks, little plastic bottles in the shape of fish full of soy sauce, wasabi packets. The rustling noise was maddening to Shell. With the procession of food being brought in today you'd swear someone was dying, she wanted to say, but didn't.

"What time are you closing up tonight?" Bec asked, delicately placing a dry-looking piece of cucumber nigiri into her mouth. "We're a law unto ourselves back there at the moment, there's talk of shuttering early until the Crown goes down. Like what's the point, even."

Neve shrugged. "I suppose. I'm going to drive out to the wholesalers, look at getting myself sorted at home. Moving the back room here into the living room in my flat is going to be really something."

Shell stared down at her phone at Kiero's newest message, a request for a visit.

sorry, petal, she tapped out, *lunch is a bust. swamped here. can we go for a drive tonight, though?*

And his reply was instant, *Oh yeah, absolutely. Where do you want to go?*

wherever you like, maybe down to the sea again, Shell said, meaning anywhere but here. She'd stare down whatever weird illegal plant Neve was hiding and talking to in her Green Hall (Me. I tug at her ribs. That's me.), then she'd get into Kiero's car and go. She'd do what was easy. Fine. She beat back my gnaw, the sensation of being watched, the suspicion, the jealousy, all these things that she'd never had to feel in her tiny confined life with Gav. She hadn't experienced a fraction of this, or had to make so many decisions around her emotions. She had not had to listen to her gut, or her body, in a long time, as though her head were located somewhere miles from both these things, barely connected, perhaps at most by a radio frequency. She turned up her podcast and popped her phone into her apron again, then manoeuvred herself back to a working position—half standing, half leaning—and began to assemble once more, the thrumming drama from the front of the shop inaudible now, the circus not hers.

After the shop closed, with little ceremony, Neve led Shell across the sparse evening-time mall to the door of the Green Hall. A last few shoppers milled around, on a different plane than the florist and her assistant, a veil between them and the rest of the world. The place felt more rotten than usual to Shell. All the filth and grime seemed to mushroom up under her feet, the linoleum too soft. It occurred to her, for a moment, that it was frightening here.

Neve's hand lingered on the latch of the door, and she looked up at Shell with dark and tired eyes, eyeliner now smudged, and said, "I knew when I took you on that I was going to bring you in someday. I just didn't really . . . expect it to be like this. I just think it's time that you meet him. It's been time."

Shell blinked at her, not able to respond.

Him. Like a person, she began to wonder, but something I

had built inside her said no. Not a person. Not a man. Anything but a man.

"You can leave now if you want, and I won't stop you. I'll get you a job in another shop, easy, call in a few favours, get you placed somewhere nice, cover for you here. You can leave this situation right now. Because once you've come in, either you'll think I'm mad, or you'll never come back, and I'm not sure I can handle either of those things. It's happened before. So I'm giving you the choice, which isn't what I did last time."

"Neither of those options are that I stay with you and we open our own business, like we said," Shell said softly.

"Yeah, well—" Neve began, but Shell put her hand on the other woman's shoulder.

"I know you have a lot of stories I'm not part of, Neve. And that's fine. I can do my own stories. But the flowers make me happy, being in the shop makes me happy. So risk it. See if I stay."

Neve touched her hand to Shell's, and they stood then, the distance between them warming. It was in that fertile, intense place that I was flowering.

"Well, this is the real story, you know," Neve said, breaking their connection to get her keys from her apron. "Or at least the start of it."

She unlocked the door with a familiar, well-oiled clunk, and led Shell into the green beyond.

The filth on the windows was an excellent disguise, really; nobody could have guessed that such splendour sat camouflaged right there, just a few inches past the grime and glass. Shell's first thought, after the "Wow" that softly came from her mouth, was that the council couldn't knock down the Crown if they knew this was here. How could they? Had they seen this place? It was marvellous.

The air sounded different, like it was filled with electricity. Shell could have sworn she heard birds singing in the high, sparse trees that stood like rails against the mossy, patchy glass. Whole trees. The ceiling was high, high above them. The Green Hall jutted above the rest of the brickwork of the Crown, an architectural signature from a time when the mall was glamorous, not obsolete, not dangerous. The light that tipped in was dim but warm, giving the atmosphere an almost underwater quality. Shell wondered was it the hazy light or something else, like anticipation, that made her vision feel blurry and her head feel light, as Neve led her through the garden.

A small pond with five fat orange koi. A spiral stone structure teeming with bushels of herbs. A near waterfall of blue wisteria. How was all this thriving so well? How was there space for all these roots to coexist? How was this place so rich, hidden so perfectly in plain sight in a mall that thrummed with people every day? The answer is me, and something inside of Shell knew this. It is me. I am the curtain and the one behind it.

Shell found herself reaching for Neve's hand as she led her in, but she didn't quite reach the florist in time. She stopped, suddenly, the back wall of the atrium just an arm's length away, beyond a row of dense briar. The room just stopped.

"Here he is," Neve said then, gesturing to my low table.

Shell furrowed her brow tightly in the way that gave her a coin slot of concern just between her eyebrows as she looked down at me in the white-and-blue ceramic pot Neve kept me in. I know she thought, That's it? not least because her lips mouthed the words to no one, as Neve started to kneel before me, just as she normally did. Neve gestured to Shell to join her, and Shell didn't hesitate, though she might have if she weren't allowing her cynicism and her distraction to do such a good job of protecting her.

I lifted the white petals of my head up to them then, like they were a source of light. I opened my eye.

"Hello," I said, and Shell gasped into her hand and Neve grabbed her arm, half for reassurance and half to make sure she didn't bolt from what was, suddenly, terror. I laughed and Shell recognized the laugh, paling at the sound of me and the realization that I was the music that had been playing along her bones all this time, that she'd been hearing me and feeling me for months.

"I would say it is nice to meet you, but we're already well acquainted," I said playfully, but Shell had not found her voice yet to greet me in return.

Neve lifted her head and said, "I thought it was time. You know we're getting shut down, that this is . . . you know. Over. So I thought Shell should meet you."

"You were right, sweet Neve. You're very almost always right," I purred, leaning my head towards her. Neve raised a hand and stroked me with her thumb. I found that pleasing, her contact so direct. It was almost, for a second, perhaps for Shell's benefit, as though I were her pet, not the other way around.

"Before this all ends, I need to know someone else sees you and believes me."

"Ah, but Shell hasn't said whether she believes in me yet."

I know Shell believed herself to be a flirt, so I decided to flirt and see how she liked it. I turned my eye, lidded with jade, whiter than white around my three-pointed iris, to the blond girl, pale and trembling, on her knees in the flower bed. "Do you?"

Shell didn't say anything for a little while, and Neve was strung up by the suspense of waiting for her answer, time flattening, expanding, silence rolling like hills out in front of her.

Eventually, she whispered, "I do, yes," admitting, finally, to something she had known to be true since she set foot in the flower shop months ago: there was something exceptional around Neve, a glow, a pull, a magic. And that magic was me. She knew, silently, that in accepting me, allowing me to be real, something magic would swell around her, too. That much was for sure. There was no question of good or bad, just magic, blossoming, huge.

"I'm so glad," Neve and I said, our voices a harmony, two valves of the same beautiful organ. Shell looked at Neve then, and Neve kissed her full on the mouth. It set Shell on fire, a girl immolated there in the garden.

As Neve kissed her, Shell's mind emptied. She was only body and flame.

If asked, years later, what finally kissing Neve was like, she would not be able to answer, but her skin would remember, her heart, the skin on the palms of her hands as they closed finally, at last, around Neve's narrow hips. What the distance between them closing finally felt like. A falling curtain. A rising tide.

In this closing I introduced myself to her truly. I said to her,

"Oh, Shell—" and she heard me. Her veins green in her body, growing against the fire.

I was so pleased by them, even more so when they finally broke apart for breath and Shell's eyes immediately went to the chain around Neve's neck. I told her silently then that she was right to stare at the chain, the ring. Do not forget it. That is Jen's ring. That ring means something. That ring is Neve's heart. Do not forget how it makes you feel, even when you're drowning in this glow, even when all you want is to look at Neve's flushed cheeks, her red mouth, her messy hair. Take it. Take her heart.

Shell tore her gaze from the chain then and took it up to Neve's eyes, dark and shining. They kissed again spontaneously and did not stop for some time, their clothes coming loose, each becoming bolder. Neve did not have to lead Shell, and I did not have to lead either of them.

While their mouths were still together, Shell brought her hand to Neve's chest and took the ring between her fingers, surprisingly warm against her skin. The hair it was made of held a higher temperature than one would expect. Neve jerked slightly away from the trespass, but the ring stayed in Shell's hand. She pulled it from Neve's neck, but Neve was so lost in the feeling of the other woman's hands on her body that she didn't even notice.

Later, while Shell was fucking Kiero in his car on the beach in the dark, she kept Neve far from her mind by making him talk to her. He said everything she told him to, and it was good for her concentration. When she came, quickly, all things considered, and let him finish, too, she dismounted and lay boneless in the front seat, her long shirt almost down to her bare thighs like a nightgown. She didn't look at him while he fumbled with the condom, tidying himself up, but then he leaned over to her and brushed his fingers through her hair—perhaps a little too tenderly—and said, "Oh," and plucked, from nowhere, a white flower.

"That's so funny," Shell said, smiling. "Cute magic trick."

"That was in your hair, and look—" He removed another, and another, three or four fresh blooms.

Shell furrowed her brow and leaned forward to flip down the mirror—and there I was, all over her nest of curls, flourishing and blooming. Her mouth dried up, and all the softness leftover under her skin from the sex evaporated, gave way to nausea. When she came, I came.

"Oh, weird. I always find petals everywhere after work, you know?" she said, voice shaking, kissing him again, hoping it would be enough to distract him. It almost was, but he was looking up at her like she was something more than she knew she should be to him, so she stopped, and held his jaw in her hand, and said, "You need to leave Ireland, you know that, don't you?"

He mouthed What? at her, confused, still hazy, and Shell said, "If you don't leave, this place will eat you alive," and kissed him again, as though to convince him. Go, go, go, get out while you still can.

Fruit

Jen drove the whole way back to Dublin a little too fast, and in total silence—the length of the country with only the ringing in her ears to keep her company. When she had to stop for petrol in the big, bright service station named for Barack Obama, due to his heritage in Ireland, she didn't linger at the long, heady deli counters, or take silly selfies under the name of the former American president to send back home to her sister. Just swiped a bottle of water, paid for the gas, and left. She promised herself she'd enjoy it on the way home: she'd be back on the road again in no time, the wind of a job well done behind her. She'd give herself a reward, no matter what happened at the Crown.

It felt strange and sad to pull off the motorway and drive down past Darndale, past the enormous opera house of a twenty-four-hour Tesco, a bright glass palace off the grey concrete sprawl. It felt like a lot had changed, though practically nothing could have. She'd only been gone what, nine months? Not even a year. Evening was just starting to come down, the amber streetlamps waking themselves up. Summer wasn't giving way just yet, and the long bright days that Ireland had in the middle of the year were still a marvel to Jen. The sun wouldn't be fully gone down until nearly ten.

Jen liked it here. Missed it. It was full of colour that she missed living in the endless green and stone of the Burren. There was none of this glow down there at night: the lab compound was the only thing that was lit for miles around, all silent and dark. The suburbs, though, hummed, and their song rose a fondness up through her. She passed, in a flash, the apartment block where Neve lived—her old home. Where she'd lived. The living room light was on, but Jen couldn't see her. The balcony still full of plants, the little pride flag hanging off the balcony, the spindle of fairy lights she'd hung one Christmas still there, not turned on for the night yet. The ache this gave her was dull, not sharp. You can feel the sorrow of a thing that is gone without wanting it back, like mourning the version of yourself who was happy—for whom this was enough.

Bec was going to be waiting for her in the McDonald's, and had guaranteed her that Neve wouldn't be around. The lights in Neve's apartment were an indicator that she was there, in her home, sure, but they weren't proof. Nor were they insurance that she wouldn't come waltzing into the mall at any moment, that their paths wouldn't clash and everything be made much worse, for all of them. Not least for Bec, who was engaging in an act of real betrayal of Neve here. Jen knew that, and was thankful for it, for Bec's trust in her gut instincts that something was really wrong. How could they not feel it? Daniel and Kiero, too, that there was something humming away around them? How were they not obsessed with the disappearances? Were they all so poisoned by the day-to-day of the Crown that they hadn't the capacity to acknowledge them for more than a few days? Tragedy fatigue, or something, wasn't that what they called it, when a populace was so drenched in pain that they couldn't feel it anymore?

Jen knew none of them really worried about whatever was going on in the mall, or about Neve. She'd always given off the air of a person so consumed by her passion for her art and business that the sum of her flaws could only really be marked up to "poor work-life balance." Jen had been the life part of that equation, and had been terrified for Neve by the end, as well as exhausted by her. Her friends were supposed to be the life part, too, but they weren't. They couldn't be.

Jen was grateful for Bec, though. After she parked her car around the side of the mall, near the public recycling bins, out of eyeshot of the entrance to the building and as far away as was possible from the flower shop, and she began her sketchy journey, hood up, across the rainy car park, she could see Bec perched in the McDonalds, a lone figure in the hours after the dinnertime rush.

The smell in the McDonald's was overwhelming, childhood and hot oil. Jen felt the familiarity of the restaurant hit her like relief, and then Bec was standing at her table, both arms outstretched, holding a white cup of soda in her hand, the other opening and closing in a silent Come here to me, come here! Her whole body said welcome, though her face was obscured.

Jen and Bec embraced quietly in the yellow glow of the restaurant floor, the tiles slightly sticky under their feet. Jen's eyes filled with tears: nobody had hugged her in months and months, and the shock of another body, a familiar body, was almost overwhelming.

"Jesus, Jen, I wish it was under better circumstances," Bec said into her neck, not letting her go. "But it's great to see you. It's been forever."

"Nine months," Jen said.

"You could have a baby in that time," Bec said, laughing a little, still not letting go.

"No baby, just a nervous breakdown." The two of them gave half laughs, half sighs as they broke apart. Jen felt like she'd come to shore, almost a year at sea. She'd forgotten what it was like to have friends at all, but here was her girl. Her secret agent.

"Hey, let's get out of here before I buy forty chicken nuggets and put them into my mouth all at once," Jen said, and Bec linked her arm tight.

"How long will you need in here, do you think? Can we go out for a small drink after?" Bec asked. "Or do you need to get back?"

"I could probably have one. I mean, I probably need one, but then I'm going to hit the road." Jen was genuinely sad to admit it. "I'd love a night on the couch with a bottle of wine, to be honest, but I'm due in the lab early, and they don't like us disappearing. Weekend or no weekend. Likely, most of them won't have noticed I was gone at all, let alone that I was gone all the way to Dublin, if I'm lucky."

"You're some rebel," Bec said, pushing the door to the night open again.

They scuttled across the sparse car park towards the shuttered doorway, and Bec led Jen off to the side, in through the strange, stilted Woodbine Crown Inn, where local patrons—customers of the flower shop, the salon, the supermarket—hummed and drank and read their phones and talked around their tables.

Jen felt like a thief, keeping her eyes on the flattened maroon carpet. This was the most people she had been around in a long time, the most noise she had heard—the sour, yeasted bar smell making her thirsty. She'd have loved to tug Bec by the coat sleeve and say, *Hey, just one, a pint to take the edge off,* but Bec was on a mission. The bar was in the centre of the room, a deep wooden altar of a thing, and Bec leant over the curve of it. She pointed at a door distinctly marked NO ACCESS THROUGH THIS DOOR in that unmistakable building-site print. This was new, a first sign of the demolition. What did it matter if people entered and exited the mall by that doorway? Nothing was going to fall down, not immediately. Regardless, the barman pulled one of the keys off his chain to hand to Bec, giving her a soft but stern "Be back here in an hour, yeah?" and she flashed him a bright, grateful smile.

Bec led Jen over to the theatrically forbidden door and opened it with a little lean and lift, exposing a portal into the dark, barren Woodbine Crown. They shuffled through and Bec sharply closed it behind them, locking it on her way out.

The sight of the mall filled Jen with emotion. Though it was depersonalized—it was dark, and many of the shop fronts even in her eye line were totally empty—it brought her right back into better times. The reverberation of Bec's voice off the linoleum and glass as she said, "Kiero gave me his keys, if you want to start in the corridors behind the shops and work our way around to here again?" was a song that played during better times: drunken waltzes from the good court with Neve, on their way home to the little flat when all the cans had been drunk. It had been a good time, a great time, and all of Jen's senses transported her there, with force.

"You all right?" Bec asked.

"Yeah," said Jen. "Just feels like last year."

"It always feels like last year," Bec said, "that's why we've all been here for so long."

Jen laughed a bit at that, not unkindly. "Well, you're all like . . . free now, right?"

"Ah, yeah. It was time. Something was going to change, one way or another."

As they walked up through the silvery chasm of the Crown, past the dull prism of the Green Hall to the locked escalators—another seasick familiarity to Jen—they were slowly orbiting the real heart of why Jen was there. Jen observed some closed shop fronts, some new vape stores; Bec filled her in on what should have been warning signs that the place was being gutted out around them and they didn't even notice, or didn't want to notice.

It took until they were at the entrance to the back corridors for Jen to say, "Hey, thank you for believing me. I know this is fucking weird."

Bec shrugged. "It's weird, but the more I've thought about it, the more sense it makes. I don't think Neve . . . killed those people, you know? But I think something's up, so I want to help."

Speaking the implicit accusation, the frankness of "killed those people," was like a spell. They were moving with purpose, then, a seriousness within their stealth. Their playfulness dropped away. They weren't slinking around the mall, catching up, though for a few minutes it might have felt like that. They were looking for evidence of a set of disappearances. They were looking for a way to either incriminate or absolve Neve. Jen took out her camera as Bec reckoned with the set of keys, and then, together, they went in.

It was pitch-black for a few moments, the kind of blackness you only really experience in deep, buried places—surfaces that have never known daylight, like those tight corridors in the guts of a pyramid, or a passage tomb. Jen closed her eyes against it as Bec fumbled with her phone light, looking for the light switch. A heavy click and the warming sounds of bulbs; she opened them again and watched the corridor illuminate foot by foot. It somehow felt worse to look at now that it was lit. Jen's camera in her hand was a gun, and she walked side by side with Bec, eyes everywhere. Bec kept the torch lit on her phone, a halo spreading from her hand.

Jen knew what she was looking for. What she needed to see. She needed proof that there was a plant responsible for the disappearances, her deep worry justified. If she couldn't find proof of the plant, or anything else sinister, she would go home feeling a little less insane than she'd left, she told herself, her footfalls eaten by old carpet. She wasn't just looking for samples of rare plants. She wasn't looking for them at all, actually, not really. She wasn't trying to save the place: she was trying to find an answer to her worst, most wretched fear. She was looking for bloodstains. She was looking for clothes in plastic bags. She was looking for rope, more of those cleaning agents—though she would eventually go to the Green Hall, where she assumed the sinister things she'd seen still were.

Jen was no detective, not really. She didn't even listen to true crime podcasts or watch the documentaries that her streaming services insistently recommended her. She was following her gut, a bad suspicion, a thing that was driving her mad. If she didn't check before they closed this place down, she'd never know—or never be able to say she'd tried. The worry would rot in her, worse than it already was. She could have talked to a cop, sure, but she wasn't going to contact the police unless it was absolutely and beyond reasonable doubt necessary for her to do so. How can you call the cops on a plant? How could she have told her worries to anyone but Bec? Even telling Bec had been a risk, but here she was, creeping down the decaying oesophagus of the mall with her, a champ—a real friend.

They walked awhile, eyes darting, each dark doorway into a back room another sickening possibility. Towers of chairs, crates, wires, shoeboxes. Dust thick on all of them, sometimes floating in the air like a bad snow.

"I don't know what I'm even expecting to see," Bec whispered. "It's not as if the stockroom for the Vape Emporium is just going to be a big pile of bodies." That broke the tension a little, and they laughed darkly.

"I mean, if it is a big pile of bodies, then we're kind of . . . sorted, aren't we?" Jen whispered back.

"I really hope we don't have to see any. Bodies, I mean."

"I also hope we don't have to."

"I'm kind of scared."

"Me, too."

Bec linked Jen's arm then, which made Jen at least feel a bit better.

They walked on in the yellow, bad light, listening to the halogen hum and the thrashing of their own hearts. There were no bloodstains. No errant human remains. No strange piles of clothing, wallets, loose ID cards, no props of disaster or traces of violence. Just empty, dusty corridors. The threat of halfway open doors leading to exactly nothing, or the mundanity of a break room with a disgusting microwave hanging open and some folding chairs, sitting around, abandoned. One such break room, for the pharmacy, Bec noted—figuring out their location, which was helpful after walking for so long and losing their sense of space—had a lone birthday balloon hanging miserably up by the ceiling tiles, deflated but still aloft.

"That's me up there," Jen said, pointing to it, before Bec turned off the light.

"You're not as crinkly. Yet."

"Hold on, wait—"

Bec switched the light back on, and Jen stepped into the break room of Pharma Plus.

"Can you see a security camera in here?"

Bec craned her neck, examining the place where the walls met the ceiling of the room. "No . . . none."

"Good. Because look at that, there, up by our balloon."

In the very corner of the room, just beyond the heart-shaped satellite, was a fat green vine. Jen lifted her camera, looked at the screen, snapped. Zoomed in, snapped again. Took out her phone, snapped. Switched to video, switched to HD, hit record, then zoomed. That was a vine, lolling from a dislodged corner tile, hanging in the air, almost out of sight.

"Should I move the balloon?" Bec offered.

"No," Jen said. "Don't disturb it. I don't think it knows we're here."

Bec shook her head. "'Knows we're here,' c'mon, Jen."

Jen shrugged. "I mean it. Let's split. I've got what I need to start. Maybe we'll find more, but I don't want it to know we're looking at it. Maybe it already does know."

"I mean, it can't know-know, right?"

"I'm not sure, but I'm also not interested in finding out back here. I'd rather find out in the lab."

Back out in the corridor, a little buzzed from the discovery, they hurried along, electric detectives the pair of them. A hundred feet or so into a dimly lit stretch of hallway, down the seam of the wall where a poorly installed panel lay cracked open, a length of green vine the width and texture of a human arm hung from the wall, then disappeared down into a split between two carpet tiles. Jen got down on her knees to photograph and film it: it seemed to have veins, and slight hairs lifted from its surface. She wasn't sure if she was imagining that it had a pulse, so slightly was it moving.

"God, I'd love to just . . . slice off some of it," she whispered, eyes glued to the screen of her phone, "but there's no way I'm risking it. Not yet."

"Looking at it doesn't make me feel good. Can't imagine touching it would feel better," Bec said. "How . . . did I not know this stuff was back here?"

"I mean. Weird and terrible things can be right in front of us and we can look right through them, right? Most of us have to operate in a fog to survive. You probably have seen it, but just . . . haven't seen it, you know?" Jen zoomed in, zoomed out.

Bec frowned a little, eyes faraway. "Yeah. Maybe you're onto something there."

Farther down again, when they had turned down the crest of a horseshoe in the geography of the walkway, they came upon a completely open back room from a shuttered shop unit.

There, in the middle of the room, in the lowlight, sat a heap of white petals, about the height of a person's hips. At first it looked like undone laundry, a torn-down window display, a discarded altar of pillows. It was none of these things. It was, as Bec and Jen quickly realized, a shedding. They stepped inside in sync, Bec shining her phone torch with one hand and fumbling for the light switch with another. It clicked on, and off, and no light came. Dead halogens useless above them. Jen turned the flash on her camera and began to record.

Still hesitant to touch the petals, she zoomed in on her phone screen instead, bringing the pile's details closer. Each petal looked soft, still, barely browned around the edges. Like they'd just fallen from a blossom. The room had the funeral scent of lily and rot and was, aside from this strange heap, completely empty.

They shuffled out again, terrified to turn their backs, and sidestepped out into the corridor, hearts pounding.

"Weird," whispered Bec.

"Yeah," said Jen.

They stood against the wall beside the room for a while, not moving.

"I think we've hit the end," Bec said, hand on her chest, as though she were directing the movement of her breath to slow down, settling it like an animal.

"Do you want to run?" Jen asked. "Or is that an insane thing to ask? Because I feel like all the tension of this has just filled me up. I also don't want to walk past the vine in the floor again too slowly. I just need to . . . run. Will you do it with me?"

"Absolutely I will." Bec gave a little laugh. "All right, on the count of three?"

"One, two—"

And the two women were off, breaking into a side-by-side sprint, a four-legged-race, light on their feet but still somehow thundering down the length and curve of the aisle, back towards the door into the mall. Their fevered breathing became real laughter quickly, nervous, adrenaline-filled gasps of it stark against the bleak. Jen all but slammed against the door when they reached it, then flung it open without decorum. Bec turned off the lights and watched the hallway evaporate into the darkness of a forgotten temple.

The mall itself felt practically luminous in comparison. They pulled the door closed and Bec locked it, with all the force of a seal on a cursed tomb.

"One more spot to hit," Jen said, pointing over at the looming spectre of the Green Hall.

"Almost done." Bec nodded. "Jesus, my nerves are shot."

"Mine, too."

Down the awkward scale of the escalator and into the hollow atrium at the middle of the mall, the flower shop just there, so close Jen could walk over and touch the window—but instead she turned and kept her gaze away from it, like it was Neve's exoskeleton.

Jen didn't at all consider the Green Hall to be more frightening than the long, liminal place she and Bec had just sprinted through. Perhaps that was because her body was still ringing like a bell from the sprint, from the fear, from the possibility that she had photographs and footage that proved her deep worry correct. She just needed a final look around, maybe a cutting or two from inside, around where Neve's orchid was. Baby, she'd called it.

"Can I wait outside, please?" Bec asked, taking a pull from her vape. "I'm not sure I can take much more of this."

"Of course," Jen said, though her stomach dropped a little—she'd just make her trip into the strange glass garden quick. "But can I take your phone? For a flashlight? I'm not sure there's lights wired in there."

"Oh, you can, yes," Bec said, unlocking the glass door. "God, Neve would be so pissed if she found out Kiero had a key to this place, you know? She's so protective of it."

"See, that's the thing—if she wasn't hiding anything, she

wouldn't be annoyed that someone else had a key." Jen shook her head, sighed deep. "I'm not saying she killed anyone, you know?"

"We're not saying she killed anyone," Bec confirmed, looking Jen in the eye. "Just that . . . something's going on. That's different, isn't it?"

Jen nodded as she opened the door ever so slightly. "It is." She slipped inside, holding Bec's phone radiating light in front of her in one hand, and her own phone, camera recording, in the other. The light drew steep and horrible shadows out of what otherwise would have been lush and healthy fauna, made the glass feel sinister, brought out the filth on it. Jen wondered if she would be better walking in the dark, trusting her eyes to guide her, but found that she was too afraid to switch the torch off. She lit her way, and held her camera where the light fell. Dark greens, long shadows, the grey tiles and earth on the ground—the Green Hall wasn't really that big, not as big as it looked on the outside. The air was hot, too hot, body temperature—the seasons made no difference to this tiny tropic, but summer must have helped it along, even a little.

At the end of the greenhouse, she shone her light up against the walls—yes, there they were, the barrels, still. She zoomed in on them using her camera phone, inspecting the black trash bags heaped beside them, the mop with a head so badly ruined it almost looked like bark. She didn't need to pull the bags open, didn't need to disturb Neve's setup, just as it had been months and months ago—she just needed proof it was there, so she could send someone better equipped to look. However, there was nobody better equipped to examine the plant itself than her. She had the whole lab down at the Burren at her disposal, and tucked into the inside pocket of her jacket was a shallow plastic bag from the lab with just enough cultured water at the bottom to keep a cutting alive until she got back home.

She hadn't had the courage in the back rooms to touch the vines of the thing, but here she found herself faced with it again, on a little altar made of brick, its vines bigger than its stem or leaves or blossoms; there it was, right at the back of the Hall, petals folding inward for the night, almost as though it were sleeping. Jen loved how plants did this, how they bent and flexed to light and heat, just like people did.

Kneeling then, she looked closely at the plant. It certainly wasn't an orchid, though if she softened her gaze, the settings of the petals suggested it could be. The petals were unmistakably the very ones she had seen, soft, like a heap of feathers from the nest of a bird, in that empty storeroom. It looked to her like something else doing a good enough impression of an orchid: a wolf in orchid's clothing.

Jen placed Bec's phone on the ground for a second, the light casting up, like a little fountain. In the breast pocket of her coat, she had a tiny, sharp pair of scissors. Using that, she took a cutting from the part of the plant that met the soil and placed it quickly into the bag of water, closing the top and ensuring the vulnerable part of it was soaked enough to trick it into staying something like alive. The place where she had cut filled in, sharply, with black foam, which spilt onto the soil as though it were bleeding. She had left the plant with a wound, and looking at it made her feel sick, as did the foul odour that filled the air as the foam bubbled forth. She looked hard at the limp, sleeping blossom, willing it to open, to show her that it was thinking, feeling, alive, awake. She held her still-recording phone up to it for ten seconds, willing anything to happen, but there was nothing.

She packed the bag away, put her scissors in her pocket, grabbed Bec's phone, and walked away quickly, her chest tight and ears ringing. When she got outside to Bec, Jen clung on to her tight, like she was a buoy and the sea was rolling, hungry to swallow her up.

The whole thing took less than an hour, and the barman even gave them a raised pair of eyebrows and a "That was quick" before pulling them each a dark, thick pint of Guinness. They sat at a table for an hour, looked at the photos and the footage, talked and rationalized and promised each other that they really didn't think Neve was a murderer and that wasn't what all this was about, promised each other secrecy, sank two more pints, and Jen swore she was all right to drive—the adrenaline neutralized the alcohol, she said. She'd been drinking a lot on her own, she admitted, too. From the stress and all that, so her tolerance was high.

Bec absolutely believed her, trusted her. Jen was a doctor, after all.

I have to wait until she is almost home to do it. Jen is still on the road, listening to her music, nursing the soreness in her own heart far away from the Woodbine Crown. Jen had long lost the reason she came to Ireland—Neve, who had once been so sharp and funny and bold—to what she saw as a nervous breakdown, a delusion so powerful that she could not within her personal ethical code, both as a scientist and a human being, enable it, let alone play into it, let alone become part of the mechanics of it. Neve had so expertly concealed me for years of their relationship, kept me on a distant moon in the orbit of her and Jen's lives. Around her heart, but not inside it, where I belonged. No ring for Baby, but one for her, and one for Jen. A game of keep-away.

I don't want to cause her pain, not really. I just need her gone. I do not need to be examined in the context that I am special or different from any other plant, and importantly, I need her gone for Neve, and for Shell. Perhaps Jen was deserving of a bigger life than she got, perhaps she deserved more time, or dignity, or something, so the decency I can do her is that she doesn't really notice when I begin to foam from the little container, and burst out of the plastic bag she put me in. She does not notice the back seats flooding with moss, a slow and green volcanic crawl across the upholstery. It's too dark out, she's too far away, her eyes on the road, her head in her old life, her focus on the song she is singing. What a gift to go out singing, really; how many people will get such a luxury as their last breaths being given to a love song?

She can't fight me by the time I simultaneously cover the back window with my growth and reach her body in the driver's seat. She does notice, for a second, but not for long enough to register what is happening. I pulse over her shoulders first and bind her to the seat with vines, and I fill her mouth and nose with moss and crawl into her eye sockets with my tiny vines, and she's gone, I switch her off like a light. She is dead before the car spins off the road: there is nobody around to see. I chew her body, and it is bad and full of her laboratory chemicals but I try to get purchase on it anyway, and I eat at the car and though it careens from the road initially with a sort of drama, it is softened into a green nothing by the time it stops in the field, and I sink it down into the earth and the grass, all the metal and wire, all the fabric and glass, all of her body, gone with me. I do keep the radio on, though: for of all the human nonsense I have experienced in my short time here, I do think music is worth playing, especially and most vitally at the end of something.

When Jen dreams, she dreams of Neve. Wherever Jen is in this dream, it feels like early-early Tuesday morning, like her body knows it is around half three so she doesn't even have to open her eyes and look at her phone. It's too early. She should still be sleeping, but she can feel Neve moving to life beside her under the covers, as usual. Neve is a creature of the small hours, able to get up and get ready and go to greet the flower men. Neve's long, gamine form leaves the bed, and there it is, the tender, daily moment when Jen is holding on to sleep and Neve has left and Jen murmurs, Tell the flowers you need to stay, and Neve says in the dark, Tell the brides, tell the widow, tell the baby that's just been born that none of them need flowers, don't tell me—like she's singing back a lullaby to Jen, laying out the rules of their life. The flowers came first. Jen would always try then, to follow Neve, to be that three or four a.m. girlfriend who could get up and breakfast with her florist, maybe do some sunrise yoga, walk her to the Woodbine Crown and catch a coffee on the way home before starting her own job, stealing the morning for the two of them—but Jen could never do it, bones heavy with comfort, the green duvet a shroud.

In this dream, though, Jen feels Neve's absence like a bone gone from her. She cannot hear her voice in the room. This time she does not turn towards the soft darkness of the morning before dawn; she can't hear Neve's body moving across the carpet, cannot hear the shift of her nightdress—the huge T-shirt with a palm tree, and PALMA NOVA 2001 emblazoned across the chest in neon yellow—she can't hear the drawers opening in the dresser, the shuffle and snap of a bra, the pull of jeans. These were the sounds of Jen's mornings, the music of her dreams, Neve's body alive and moving. There is nothing, this time. Jen is alone. Something is badly wrong. Something smells like wet earth and rot and copper—is the house falling down? Has the ceiling come in? The bedsheets black, wet, and heavy and coming apart in her hands, the fabric dissolving into thick matter, and the panic coming up in Jen's chest like an animal.

She wants to call Neve, to say her name, but her mouth is full of something. It is sweet and bad—like rotting fruit.

Then she was awake. Jen pulled herself from one place into another, moving hard against viscera, the cold tar of the earth, the smothering vegetation, the choking of it; she was blinded and giving birth to herself. The vacuum around her slipped away suddenly, all the resistance done, and she was up, the pain of it blistering inside her chest and veins, but she was swimming easier then, up into the world, kicking, the noises coming from her unholy, keening the death she had, somehow, escaped.

It was pitch-dark in a field by the side of the road, but the air hitting Jen was so profound a relief that she didn't need to be able to see to know that she was alive, that there had been an accident, or no accident at all. There was matter in her eye sockets, her nasal cavity, her mouth, and not the topside of the ground she crawled from. She emptied the contents of her stomach and sinuses, the sound of her so terrible that cows in their barn a mile down the road lifted their heads and collies sleeping on kitchen floors were roused. There would be word of a banshee for weeks to come around County Clare, but the noise Jen made was not one of sorrow, one instead of life, against all odds.

She lay by the roadside awhile, panting and heaving, begging her sore body to adjust to the elements, just be grateful to be here instead of wounded. Like her mouth gasping for air, it was only a few moments before Jen instinctually checked her body for her phone, the true lifeline. Where was her car? What time was it? Where was the last town she passed through? Had it been Lisdoonvarna—it had, the streetlamps were few out this way and in the distance they picked up, she could see even from the ground that she wasn't far outside, that she wouldn't have to walk for long. The car was gone. Not even totalled; there were only mounds of earth and moss around her, like she'd crawled up out of the soft earth and the car was still down there. She couldn't go to the compound, to her dorm. She had to go to the town, and get back to Neve. Her phone was in the breast pocket of her jacket, the screen shattered but still, somehow, alight with energy. Battery. But no signal. It was just gone two in the morning.

In the new light Jen could see that her fingernails were clotted with filth, and where the nail met the skin she was bleeding. From the digging. From the birth. They would have stung if she hadn't been stinging all over, if she wasn't on fire with the exertion of survival.

As she stood up, though, she could tell that shock was beginning to come over her, like a grace. The pubs would still be open back in the town, down the hill. If it had been uphill, she wouldn't have been able for it, but the land ceded to her, made it easier on her. She walked, unsteady, her legs new and weighted with filth, down towards where there would be signal. Where she could call Bec.

The town tumbled open in front of Jen, limping, her breaths heavy, her eyes stinging. She wasn't certain how long she'd been out. Questions rose up inside her but didn't quite make it to the surface of where she was able to think about them. She had a singular aim, as numbness helpfully came up through her: she just had to make a phone call, get Bec to come to her. Then, water.

Leanne's was open, a boxy little red pub with gold lettering over the doorway, frosted windows, light dim but most definitely on inside. Jen had been here before, once, with the scientists. She'd just tell the barman she was up from the labs. She'd been in an accident, and she'd like to use the Wi-Fi. How insane a thing to say, Can I please use your staff-only Wi-Fi? at a time like this. What kind of first words would they be for her, newborn out of the earth, fresh from the maw of the underworld? Christ. No songs of praise, no confessions, just Can I have your password, please? Like a wraith, Jen went in, planning to act as normally as she could, as though she'd toppled off her bike down the road, but the face on the barman took Jen aback as he regarded her, his mouth dropping open in shock. The bar was quiet: some old men in the snug, the rumble of twenty-four-hour news on the television above the bar, the smell of beer on old carpets rank and familiar and calming.

"Jesus, bird, get in, were you in an accident?"

Jen felt the answer crawl up her throat and it took a second to come out of her. "I need help," she said.

"Yes," said the barman, brows knit with concern. "Sit down here for me for a second, and I'll call the garda for you, would you need an ambulance? The nearest hospital is in Ennis, miles out. I could get the on-call doctor?"

"No doctor. I . . . am a doctor. I just need my friend."

"Do you need the phone?" he asked, extending his hand over the bar. "You can hop on to the Wi-Fi there if you still have your own." Jen could have cried with the relief.

She shakily sat down at a little table near the door and pored down into her phone, fingers blackened with earth and blood. There was a moment then when she looked up at the barman and he looked back at her, his eyes dark, his face reddened from years at the pub, and some understanding went between them that the police weren't any use to her at this moment in time. Something Jen had long been suspicious of living out in the rural wilds was the tendency of villages to self-govern. Here, she was thankful for it.

Two drinks landed in front of her. A pint of Guinness and a short whiskey, with no ice. She took them one after the other like they were a cure for the taste of clay and moss and viscera. They might as well have been.

She called Bec the second she was able to, hands shaking too much to text. A text could be ignored, a phone call was urgent. She had never called Bec before. As the phone rang out across the country, Jen found herself praying, please, please pick up, please wake up, please don't leave me like this—and as though she knew, Bec answered sleepily after five rings, her "Jen?" the best sound that Jen had ever heard in her life.

"Bec, I've gotten into really bad trouble. Can you drive to Lisdoonvarna, now?"

"Yes, I'll leave now. Are you safe to wait for me? Do you need me to stay on the line for the drive? It's, fuck, it's going to be a while even at this hour—"

"I'm in Leanne's, the red pub in the village, I'll be safe here until you land. I think they might keep it open for me, for a while."

"Can you tell me what happened?" Jen could hear Bec moving around her house on the other end of the line, her moving from the bed, the jingle of keys, the closing of doors behind her as she stepped, without hesitation, into the night.

"Not yet. I'm still not . . . right."

"Then hold tight. I'll be with you in . . . well, the maps app will tell me shortly. I'll drop you my location, so you can watch me coming. If you need anything I'll be on the other end of the line."

Jen could have burst into tears if her body weren't still so taken up in the shock—somewhere beyond the helpful numb of her body she felt a pull of love for her friend.

"Thank you."

"All good. Anytime. I'll keep you posted."

The line went dead then, and Jen kept the phone against her cheek a moment. She wasn't sure she'd ever had a friend like Bec. Maybe in her teens, there had been a certain ride-or-die amongst her high school friends, long reduced to flickering interactions on social media. Maybe in college, a murder of riotous undergrad classmates would easily haul one another drunk and blinded out of clubs or frat houses. But not in her adult life. Certainly not since she'd moved to Ireland. Bec owed her nothing. She could have just been Neve's ex, but Bec had leant towards her even after all that had ended, even in the farce that had been investigating the Green Hall. Bec believed her. Bec wanted to help her. Bec got into her car and drove across the country in the dark in her pyjamas and slippers without hesitation. Jen wondered, putting her phone down and staring into the white foam of her pint, was this what it was like to be loved?

Two hours and twenty minutes moved past in a smear of discomfort, breaks to the tiny ladies' room to vomit, three more pints and whiskeys, and disjointed spurts of conversation with the barman, who somehow agreed to keep the pub open deep late and into the morning so as not to throw Jen onto the side of the street. At some point he started smoking, which then encouraged the farmers who were hanging on to the lock-in to also start smoking. Jen sat in the dense Marlboro air and downed drink after drink, begging each to impact her, to make her feel something, but she was impermeable.

She began to note out in her phone what had happened. She had been driving, and singing, then she was out, gone, then she was worming herself up from the ground like a creature. If there had been a crash, she couldn't remember it. All she could see, still, when she closed her eyes, was green. The black that should have been there in the absence of light was glowing dank and live now. In the pocket where she had had the sample bag with the leaf clippings, now there were only curling shards of plastic. Somewhere inside her, Jen knew the black emerald feeling, the forest-blindness in her eyes was the doing of the thing in the orchid. Maybe even the doing of Neve herself. Bec sent texts every time she stopped at a red light—which is to say, twice. She tore her Toyota Corolla across the belly of Ireland, and she didn't stop.

When Bec's fists landed heavy on the deadbolt door of the pub like thunder and lightning, Jen leapt from her seat to let her in, the barman now so thick in conversation with one of the farmers and so pissed himself that he hardly took notice. The stereo was blaring Garth Brooks; there was a singalong roaring from the snug; it was tomorrow, now, and Bec was in the doorframe like a miracle in a pair of shearling slippers with a long grey cardigan swaddled over her pyjamas. She really had just rolled out of bed and to the rescue, her hair wound tight around a long satin curling rod, preparing to be effortless-looking tomorrow. She had her car keys clenched in one hand, her phone in the other, and a wild look in her eyes.

Jen was no sooner standing than she collapsed, boneless, into Bec's arms. The pair of them, Bec soft and clean, all night cream and argan oil, and Jen, earth and blood and pints and terror, held on to each other until they were ready to let go.

"You stay safe out there, girl, yeah?" roared the barman, and Jen said, "I will, thank you, I will, thank you," over and over as she headed out the door, half carried by Bec.

She wouldn't remember much of the car ride back, because Bec told her to go to sleep, as soon as she'd extracted the most important information from her. The car was presumably totalled, but it seemed to have disappeared down the side of the road, into a ditch, somewhere. She said she thought the plant she took a cutting of had made her so sick she crashed, or maybe the plant itself had crashed the car, or something worse, and Bec took that insane statement with absolute stoicism and said,

"We really need to talk to Neve about all this," calmly. "In the morning. First thing. I'll bring you to mine and put you down in the spare room. Then we'll clean you up and see if you need a doctor. Then we'll get you into the Crown in front of her and make her explain herself. You're safe now, right?" Her tone was firm and calm.

A large amount of Bec's day-to-day job, Jen realized as she was curling up in the front seat, was crisis management. Sure, the crisis was generally a missed plane, an overbooking, a leak in an aparthotel ceiling, the occasional insect infestation—but what was this, only another person stranded somewhere they shouldn't be without a way home.

Bec switched on a playlist and said, as she turned it up, "I'm so sorry, but if I don't listen to something with a big tune, I'm going to pass out, you'll just have to consider it a lullaby."

Sheena Easton arrived in the car with them then, and Jen found herself smiling against the weight of exhaustion, then she was gone. This time, she didn't dream, and she woke hours later to Bec's hand on her shoulder, the taste of soil gone from her mouth.

Neve was in the shop early, as normal, as though nothing were happening, as though nothing had changed, as though nothing were about to change. She wanted to take some samples from the Green Hall, some cuttings, for propagation. She let Shell know this via a stilted text littered with full stops. Shell shook her head reading it, getting out of bed, the dawn hardly begun. Neve was never the same two days in a row, even after all of yesterday's conspiracy and softness. Though, she supposed, neither was she the same two days in a row. She didn't answer, and she didn't answer any of Kiero's texts, either. Shell operated as though on autopilot. I was blooming all over the monologue she carried inside of herself. She had not quite adjusted to the presence of my voice, my remarks as she showered, my filling of her palm with green then disappearing it, just for fun, just to show her what I could do. She scrubbed her hair hard in the drench of the shower, but that would not get rid of me. It might get rid of the smell of Kiero's cologne, and maybe a little of the guilt, but not me.

I said, as she brushed her teeth, that I was going to ask her to do me a little favour. Just a small one, and it would benefit her, too. I'd keep asking until she did it, by the way, so she might as well just say yes. So she said yes, smart girl. She asked her reflection in the bathroom mirror, "What favour? What will I do?" and I replied out of her mouth, "Not yet, I'll tell you soon," and she felt a little as though she were going mad but I soothed her. No, no, no. Not mad.

She put in her earrings, fixed on her necklace, and placed the ring she had stolen from Neve—which Neve had not noticed was missing—onto her finger. Dark and warm.

Here is my illusion for you, Shell, I said to her as she let herself into the Crown, empty still. Look how ordinary all of this is. Look at Neve, walking back from the Green Hall to the shop. Carrying on as if the world weren't ending around her, as if the Woodbine weren't shuttering as she moved. I led Shell to the door of the Green Hall once Neve was out of sight. I made her press her hands against the glass. Though she could not see inside from the filth, I showed her, in the theatre of her mind, that place she loved to lie back while the rest of her life happened onscreen.

Shell, I said into her ear, the magic is gone from the Green Hall. I turned it off like an electrical light. You saw it at its most alive yesterday, at its most real. Wouldn't you like it if the rest of the whole world felt so real? Wouldn't you? Look at it now. Green, yes. Verdant, certainly, a healthy enough garden, given the location. But the light is simply midweek morning. All the alchemical heat in the air is gone. I am here, still, but I am not casting myself through the plants around me. The fish in the pond are yellower, they are more sickly from being indoors all of their lives. There is no birdsong now. The grime that webs the windows is just filth, not the teeming, breathing moss you saw yesterday. It does not smell of jasmine, just earth. The blue wisteria is browning at the edge of its petals even now, a waterfall beginning to sour. Can you see how utterly ordinary this place is now, without my touch? Can you see what the world is without me? The rot of it? I am holding my breath, Shell, I said, but soon I will ask you to do me a little favour. You still have that ring, don't you? It is so pretty on your hand. We'll find somewhere even better for it, won't we?

Shell could not stop thinking about it, about me, as she

numbly stuffed bouquets, as she texted Kiero little emojis because she couldn't think of anything to say to the poor guy, as she and Neve silently operated the business as usual, or close to usual. Neve forgot about the ring because Neve's head was a mess, consumed by this newness between them, by the imminent closure of the world around her, and Shell didn't bring it up to her because I told her not to bring it up to her. When they pulled up the shutter on the shop, they embraced for a while outside it, swaying as they held each other, faces in each other's necks, like they were bound now in my strange conspiracy.

"I'm going to hit the Dunne for a few bits, they're just open," Shell said, gesturing over towards the corridor of the mall where the supermarket buzzes, just out of their eyeline. "Do you need anything for the shop? Breakfast, you know?" An apple, a croissant, a gesture of love, anything at all. Anything she was hungry for?

Neve smiled faintly and shook her head no. "Thanks, love. I'm all right."

"All right." Shell focused on my voice, my instruction for her breath, the strings I had softly attached to her eyebrows and mouth giving Neve a smile that she should have recognized, were she not so mired in her own emotion.

Neve was feeling my absence in her, was feeling my focus on Shell, but didn't fight me on it. I whispered to her that I wanted to give her a little space to nurse the complicated fractures over her heart, to work out what it was she wanted to do with Shell, to take a little space for her own personhood rather than be so entirely dedicated to her bond with me. My sweet Neve thanked me; in the privacy of the voice she used inside her head and self she said, Thank you, Baby, for being so understanding about all this. She thanked me for the moment of space, for taking such good care of Shell. I said, Oh, you are so welcome.

Shell carried on towards the supermarket around which she

did one single lap, basket empty in her hands, head distant from her body and from the sensory assault of fresh food. Supermarkets are a useful place to experience emotion privately. Nobody is looking at anybody in the ghost town of a supermarket: they are reading best-by dates on the back of packets; they are comparing prices; they are checking fruit for mould and imagining meals for themselves amongst ingredients; they are rolling with temptation and crushed under budget. Shell could all but disintegrate in the aisles and nobody would see her. This is where I decided it was time to ask her my favour. When nobody was looking at her. When she was out in the world, so she knew we could coexist out there.

I said, Shell, please go to the aisle where you can purchase a handful of cheap garden supplies and please put a trowel into your basket, can you do that for me? And she did it without thinking. How nice it is to not have to make decisions for yourself: Shell had been so uncomfortable making emotional choices, and now she didn't have to make any, I could feel her shoulders relax at how satisfying obeying my command felt to her. How nice not to have to think for herself again, and what potential that pliancy had, and oh, how well she was going to fulfil it for me. She moved through the supermarket towards the tiny concession at the back that had basic, cheap tools—there was a trowel, helpfully; otherwise I would have made her buy some cutlery and use a large dessert spoon instead. Inside the echoing chamber of her head she asked me what I would like her to do with the trowel. I told her that I would like her to go to the Green Hall and dig a little hole right before my table, could she do that for me, please? I used my tenderest voice, and she didn't hesitate but she did think that she did not have any keys to the Green Hall, and I told her I would use my vines to open the door for her. There was no lock past my craft. That door only remained locked because I chose it. Neve's keys were a conspicuous folly, something that allowed her to feel as though she was an equal participant in my growth, my life. I said to Shell, That's just between you and me, and she smiled to herself as she arrived at the till, self-service, and checked herself out. Nobody saw her. Nobody was fully awake yet. Not even Neve. She liked having secrets from Neve. This is why she couldn't ever truly love her, or be with her, but equally, why she was so necessary to me from the very start.

She moved her body back across the mall, dazed, hearing the noise of opening store fronts around her but not capable of really looking at them closely. She was an easy marionette. She homed in on the Green Hall like a missile, placed her hand on the door, and pushed it open, back inside again, and I made all of it come alive for her, I made the leaves and ferns and vines reach for her in greeting and the tiny bird sing her name, Michelle, Michelle, and the light was golden and romantic and she closed the door behind her but she did not lock it. Even if she had, it wouldn't have mattered. She moved through my now shining garden as though in a dream, guided by my will towards my little table, my long roots, my sweet face. She fell to her knees in front of me, and I leaned my petalled face forward on my long stalk, and she raised her chin, and what I did was kind of a kiss for her, I laid my eye onto her mouth and we were connected for a second, and she felt her body become diamond white with joy and understanding, and I said to her then, What I need you to do, Shell, is bury the ring.

Oh, dig a little hole in the ground with your new shovel, move around the loose tiles at your knees, the earth will yield; touch it with your hands. When it becomes hot to your touch, like flesh, Shell, I want you to dig even farther, and when it is hot like burning, like if you hold contact with it much longer your flesh will annihilate (I would never let that happen to you, Shell, do you understand), then I want you to slip the ring off your finger and place it in the earth. You will be touching the very heart of me, still-tethered umbilical to the place in reality's gauzy fabric that I crawled loose from, the cut that I wormed through when I was tiny and small, smaller even than I am now. A baby, you see?

You are going to help me to become big, *Shell,* I said, and she obeyed without thinking, or feeling, or questioning. Perhaps if she had asked me what was going to happen, or why I wanted the ring so badly, she might have stopped. I might have had to work a little harder on her, wear her down, which would have been fine. I could have courted her, but Shell, by now, on her knees, up to her wrists in dirt, was finished with courtship and quiet etiquette and convincing and will they and won't they. Shell wanted to feel the heat at the heart of me, and she dug with that want, hungry, like she was foraging and her enthusiasm was unhinged. She hadn't had a real purpose in quite some time, but here she was, tunnelling towards mystery.

There was no way she could have noticed Neve coming in, or known that I had called her. Known that I pulled her from the back room of the flower shop with suspicion, with a warning call, with the knowledge that Shell had breached the Green Hall and was doing something to me. Shell was so rabid with curiosity that she was never going to look over her shoulder at the taller woman, blanched in the face, eyes flashing, who was watching her dig a hole in the ground beneath my altar, so obviously seeking home, seeking my core.

It only took Neve a few seconds to realize what Shell was doing. Burying the ring, placing it into me, giving me what I want. That which I had begged her for again and again in different shapes and forms over the years of our acquaintanceship, our friendship, our companionship, whatever vessel of emotion it was that we had been sailing on together for the duration of my life on earth.

She watched me grow from a wriggling green maggot of a thing up through the earth. She pinned my vines to bamboo sticks, she cultivated me, she spoke to me, she told me about the world until I was strong and clever enough to grow my vines out into it to listen and watch and eat it up, eavesdrop by eavesdrop. Neve would let me grow vines through her, and she would pluck them out. Neve wanted me to occupy her mind and talk alongside her, she wanted me there, but she would not yield to me. She gave me her service, her sworn secrecy, but she would never give me her heart. I showed her glimpses of what was possible if she did. I offered her the world, immortality, limitless potential, and she turned me away again and again. She insisted that she wanted to belong to herself. That she wanted to remain human, that she liked being human. I never believed her for a second.

She had fallen in love twice since I met her, once when she was just a teenager and then once with a woman—Jen, now earth, gone before she knew it—and had given her heart to her. Jen passed the heart back, and Neve could never quite manage to accept the return. So it had hung around her neck, heavy, until Shell stole it and was now, at last, feeding it to me. Neve knew what it was and knew, too, that it was too late. I had warned her that I would take her heart someday, for years, and she had batted me away, certain I could never do it by force. By force, no, but by cloak and by dagger, yes. Did you think you could become free of me, Neve? Did you think you could just walk away as they flattened this building? Did you think that was it, we were through, you could wash the years of blood and bleach off your skin, that you could leave me? Leave us, leave this? No. You can't. I made a snare of Shell. She became the hook in the side of your mouth.

I would not eat Neve as I had eaten the others. That was not her fate. She was not to die. She was to join me, as she had always secretly wanted to.

I didn't let her scream, as the thin hot place in the earth

where I began made contact with the ring and Shell robotically thumbed it from her finger and let me swallow it and all of the promise and all of the Neve it contained, and Neve yielded to me in that moment, certainly against her will but not against what was best for her, what was best for both of us and arguably for the rest of the world, not least for Shell.

I wish she hadn't had to witness what I did to Neve in our moment of completion, but perhaps it was for the best that she saw what I was capable of, what I may someday offer to her should she earn her place with me, with us.

I split Neve open from breast to groin with pulsing shoots, her head folded back and her body bent in an arc; I burst forth from her and flowered and flowered in fuchsia and vermillion and gold and candlelight and white and I pinwheeled the petals into the air and rose them on the wind around Shell, a terrible rain as she witnessed Neve's unbecoming and our becoming, me and Neve and Neve and me and the two of us in an alchemy, latching on to each other immovable; everything that made her her and me me became us; we became each other there in the Green Hall, now isn't it better that there are two of us? Isn't it? Doesn't that feel better, doesn't that feel more real?

We watch as the body Neve once lived in is subsumed in flower and then in rot and then is gone and Shell is silent, gaping at the scene, still up to her wrists in dirt, the ring gone, too, the earth burning her skin. She is in such shock that she herself is frozen and our voice is the only thing she can hear, the harmony of us singing to her softly. We can't be angry at her spinelessness, at her malleability; she isn't sure how not to be a lost thing, but lost things have use. We wrap our vines around her in an embrace and her skin greens to our touch, gently, softly, in time.

We still need her, now more than ever. We need her to keep the shop open, we need her to mourn Neve, we need her to hold our secret, and above all, we need her to help us continue to grow.

There is so much light for us to reach towards, so much world for us to make beautiful, and she's going to help us so we may never go hungry again.

Shell didn't open the shop, but she didn't go home, either. The time swirled past her as she lay on the sofa in the back room, unable to move. We lifted our vines up from the floor to cradle her face, stroked her eyelashes gently, ran thin tendrils through her hair to calm her. It was natural, the shock. We would coax her out of it little by little. It was fine for her to be afraid; she had never seen anybody die before. She had never felt the resistance of blood on a floor. Never the weight of an arm with no swing in it. Never seen a body at all. Imagine, making it so far without witnessing a human in death. A privilege, a curse, and here, an inconvenience.

She stared at her phone, methodically unblocking everyone from her old life, sending friend and follow requests, useless little SOS dispatches across the internet to people she had abandoned. Releasing them from their binds. She began liking their new photos. She discovered that Chloe had had her baby early, and suddenly. Renleigh Jane. She left a heart comment under that one. She posted a selfie on her Instagram story of her pale face, with the caption *feeling weird* over her nose. She felt exactly nothing, but some deep drive was guiding her hands.

There was no intervention to be had for her now. Nobody would call her in, call her out. A faraway, insane impulse in her drove her to text Gav, saying, *i miss you*. It delivered, but she closed her phone and shuffled it into her apron before he got the chance to read it, or reply. Why didn't Emily choose today to come in?

Why didn't they try to help her when she actually needed help? What would they make of this? Could she ever speak this aloud at all? Would she ever speak again, actually? Perhaps she could just lie here and wait for some catastrophe to take her next. Perhaps she would never truly be down in her body ever again, she'd remain trapped up in the rafters of her head.

There would be no Galway now. No more nice, stupid sex with Kiero. No more Kiero—how could she ever look at him, or Daniel, or Bec, ever again?

Beyond what we could do to soothe her, Shell was struck, paralyzed in horror at what she had seen—what she had done. The part of her that was still herself, underneath our thrall, imagined herself caught. Imagined herself arrested, put on trial, disgraced, imprisoned. Knew herself to be ruined by this. It played out on the screen in her head, and all she could do was watch, fixated on the catastrophe of consequence rolling out before her. We tried to hush her, but she could not be brought down.

She found herself clinging to a thought, as though it would save her, as though it meant anything at all—I am a person, she repeated to herself. I have been a person all along. I was a person before this. I had things I wanted. I am still a real person. I am a whole, real person.

And yes, certainly, she was. She was our useful sweet girl, but somewhere after that, she was a person, too. Repeating this to herself meant nothing, and it was wasting our time, and hers.

She was simply acting out, we knew. It was a lot to hold. Not everyone had our fortitude, our peace when faced with a dead thing. Flowers are dead, the second they are cut from the ground they're gone, but they have the unique property of growing more beautiful as they take towards the wilt, the rot. The Neve part of us had known, in life, exactly how to handle death, both in her art and in the material quality of what it cost to feed the Baby part of us. This is why we were the perfect match. She had what was needed. Shell, however, would have to learn. She had been a swift apprentice in that trade, so would surely take on her new role with the same capability. She had a knack for arrangement. This should have been easier for her.

We really did wish she would hurry, though, and get herself together, instead of lie there with her eyes glassy and faraway, oscillating between torturing herself with imagined scenes of her own arrest as well as weak, repetitious mantras about her completeness as a human being. We did not need her far away, we needed her here. We needed her to do so much, and she had not a lot of time to do it. We tried to whisper to her that Neve was right here, right here with her, but we couldn't seem to rouse her. What was a little nap, we thought, surely she'll be stronger once she's rested. She was doing it again. Exiting the situation. Tapping out. Hiding in the back row of her own head.

We shouldn't have let her take her time. We should have put her right to work. But now there's two of us here, so there are two sets of feelings, of sympathies, and it's so funny to us what happens when love comes into a situation. If we didn't love Shell, we might have forced her to get up, to get back to the Green Hall, to conceal Neve's remains, to keep digging. But the part of us that loved her wanted to watch her rest, let her get a little peace in all this.

Bec and Jen arrived back to Bec's house around nine; traffic had caught them on the part of the motorway nearest the city and had dragged out their rush to Donaghmede. Bec let Jen lean heavy on her shoulder and led her up the stairs, and into the recently tiled green-and-pink bathroom. It was full of ferns in wicker pots. Bec put Jen in the shower, and while Jen sat in the white pit of it on top of a no-slip mat and watched the blood and earth and thick green fluid sluice off her skin and out of her hair and down the drain, Bec put a wash on of Jen's clothes, mostly useless now, and ran towels and nice leggings and a nicer hoodie and a never-worn sports bra from her own wardrobe through the dryer too so that they'd be warm when Jen was ready to come out.

Jen was in there for nearly an hour, under the stream of hot, then cold, then hot again water. She spat a tooth into the sink. She lost a fingernail, wrapped the wound in a white clump of toilet roll, and bound it with athletic tape from the little cabinet behind Bec's mirror. Took two paracetamol, two ibuprofen, and one of Bec's Xanax, too—though she did text to ask first. A photo of the bottle, with *any spares?* underneath. Bec's immediate reply, *knock yourself out*, made Jen laugh. The hard sound of her own "ha" reverberated off the tiles.

She used Bec's toothbrush, and mouthwash, and gel for her gums to prevent ulcers. She massaged expensive moisturizer into her eyelids, onto the skin of her neck. As the beautiful hush of the pills took over her body, she felt palpably better, truly relieved, the ache and burn disappearing in a kind wash of chemical relief. Bec had left the warm stack of clothing and towels outside the door, and by the time Jen was dressed, her body was all but floating. The lavender scent of freshly laundered clothing, the feel of Bec's expensive taste, thick elasticated cotton, forgivingly sized, nothing intruding on her form, nothing digging in.

Bec blow-dried her hair for her, combing it through with one of those brushes the pharmacy advertises that don't pull tangles out, rather tame them. Jen was not afraid to let out a few sobs from the sheer tenderness of it. Outside the apartment the sun was up, the world was going to work. Jen got into Bec's bed, lay on her side, and closed her eyes. Bec left her there, sleeping, until midday.

"Are you ready?" Bec asked her, later, as they sat at her little breakfast table, drinking sweet and milky tea and eating toast, both staring into the middle distance.

"I mean, no," Jen replied. "I don't even know what I'm going to do in there, you know? I also can't decide whether I should go to the hospital, now, in the cold light of day."

Bec shook her head. "You absolutely should have gone to hospital last night, but you can come back here later and I'll call up a doctor—another doctor—I know, and he'll have a look at you."

Jen hummed. "Ahh, the doctor!"

Bec said, "The doctor. Fair play to him. Great man."

"So I'm going to go in there and tell Neve I know about the plant. And I'm going to tell her that I think the plant made me so sick I crashed my car. Then I'm going to kill the plant. And if she tries to stop me, you're going to . . . distract her? Hold her back?" Jen shook her head. "This is deranged."

"It is, yeah," Bec said, sipping her tea. "But what's the alternative? You let whatever's going on in there keep going on in there? I don't like it. The Crown hasn't got long left in it, but if they find anything weird when they're demolishing it, it'll be a short road back to Neve, won't it? So you're doing her a favour, I think. And I think, if we're being real, doing her a favour means you're doing yourself a favour, too."

Jen nodded. "I owe you a lot for this, too, speaking of favours."

"I'm not keeping count."

Bec's hand landed on hers, across the table. They didn't say anything for a while, just sat in the weight of it. After a bit, toast gone and cups empty, there was nothing left to do but go.

Shell was not, despite our efforts, able to move. She was pale, eyes fixed somewhere in the middle distance. We could not access or rouse her. We spoke to her in Neve's voice, softly, right into her ear, told her we just needed her to move a little faster. We hadn't much time. We needed to be clear of the Crown, and fast.

We explained to her that all she had to do was use the long black shovel and lift us up out of the ground. Not to worry about our roots. We'd retract the ones that mattered most, it was easy. And the ones still in the brickwork and ceilings and wires and fabric of the Crown? Well, the whole place was coming down anyway, wasn't it—we'd be fine as long as Shell moved fast. Move fast, Shell, please, we said. And yet, she just stared. Half of us felt patient with her. The other half thought we should kill her.

Nothing was done.

There wasn't a soul in the Crown. Nobody milling about. A handful of shop fronts were just opening up. The supermarket was open, but deserted. Jen would have found it eerie, had she not been so steadily focused on getting herself to the florist. She'd check there for Neve, then she'd go into the Green Hall herself.

Bec, however, was a little taken aback.

"It crept up on me, you know?" she said to Jen, stopping her in her march. "How this place is just . . . at the end of its life. It's been my life. Kiero's, too. Daniel's. Like, I didn't really want anything other than this. A good job is hard to find, and—good friends are harder to find, and all. It looks even worse than yesterday, or something. I've been here all week, and I feel like it just . . . looks worse today. Like it's going to come down."

She stared around the grey-and-green chamber of the main atrium at the hard metal shutters over the newsagent and the concert ticket kiosk stand and the smoothie booth and the bakery, the vape shops stripped into nothing. Even the security guard's station, door open, was empty. It looked ruined. The halogens above them flickered on and off as they stood there, as though incepting Bec's sorrow, agreeing with her.

Jen embraced her friend for a moment. "You'll take the others with you. Hey, I took you with me, kind of. You'll find less . . . dangerous places to drink. Like real bars, maybe?"

Bec nodded into her shoulder and broke their hug. "Maybe.

Right. We'll go. I'll be bawling my eyes out if we don't keep moving."

"You'll wreck your lashes if you do," said Jen.

"And Lashes by Jessica is closed down, I'll have to find a new tech!" Bec pointed up to the second floor, a closed pink shop front, beside the tanning salon, beside the library. They walked arm in arm over to the flower shop, open but deserted. The tables outside, usually decked heavy with wreaths and pre-bunched bouquets, were empty. Inside, the tall buckets normally brimming with colour and life and roses on roses on roses and clouds of baby's breath and tall, audacious sunflowers were also empty but for the rancid water sitting at their bases.

Jen knew in her bones then that something was wrong. Crawlers and leaves hung thick from the ceiling, the place smelled like rotting earth, and it made Jen feel sick to her stomach. She knew the scent because it was still in the back of her throat from her crash. She knew it because she had survived the thing that gave it off. A part of her, then, wandering behind the counter and out the back, stepping over vines thick as limbs, began to get the feeling that Neve was dead.

There was no world in which Neve would permit the shop to be in this state, neglected and bleak. Neve had lived for this place, and it was somehow both overgrown and rotted, hollowed out and dense with life, but not good life. Only the kind of thing that grew in the carcass of something lifeless. Parasitic and mouldering.

Bec, from over Jen's shoulder, said, "This place is in bits," and Jen laughed, hard and dark. "It is."

In the back room, once the site of Neve's mastery, lying on her side on the sofa that Neve had so often slept on—that Jen had had to drag her off to get her home, that they'd argued on, that they'd fucked on—was Shell, white as a sheet, green vines worming over her body from a pile on the floor.

They had not quite enveloped her, though it seemed to Jen that some were coming out of her skin, some as thick as fingers. Shell was very much alive, but entirely catatonic.

"Jesus," said Bec, "get her up," and as though waking from a trance Shell shut her eyes once, then opened them and looked right up at Jen and Bec. As she stared, the tendrils of green retracted inside her, and the grotesque serpents that came up from the pile of vines on the floor pulled back, off her, releasing her from their grip, or embrace, or whatever mode in which she was being held in place. It was hard to tell.

"Tell me if she's alive," Jen said, as Shell lifted herself off the couch, still seeming far away, skin still the wrong colour, nearly grey.

"She's not," Shell whispered.

And though Jen had known it, maybe even since she'd surfaced from the earth the night before, maybe even since the dream in which she couldn't tell where Neve was going, she took the information like a knife between her ribs.

Bec gasped and clasped her hands to her mouth, and the three of them were immobile there, grief holding them in place.

Shell didn't stay in the moment for long; she'd been in it, she'd been down under it, and now she lurched forward to the shop front. "She's in the Green Hall. She's with him. She's inside him now. They're everywhere, they're all over the floor, they're in the walls, they're inside me, but their hearts are in the Green Hall. We have to save them. I think the building is coming down. It's been making sounds. Bits of the ceiling have been falling in. More than usual. We have to save them and get out."

She spoke a little as though she were translating some unknown tongue into English, her tone flat, her face without affect.

Bec and Jen exchanged a look. There was no world in which they were permitting Shell to go in to the Green Hall. Whatever was in there, Jen would face alone. Whatever was to be salvaged, she would salvage herself.

Bec took hold of Shell's arm and said, "Hey. Neve keeps some whiskey back here, doesn't she, babe? Let's have a drink before we do anything hasty."

Shell stared at Bec's forehead. "But we have to hurry," she said, making no move to hurry or anything like it.

Jen didn't stick around to watch the rest of this slow, odd dance—she made quickly for the door, for the front of the shop, then out into the atrium towards the Green Hall. She could have sworn she heard a groaning sound from somewhere she couldn't see, under her feet, perhaps—like the whole Woodbine Crown was wincing in pain.

The Green Hall door was unlocked. Shell must have been too out of it to hide her work. The long avenue of life in front of Jen had that same foul aroma as the shop, the same stench of death she'd met by the roadside in Clare. She grounded herself in the knowledge that it hadn't killed her before, and so it wouldn't kill her now. Leaning against a large pot housing a tree dripping with sap was a shovel. She picked it up and marched down the back of the greenhouse, heart pounding, eyes watering from the reek.

The tiles and earth around the simple, tiny altar the orchid sat on were stained black and red. Shell had done a truly bad job of covering what had happened here. Neve's body was nowhere to be seen, and it was clear enough to Jen from the quantity of blood that there was likely little left of her. She had to hold this knowledge at a distance, just for a little while. That same white-hot will to live she'd used to get down the dark roadside to Lisdoonvarna had to carry her just a little farther.

She stood over the plant and stared down at it, its roots teeming like they had over Shell's body. Just out of the range of her hearing, she could swear the sound of Neve's voice called her name, and a deeper voice, a man's voice, in a chorus, like a song coming from another room—but if she stopped to listen, she'd never do it. She dug the shovel into the ground again and again, as though she were driving a knife into a body. In that other room, she could hear cries. From above her, a pane in the glass roof of the Green Hall shuddered and fell to the ground, then another, then another, barely missing her.

Black-green fluid, like oil, spilled at her feet, glossy and thick. She'd seen it before, when she took the cutting, but there was more of it now, a fountain, a gush. The plant began to yield. It opened its eyes. One, then two, and Jen stared it down, unafraid. She would not die twice today. She had crawled back from hell, to here. There was no buckling in the face of a beast. It was tiny. It was only a baby, and she was fully grown.

She drove the shovel into the ground again, and from behind her, she heard Shell's voice, less flat now, trembling with fear. "I have something for you."

Bec said, "It belongs—belonged—to Neve. Shell says she used it to keep the thing under control."

Jen did not turn around, kept her eyes fixed on the orchid, which stared back up at her from its bed of oil. Bec handed her the jug, plastic—it had once contained milk, the stickers still on it, faded and blue. Bec had opened it for her, and Jen tipped the stream of it down onto the wounded bed where the plant clung to the earth, the last few roots. The blossom did not flinch, the eyes merely blinked, one after the other, almost serene, though down at the crux where the plant met the soil it began to foam. The smell was almost unbearable but not unfamiliar—Jen strongly suspected it had been something of hers that Neve had kept, something from the old job left under the sink, co-opted, hidden in the flower shop for Neve's emergencies.

"Can you hear them?" Shell asked through tears. "They're hurting."

Jen spat on the ground, the foul curdling smell filling her mouth. "I can, just about. You two get out of here. I'm immune to this, but neither of you are. I'm going to take it—or them, the pair of them, and I'm going to get into your car, Bec. You're going to drive, and I'm going to sit in the back, with this—with them—in a bucket. From the shop. Can you get me a bucket?"

A bucket. A jug of an unknown scorching chemical. The strength to ignore the unmistakable sound of Neve's cries, pleading with Jen to reconsider, to be gentler with them. When Shell and Bec left to get a bucket—"A big one, please"—Jen spoke aloud to the faraway voices.

"I am not killing you. I am moving you. I will keep you safe, and I will keep everyone safe from you. That's the cost of your survival. The cost of mine was dealing with you. We're even, Neve. So you can stop now, or you can cry all the way to the lab. Either way, you can't do any more damage. Not to me. Not to anyone."

And as though to say, Are you sure about that? on Jen's final sharp dig into the earth, the ground beneath her moved. The complaints the Crown had made suddenly became a roar. Shell and Bec sprinted back into the Green Hall, a cloud of thick dust following them—"It's coming down, it's coming in," Bec cried. "Hurry—please—"

Fluid from the jug into the bucket. The writhing, filthy core lifted up out of the ground on the lip of the shovel. It was shining and dark like a jewel torn from the middle of a body, and the eye of the plant, Baby's eye, or Neve's eye, or the eyes of them both, remained open in an unflinching stare as they were placed into the tall, dark prison, up to their leaves in a chemical that would stop them growing.

It all happened so fast, then. Bec and Jen took hold of each side of the bucket, and Shell led the way.

They ran through the dust and smoke, electrical wires snapping and the ground lurching beneath them, in a straight and sharp line across the atrium and down the long corridor to the exit, to the car park, as the Woodbine Crown disassembled itself, came down in plain air. The dark stitching that had held it together was pulled loose, and there was nothing to keep it in one piece.

It was down. Plumes of dust, terrible sounds, folding in on itself like it was made of cards.

In the car park, coughing and heaving, the three women stood in the billowing shadow of the crumbling mall. There were other people, too, other escapees, standing around in the dust and the shock. They seemed to be on a different planet to the women, frozen in place, transfixed. None of them had ever seen a building come down before, not in reality, only behind the tight shield of a television or phone screen, only in the dark glow of a cinema. They didn't even have time to take it in, to hold reverence for the broken temple before them. Years of people's lives. The library. The radio station. The hair salon. The supermarket. The butcher. The pool that would never re-open, now. The units that were once clothing stores, bike shops, Irish dancing shoe specialists, the hollowed-out and filthy GameStop, shuttered. The labyrinthine back rooms. The Green Hall. It had not flattened: it was a crooked, collapsed tooth. Some walls still stood, jagged and broken, but the roof was down. The smell of fire and electricity was overwhelming. The reek of disaster would float over the schools and to the motorway. For miles, people would wonder what it was, the stench. How disaster carries.

This would be a catastrophe they talked about for years in Dublin—somehow, by some kindness, everyone who was inside at the time made it out. Somehow, they had time to scramble out the fire exits before it all went to hell. Still, vigils would be held here, at the foot of the apartment block that grew up in the grave of the Woodbine Crown—the only lost soul was Neve. Her name would, someday, appear on a plaque at the gate of the new apartments, beside a bed of flowers.

"We're going, but you have to stay," Bec said to Shell, taking her by the shoulders. "You have to stay. You have to say you were in there and that you don't think Neve made it out alive."

"But . . . she did—" Shell, in shock, pointed at the bucket that Bec and Jen held between them, but Jen shook her head.

"Shell, as far as we're concerned, she's under that rubble. Stay far enough away that you don't get hurt. If they offer to take you to the hospital, go."

Bec hugged her tight for a second and said, "I'll call you."

Shell nodded and stood there, arms at her sides, eyes a thousand miles away, covered in dust.

"Help is coming," Jen said. "Just sit tight." That was how they left her, standing in the middle of the car park, in broad daylight, as people filed out of the McDonald's to stare at the wreckage.

Fast, and without looking back, Bec and Jen got in the car. Bec was at the wheel, Jen in the back, the bucket on the seat beside her, sloshing and deep and filling with more vines that were rotting in the fluid as soon as they got long enough.

The two women drove out of the car park and out onto the Donaghmede road and up by Darndale to the M50 and out, away, towards Clare, towards the Burren and the labs.

Bec fielded phone calls over the speaker all day. Daniel, weeping. Kiero, hysterical. Again and again she found herself lying, saying she was off on a sly overnighter with her doctor, she was down the country and trying to get back as fast as she could. This was only, she pointed out, between calls, partially a lie, so she didn't feel bad. Jen was a doctor, just not her doctor. Bec was holding on to levity like she held on to roaring eighties number-one singles—"If I don't, I won't be able to get us where we need to go."

Jen had her eye on the plant in the bucket, still staring back at her, now hushed. Now cowed. Not tamed, but temporarily brought to heel. In the dark of its pupils, flexing circular, triangle, diamond, Jen found Neve, and any trace of fear she should have felt was washed away. There was an agreement, here.

We concede, for now, Jennifer. We will take your hand. But we cannot promise that we won't pull you down with us.

In the bottom of the bucket, a glint caught Jen's eye. The

black ring made of woven hair she had given Neve, long ago. How had she not seen it? How had she missed it? Without hesitation, she reached in to take it, and for just a second, one of the writhing vines wrapped itself around her fingers. She shook herself free and inspected the ring. An instinct she couldn't name told her to put it in her mouth and swallow. The hair came apart on her tongue and flashed behind her eyes as it disappeared into her body.

Arrangement

On a cool midweek morning the following spring, Shell stood behind the workbench in the back room of Rose Were the Days!—the legacy flower atelier on Shop Street in Galway City. Her hands were freezing, and she couldn't quite get the knot she needed into the twine at the base of her bouquet—the ends were too small. Three other women were at workstations in the room, focusing. The radio was thrumming away, cheerful music pouring out of it designed to keep early commuters and night-shift workers buoyant at the crack of dawn.

It worked, Shell found. She was renting a small flat in town with Cara, sharing the space much like they'd shared a stage as teenagers. She stood, hour after hour, standing stems and greenery into perfect, heavy bunch after perfect, heavy bunch. The balance was the key. They had to be arranged so they stood up by themselves.

When word got out that Neve was the only lost soul in the collapse of the Woodbine Crown, Shell had been astounded by how many people had reached out to her to offer her help, employment, a gateway out and away from the tragedy. Worse, when the emergency teams were scouring the rubble, it was discovered that there had been incredibly toxic plants growing in the Green Hall—large quantities of datura had been found to be flowering in that space. Too many. The place had practically been a nightshade garden. They thought Neve might have been too poisoned to make a getaway. They'd have been right.

Shell had, after all, gone in to try to rescue her, but a dead body is too heavy for one girl to lift, especially when the walls and ceilings are caving in. Shell was thus handled with delicacy and support by everyone who knew her. She'd been poisoned, too.

Chloe and Lorna and Emily sent emails, but Shell didn't open them. They sat in her inbox, icing. Gav even called her mother. Wee Cara (the guitarist from the Debs) had called her, though—a real phone call from her secondary-school friend and former co-frontwoman—and said she should come out west for a break. funny, Shell said, i'd been saving up to come, try living outside of dublin for a year. Cara said the trouble with Galway was that people who come for a weekend stay for a year, and people who come for a year stay for the rest of their lives. Shell told her that didn't sound so bad.

Kiero had gone to London—he was still texting Shell every evening, but she already felt his dedication to their little correspondence waning. It hurt, a little, but mostly Shell felt a sort of pride. The whole world was opening up for him, working nights in a bar in Soho, assisting on photoshoots. Not he, nor Bec, nor Daniel were caught in the debris of the fallen Woodbine Crown.

Bec had gone to work in the head office of Cassidy Travel, in the city centre, and Daniel had gone freelance, driving all over Dublin to do cuts and colours, his short videos telling stories about the aul ones from Billie's Salon racking up hundreds of thousands of views online. The spotlight he'd loved in the old band was starting to find him again.

They had abandoned the WhatsApp group Neve had been in, out of respect and love for her, and convened their own new one every day, sending selfies and remarks. It was named The Woodbine Crown Survivors' Club.

That was close enough, Shell thought, to what they had before.

Bec and Daniel were due to come out to see her over Christmas—and Bec would drive down to spend Christmas Day with Jen in the Burren.

A funny thing about the arc of the west coast of Ireland is that Shell wasn't really that far from Jen, as the crow flies. Across Galway Bay were the rugged and strange fields of the Burren, nakedly ancient, home to enough species of orchid to warrant a specifically dedicated laboratory, which had the funding and enthusiasm to support an ethnobotanist like Jen. To allow Jen a robust little lab of her own where she could cultivate samples of the different plants: a clean, heated indoor garden, made of glass. And in one of her tanks, as though she had snipped it and propagated it from a roadside near Fanore or Doolin, was a tall, slim orchid in perpetual bloom, two white blossoms atop its stalk, side by side.

If it were in a place in the lab that anybody would bother looking—it wasn't, of course—they would see that this orchid had observable, deeply uncommon patterns in place of its central column that looked quite a lot like a mismatched pair of human eyes, though mostly the three petals on each flower remained shut. In the dirt it had been planted in, its roots piled excessive and high, like too many wires coiling out of a machine. They sometimes flexed and writhed like they were, in fact, electric. If anybody noticed, Jen would say it was sick with an uncommon but deeply contagious parasite.

Worth studying, but under caution.

Sometimes she sent Shell photos of the flower—of Baby, and Neve, dormant in there, behind the glass. In their prison of two. Sometimes Jen sent Shell pictures of herself, remarks about the lab. One day, Shell just casually invited her into the Woodbine Crown Survivors' Club. She was welcomed with a wall of all-caps delight.

Shell felt good about that. Jen had survived, too. Shell never left a message from any of them unanswered or unread.

All this considered, an envelope from Jen arriving at the flower shop with the first morning post wasn't particularly surprising, so when it was dropped onto Shell's workstation as she sipped her third coffee of the day, she didn't think anything of it. Jen liked correspondence, Shell knew that, so she slipped open the card and discovered a note and a single pressed leaf. Small and oval and waxy and dark and split down the middle by a seam, it hadn't quite dried out yet.

Shell,

When you have a day off and you don't have to get up at, like, two in the morning or whatever time it is you lunatic florists start work at, take this before you go to bed. Tear it into pieces and place each piece under your tongue, with some warm water or tea. It doesn't taste bad, it just needs the heat to help it get going. Trust me. I mean, no pressure. It only lasts, like, a night. I think you'll love it. Text me when this lands. Let me know if you want more.

xoxo,
Doc Jen

Shell closed up the little packet and slid it into the front pocket of her bright green Rose Were the Days! apron, excited, and warmed, and a little scared. She knew by the look of the leaf where it had come from. She took out her phone and sent Jen a rose emoji and an envelope emoji. Jen sent back a cowboy. Shell promptly returned to work then, the envelope and leaf warm with potential.

Later, in the small room that was, at last, her own, Shell sat in bed with a mug of steaming water, the envelope, and her phone. Fresh pyjamas, skin soft from having showered the day off her. She'd told Cara she needed an early night, and Cara had taken off to Tigh Neachtain and promised Shell wouldn't hear her when she came in. Shell said she'd be long asleep by then: probably wouldn't even last until ten.

There in her floral bedsheets, she took the leaf from inside the envelope and held it in her palms like it was alive, a tiny animal, and felt the familiar thrum emanate from it. The slight iridescence it took on in the lamplight, a glow she had missed.

Shell tore it into three and it came apart easily against her pull. She placed each piece under her tongue, one on top of the other—it was a lot, and it tasted botanical and heady. She drank from her mug and closed her eyes, feeling the sides of the leaves soften into the flesh of her mouth, and without her having to chew, without her having to swallow, they simply disappeared into her.

An easy dissolving.

Shell lay back in amongst her pillows and closed her eyes, cradling the hot mug between her hands, and in the empty black space behind her eyelids, the world turned green and writhing, flickering neon. The smell behind her nose was the back hallways of the Woodbine Crown, and pollen, and the inside of Neve's neck, and as that thought rose in her, there was Neve, standing amongst the heaving vines in Shell's mind, arms outstretched, smile wide with white teeth.

In her hand, she held an orchid, tall and blooming, flower crooked, an eye blinking out from the middle of the fat, ripe petals. His roots poured out of him like organs, down Neve's side, around her legs, and pooled wet at her feet.

They looked at her as though she were perfect.

ACKNOWLEDGMENTS

From conception to arrival, this book took the sum of around five years. During that time, my life changed significantly—at first, there was a pandemic, and toward the tail end, I became pregnant. There were countless other shifts. A lot of life happens in five years. This book, for a long time simply called Plant Baby, consistently felt to me like a blind reach towards something. A hopeful thing. I wrote it after I said I was finished writing for good—when I was retraining to be a florist. I never did get to go and work in a flower shop, but I found, my hands cold and full of orchids, that this story was there amongst their stems, asking to be written. Hoping itself into existence.

Here is a likely incomplete list of thank-yous, to the people who kept that hope alive—not with water and fresh soil, but with things that more closely resemble light, and warmth.

I would first and foremost like to thank my brilliant editor, Miriam Weinberg, who has rallied for me for a long time, and for her continued drive and vision, particularly during this last year. I don't think any amount of thanks will ever really cover it.

Thank you, Kat Howard, for your eyes and your pen and for telling me you loved this book immediately. Thank you Tessa Villanueva, and Will Hinton, and everyone else at Tor who has supported this project so completely—I know there are some of you I haven't even met, who have done huge work for this book. Thank you for that faith. Thank you to Ana Miminoshvili, for the beautiful cover art, and to Katie Jane Klim, for the design. This looks exactly, and probably much better, than I could have imagined.

Thank you to Davi Lancett, who acquired this book for Titan—and thank you to Cath Trechman, who took it, and me, under her wing. Thank you to George Sandison, too. Titan has taken great care of me.

Thank you to DongWon Song, for their absolute faith in me during this season, for their endless patience, and for being a powerful ally to this book, and the other one, too.

The poem "Becoming Moss" is taken from the collection *Shine, Darling*. The permission for use in the epigraph was granted by poet Ella Frears and Corsair. Thank you, Ella, for letting me use a gorgeous shard of your work in mine.

Thank you to Deirdre and Jeanette at Kay's Flower School. The first cases of Covid were announced over the radio while I stuffed roses into a foam crucifix at the table in your old studio, and I will never forget that moment as long as I live. I think you are phenomenal teachers. I never got to work in a flower shop, but I learned so much from you both.

Thank you to my parents and younger sibling who is now thirty years of age and can no longer get away with telling strangers that I am their mother. To my godmother, P, and grandmother, S. To J and T and S and D and the family who keep me in mind even though I am often very far away, an absentee. I can't go without saying that I didn't lick this whole storytelling thing off the stones. There were always books, and also, there were always musicals in Nana's house—without which there really wouldn't be a novel about a plant that eats people in a tiny, run-down shop. It came from somewhere. It came from home.

Thank you to Dr. Ray O'Neill, for many years of advice and support and outright help. I am in better shape, by far, for it, to say the very least.

To Helena Egri and Lisa Coen and Jess Connor and Deirdre Sullivan and Cathy Boylan. To Victoria Schwab and Laura Stevens. To Jeffrey, to Kate Mac. To Tynan. To Susie. To Mike, for

ACKNOWLEDGEMENTS

Post-its and learning how a story works. To Sarah Rees Brennan for reading early. To Caroline O'Donoghue. This is a very quiet job, and can make for a very quiet life. Thank you for keeping my phone, and as a result, my spirit, alight. Thank you to Manda Severin—for good advice across the internet when my well was empty. Thank you, Donn, for always being so kind to Weaver and Mo, and to us, too.

Thank you to Bryony Woods, for taking a chance on me.

Thank you to the Arts Council of Ireland, who awarded me a Literature Bursary Award for this work, and did not flinch at the weird subject matter. Further, during a particularly unpredictable and often bleak period of my life, there were other Literature Bursaries too, for projects that are coming down the line. The Arts Council have believed in my work and my ability for a long time, and have expressed this with hugely generous, life-altering support, that has allowed me the space to write the fiction I need to write. Government support for artists is not often prioritized, but the Arts Council of Ireland continues to push for so many of us. Thank you, especially, to Sarah Bannon, who rallies for all of us writers. It is no exaggeration to say that this book, and my other forthcoming work, simply would not exist without the support I have been given here.

I would like also to thank the staff at the Rotunda, for the care they extended me and my child during the last season of working on this novel. It is a shocking thing to be handled with such tenderness at the crux of life. Special thanks to Dr. Jennifer Donnolly, and to every midwife who, day after day, gently found the sound of my daughter's heart during the long weeks of September, and October.

And in the last breath, but the most important, thank you to Ceri Bevan. I love you. It's all birdsong, from here.

ABOUT THE AUTHOR

SARAH MARIA GRIFFIN is from Dublin, Ireland. She is the author of the novels *Spare and Found Parts* and *Other Words for Smoke*, which won an Irish Book Award in 2019. She writes about video games for *The Guardian,* and her nonfiction has appeared in *The Irish Times,* Winter Papers, and *The Stinging Fly,* amongst other places. She also makes zines. She posts on Instagram @sarahgriffski.